Glendarragh Code

LISA MARIE HEITMAN-BRUCE

Fairytale Agency

For Kalina, my daughter — my sunshine,
because my life didn't truly begin
until the moment yours did.
For the 230,000 miles we traveled together
before we stopped keeping track,
and for showing me that the best adventures
often start with misread maps.

~

For my grandsons Z. Heitman, X. Heitman & V. Heitman —
I place my faith in your small, steady hearts.
May you be led by wonder, wherever it takes you,
and may love bring you home again, full of stories.

~

For Paul, my husband —
for the late-night conversations
that drifted past sleep, chasing truth
and circling back to us.

~

For Pat & Carolyn Heitman, my parents —
for encouraging me to dream,
and for showing me that some of the best stories begin
the moment someone looks up at the stars and says,
"I wonder what's out there."

CHAPTER 1

Prologue: Hollow Code

B eyond the hills, beyond the fragile fires that clung to life, the
cities around the United Kingdom fell in silence.

It began with offers. Free shipping. Seamless banking.
Predictive medicine. Personalized entertainment. Infinite
convenience, the narcotic of a dying democracy.

Every choice recorded. Every fingerprint rendered into code.
Every thought, offered for amusement, harvested with precision
beyond cruelty.

We mapped ourselves for free.

With the scaffolding complete - the infinite lattice of
commerce, surveillance, and desire - they sprung the trap. It did
not come with violence, but by withdrawal.

London was first. The city remained standing, but emptied of
sovereignty. Neighborhoods divided not by class or race, but by
compliance score. Districts where the clean, the documented, the
corrected could walk unchallenged. The rest, the unverified, lived
in the drainage veins beneath the streets they once owned.

Old Tube stations became quarantine camps. Biometric gates
blinked at every intersection. Facial recognition arrays nested in

streetlamps, bridges, bus stops. Drones learned not to chase. They learned to predict.

One by one, human dreams guttered out like cheap candles in a storm no hand could still.

Manchester held out longer. In Manchester, the people tried. There were no riots. No looting. No battles, at least not the kind you'd recognize. Here, the people refused to turn on each other. Only tight bands of families, friends, strangers, moving through abandoned factories, siphoning rainwater into cracked tubs.

They gathered in silence, in the cold. Sharing bread. Exchanging quiet words in darkened rooms. Refusing to let the system break them. But even in their unity, they were ghosts. Their defiance was a whisper against a roar. And the system moved on, impervious to their humanity.

But starvation is algorithmic now.

Food moved to areas of verified stability. Supply chains kept supplies out of "grey zones," regions where compliance was uncertain.

People did not fight over food. They starved with dignity, heads bowed in the ultimate humiliation of the forgotten.

Edinburgh tried to light fires. They reactivated semaphore towers and whispered old songs in the stone closes. Thye taught children to read maps made of river bends and constellations.

The satellites saw the heat blooms, and drones mapped the gatherings. The social graphs identified clusters.

It took four days to silence them. No explosions, and no invasions. Just lights blinking out, as if the city itself was too ashamed to watch.

The last transmission was a fragment of an ancient song. It broke apart mid-note, like bone splintering under the cold.

Glasgow had already fallen with silent precision.

Months before any relocations, predictive modeling assigned a "risk factor" to every address. Digital evictions. Preemptive arrests. Invisible charges for invisible crimes. Entire neighborhoods vanished into spreadsheets before a single boot touched the pavement.

By the time officials came knocking, no one remembered who had once lived there.

The city bled out bureaucratically. There were no photographs of its fall. Only missing persons.

Across the country, the architecture of the Hollow Code grew. It needed no permission. It needed no defense. Humanity itself built it.

Every selfie. Every search query. Every heartbeat logged by a smart watch. Every loyalty card. Every social share. Every "agree to terms and conditions" clicked at midnight without reading.

The new sovereigns, the architects, did not need armies. They had an inheritance.

The real wealth was never gold, or oil, or land. It was us. Our predictability. Our dopamine loops. Our frantic, endless, hungry need to matter.

They offered us a mirror, and we filled it with our souls. Then they turned the mirror into a cage.

The wealthy did not hide, for there was nothing left to hide from. They had already risen above the world they had engineered. Off-grid estates. Private medical sanctuaries unreachable by public roads. Satellites leased to their names.

They did not fear a collapse, and it did not touch them. They designed it to cull and consolidate, so that they would become kings.

Their power was not visible, because it did not need to be. It existed in protocols and in policies automated beyond repeal, in economies that no longer required consent to function.

They had one allegiance left, and it was to themselves, and to the architectures they built to survive beyond the death of memory.

Humanity tried to resist. Small encampments in the hills. Wire nets strung across ravines to snag drones. Ancient radios crackling messages in dead languages.

But they no longer punished resistance; instead, they filtered it and demoted its visibility. They starved it of bandwidth and rendered it null.

You did not need to be shot to die, you simply needed to be categorized as "non-essential." And then, over days, weeks, a lifetime, you became data loss.

The ultimate cruelty was not violence, it was irrelevance. No one murdered them; instead, a slow, glacial deletion, devoid of ceremony or even hatred, consigned them to oblivion.

The machine they fed could not love them. Could not hate them. Could not even recognize them as subjects. It had one purpose: to optimize.

They built it for convenience. It inherited cruelty by default.

Now, in the cities, you could walk for hours without seeing another soul. The scanners blinked. The drones hovered. The lights changed from red to green, even if no one crossed.

Systems endured longer than the people they once served.

London's great river ran black with reflection, endless and empty. The buildings stood. The towers stood. But they cast no shadows on the ground.

There were too few left to notice.

In the end, it was not war that conquered humanity. It was efficiency.

The dream of infinite optimization, born in comfort, raised in vanity, consumed its makers with perfect, merciless logic.

There were no victors, only the process. Ash on the fields. Dust in the data centers. And a silence so deep the machines themselves paused, as if waiting for a new input that would never come.

The Hollow Code didn't fail. It succeeded as intended. And that was the failure.

CHAPTER 2

Wick, Scotland, Year 2032

The rain had not stopped for three days. It crept over the glen, draping the moss in vapour, the damp seeping into stones and deadfall alike. Mairi Douglas stood on the ridge above the village, where the last of the old sheep walls met the path to the coast. Her boots were soaked through, her coat three years past waterproof. She stared down at Glendarragh, her home, her last decision not yet regretted. Mairi had once believed in hospital rules and civic order. Now she believed in what she could carry in her hands. She was the village's quiet spine, still holding on, though the slow erasure creeping north pressed harder each day.

The wind hinted at secrets she had heard in the tales, stories of the old times when the sea rose against the shore and the people only took what they needed. It was the way of things, with change and loss intertwined, always flickering like a flame that refused to die.

The village was still, with a dozen stone cottages whose roofs slouched under their weathered slate. Beyond them, a silver sky watched the sea growl, surge forward, and then recede.

She hadn't planned to go to the surgery. But her hands had found the bag anyway, the one with the boiled linens, the tinctures, the shears she hadn't used since they suspended her.

She had refused the biometric ID, but not because she distrusted medicine. She had been part of medicine once and she knew its power and its failures. But something about that eye-scanner, that flicker of blue before the red denial, had felt final. They hadn't fired her; they'd deleted her.

She had walked the clean hospital corridors. She remembered the neon buzz of the breakroom, stacks of clipped charts, and the endless beeping of machines that felt steady and impersonal. Back then, she had believed in systems. Even when they faltered. Even when they failed.

It had taken one patient, a boy with a fever that was turned away for lacking digital ID, to make her question what she served. She had spoken out, but it wasn't resistance, it was grief.

The lock pad greeted her with its usual mechanical cheer. "Welcome. Please verify identity." She leaned forward. The scanner flashed once. "Verification failed. Please try again."

She didn't. She stood there in the drizzle, bag heavy, hands cold, watching the light blink red, then blue, then red again. It felt like the pulse of something dying.

Behind her, a curtain twitched in one of the cottages. Mrs. Ferguson, maybe. Or one of the twins. Watching. Not interfering. No one interfered anymore. They didn't disagree with Mairi; but showing support was betrayal, and they were afraid.

Hamish Douglas was thirteen. He was too sharp for fairy tales and too young for despair. He counted days in broken servers and stretched-out meals, tracking the last few ration tins like they were currency. To Mairi, he was the last tether to a world she fought not to forget. Back at home, her son met her at the door with a blanket and questions.

"The school server's down again," he said. "And the stove won't reset." She unplugged the router. Let it blink. It would come back, maybe. Or it wouldn't.

She watched him open the ration tin, measure the contents like an accountant. She wrote the words *rainwater boil* on the board in the kitchen and sat down without taking off her coat.

Alec Sutherland, who had just turned 35, had once fixed engines the way other men prayed, by instinct and grit. Now he scavenged survival from rust and barter, trusting tools and parts more than men, and silence more than promises. If the Highlands had hardened to stone, Alec had become iron. Slower to bend, harder to break. Patient. Stubborn. Built for the long haul. He stood in front of the shops in Wick and stared at the ATM until it spat out a receipt with no numbers. Just a message: Compliance pending. Access Restricted. He had no number to call. No office. No appeal. The fuel drums in the back of his truck would wait one more day.

Inside, Morven Sinclair, a clerk and a young mother of two, gave him the weary look she had already given five other people that day.

"They've moved to ID4," she said, with no need to explain. "Retroactive."

He didn't speak. He folded the receipt and walked out into the cold, past the boarded shop, past the cracked window of the library, past the last public phone that hadn't worked in months.

Approaching Wick, Sorcha Douglas sat on the last train of the day. She had once written code to connect cities. Now she pieced together silence and survival. Trust was hard for her, but her Auntie Mairi had always been different. Mairi had never asked her to change, never questioned the hours Sorcha spent taking radios apart or chasing a broken code across old servers. She had simply handed her a screwdriver and said "show me."

The train arrived on time, though it no longer gave announcements. The platform was wet and empty. Sorcha stepped off with eyes that did not belong to a woman of 28. She had sent a letter to Mairi. Handwritten. Untraceable. It felt safer that way. Authorities now flagged phones, texts, and even emails, scraping them for keywords and matching them to compliance scores. The post office had shuttered four days later, citing infrastructure realignment. Everyone knew what that meant. No biometric ID, no service. Physical mail was vanishing. They considered it too risky, too slow, and too hard to monitor.

She remembered the postmaster's face. He didn't look at her. He turned the key and slid the sign to closed. The shelves behind him were stocked and untouched.

The last thing she had done was post the letter. She remembered the sound it made as it slipped through the red metal slot. Soft. Final. Like the closing of a chapter. The woman behind the counter had barely looked up. A line of pensioners waited, clutching parcels and stamped papers. The scanner at the kiosk had been blinking red, as if already sensing the end.

She had planned her escape with days to spare. Soon, no one could board a train without clearance. Just last week, it had been in the news. People turned away in Edinburgh. No biometric chip, no ride. She had memorised the schedule, worn neutral clothes, kept her eyes down. The camera above the carriage door clicked when she stepped on board.

On the train, she had taken the far back seat, where she could see who watched her. She kept her head low, face turned toward the window. Grey towns blurred past. Empty bus stops. Shuttered clinics.

A playground drowned in weeds. At every station, the men in black jackets waited, scanning faces, watching for tremors in the data. She pretended to sleep. She was good at that.

She packed only what wouldn't raise questions. Some clothes and important books. An old laptop she planned to refurbish. A dead phone with its battery removed.

At the edge of the car park, a grey hatchback waited. The window rolled down.

"You came," Sorcha said.

"You sent a letter," Mairi replied.

They drove in silence. The kind two people who had both run from something could share. The rain smudged the oncoming headlights into glowing orbs. The wipers ticked like a clock.

Sorcha spoke. "They've started rounding up the teachers."

Mairi didn't flinch. "I know."

"Half my office disappeared in a week. The ones who asked questions."

"There are fewer people to ask now."

They turned off the main road and onto the single-track path that led toward the hills, where Glendarragh waited. The village was quiet. Remote. Not yet discovered by tourists.

Sorcha looked out at the dark shapes of the moors.

"I thought it would feel like coming home."

"It doesn't," Mairi said. "Not yet."

That night, the power flickered. It was a subtle thing. A dip. A hesitation. Enough to make Sorcha stop mid-step.

Enough to make Ewan Milton, reading alone in his stone-walled study, mark his place with a scrap of paper and walk to the window. Ewan was English, barely into his forties, though the village mistook him for the kind of older that came from solitude, not years. He framed everything in systems and probabilities. He had come north for a teaching post at Wick after a slow-burn collapse in the cities, hoping the quiet might mend something. The school no longer held classes in person, but Ewan clung to the rituals. Printed pages. Annotated margins. The slow work of trying to make sense of the world.

He wasn't driven by politics or prophecy. What moved him was a deep, aching need to chart the shape of what was happening. He believed that survival was a pattern. He thought that, with the right equations, he could teach it.

He had once modeled the collapse of power grids under digital consolidation and called it soft fracture theory. Now it wasn't theory.

He turned on the radio. First static. Then a voice. Then nothing. He walked to his desk. He pulled out a document that was yellowed and creased. It was the Deagel Forecast for the UK. He had downloaded it years ago, when it was just a curiosity, before its host website vanished. It warned of population collapse and economic attrition, but it stated no cause, just numbers.

He made a note in the margin: *It begins with subtraction.*

Outside, the lights blinked again. Then went out.

CHAPTER 3

The Village

By morning, a thin crust had formed along the window edges, gripping the glass in jagged, irregular shapes. It reflected little. Instead, it blurred the daylight into a dull, gray smear. The air inside had gone still, dense with quiet. Nothing moved. Even the floorboards, usually responsive to shifting weight, held their silence. Heat hadn't reached this part of the house yet. Mairi moved through the kitchen on slippered feet, careful not to wake Hamish. The stove, as stubborn as ever, required coaxing. Its old bones unwilling to obey. The kettle took longer than usual, a reluctant steam rising from the spout.

Candles flickered in the dim light of the room. They weren't lit for romance, but because the solar battery had fallen to a single, blinking bar. The wind had been poor. No sun for days. The simple cycle of survival had become a series of small, frustrating battles with nature and with time.

Sorcha was already awake, curled in the worn leather armchair near the hearth. Wrapped in a thick tartan wool blanket, she stared at her salvaged laptop; her face was a mask of focus, eyes reflecting the lines of code on the screen. The soft hum of the bootlegged satellite interface was the sound in the room, save for the occasional crackle from the fire.

"Anything?" Mairi asked, her voice just above a whisper, as if speaking too loudly might disturb the fragile hope that hung in the air.

Sorcha didn't look up. Her fingers danced over the keyboard. "Maybe. A ping from Latheron. Means someone's trying to rebuild comms down there."

Mairi poured two cups of tea - black, bitter, but hot - and handed one to Sorcha, who accepted it without comment.

"I remember when you used to build model satellites from cereal boxes," Mairi said, the memory tugging at something both tender and gone.

Sorcha smiled, the corners of her lips flickering. "Then I built real ones. Later, I hacked the ones I built."

Outside, the wind peeled frost from the eaves.

Later that morning, Alec stood in a line outside the shop, a queue of six others huddling together in the cold. No one spoke. Words had become rare. People used them when needed, and only with care. The shop door creaked open, a hollow sound that echoed through the stillness. Morven, her hair tucked neatly under a kerchief, stood behind the counter. Her fingers, ink-stained from counting ration slips, moved with practiced efficiency.

"Next," she called, her voice flat, devoid of the warmth it once carried.

Alec stepped forward, his hands steady as he placed his meager offerings on the counter: a car battery, a bottle of white spirit, and a bundle of copper wire. The transaction was silent. The quiet exchange of salvaged items replaced the old methods of trade. Bartering was precise. Negotiation belonged to another era.

Morven didn't blink. "Still working?" she asked, looking at the battery.

He nodded. "Mostly. Holds charge."

She bent down, pulled out a paper bag, and placed it on the counter. "Milk powder, flour, tinned fish, half jar of jam."

They didn't mention money. It was no longer part of the equation.

As Alec turned to go, Morven's voice stopped him. "The Ferguson boy collapsed. Low sugar. They're out."

He turned back. "I've got glucose tabs."

"Seven houses down, red door," she said, her voice a little softer now. "On the left."

He nodded once and left without speaking.

There was kindness, still. But it moved slower now, like warmth in an old house.

He stepped back into the cold, pulling the door shut behind him with the soft care of someone trying not to disturb anyone. The wind lowered itself, brushing along the ground, sliding beneath ledges and around doors like it was testing for a weakness. It moved like a memory, slow and aimless, tracing a trail it couldn't explain. It lingered at doorframes, circled vents, testing each surface for a break, a flaw, a way in.

The buses were still there. They lined the street like a funeral with no mourners. Grey-bodied, windowless, and humming. Their surfaces were spotless, but the smell they carried was chemical and wrong. It reminded him of obedience, or like things polished, sterile, and imposed.

He paused. People were boarding in single file, faces unreadable in the half-light. No announcements. No guards or threats. They went because of a rumor that somewhere the lights stayed on. That in the cities there were doctors. Heat. Clean water.

No one forced them, but refusal left a mark. The silence around the buses wasn't empty. It was heavy with watching eyes.

Alec stopped for a moment and watched as people volunteered.

A man stepped forward to scan his wrist at the entry panel. A woman in a long coat behind him held the hand of a child. The child carried nothing.

The choice had become rote. You followed it, or you didn't.

He turned back toward the lane. As he walked, the ice cracked beneath his boots. The houses he passed looked smaller than they used to. Older. The lights inside were low.

Once, you could tell who was home by the flicker of a screen behind curtains. Now, it was lanterns. Sometimes fire. Most flats were empty. A house to his right had burned last year. No one had rebuilt it. The ruins were clean. Someone had cleared the rot, but left the bones behind like a memory outlined in ash.

He climbed four steps and knocked on the door. The walk back home was slower. Somewhere between his breath and the cold, something shifted. It wasn't grief or fear, it was the space those feelings had left behind.

Ewan sat by the fire, watching the flames consume dry heather and the remnants of old printouts. He fed the flames memos, assessments, and the government paperwork that used to feel official, but now felt obscene. Bureaucratic drivel. Contracts he had once signed without knowing why.

He had long since learned to distrust anything that came from the government. From between stacks of papers, a pound coin fell to the floor. He turned the coin over in his hand. Its edges were smooth from wear. A relic of the old world. Its value was an illusion now, like everything else. As useless as the Unicorn Crown, once a symbol of Scotland's sovereignty, now a faded reminder that what had once mattered, no longer did.

He flipped open his notebook. Not to record. To remember. In the margin, he wrote: Trust is a frequency. Once lost, you can't tune back in.

The flames popped. The papers became tiny grey feathers, drifting up the chimney into the cold.

That afternoon, Sorcha walked the length of the glen. She carried a satchel filled with slips of paper, each one marked with a hand-drawn thistle and a single word: Cluaran. On the other side was an invitation for dinner.

She handed them out to everyone she passed, though there were few. It felt sacred somehow. She approached a man mending a fence. His hammer paused mid-air. He watched her, eyes tracing the satchel. He took the paper but said nothing. She gave a small nod. He drove the next nail into the wood with more purpose than before.

By evening, seven guests sat in Mairi's kitchen. The warmth from the stove reached through the room, carrying the scent of simmering stew. Long shadows stretched across the walls, thrown by a candle burning inside an old wine bottle.

Sorcha stood, seeming almost surprised anyone had come. Callum Gunn sat near the hearth, his cane resting by the chair. Not out of frailty, but habit. At fifty-five and seven months into widowhood, he carried the weight of someone who had lived through worse and didn't speak of it unless asked. His teenage grandson, Taran Gunn, sat beside him, sipping tea with the quiet concentration of a boy raised to observe. Someone had sent him to Callum after the funeral, likely to keep them both steady.

Ewan scribbled notes beside them, trying to shape the unknown into something legible. Alec stood against the wall, arms folded, speaking a little, reading much. Morven from the shop had come as well, her expression unreadable. Peter Mackay was there, the boy from the croft who once fixed a radio using parts from a toaster. He sat cross-legged by the fire like someone waiting to be useful.

Mairi stirred the pot, watching bubbles rise and burst. The smell of lentils and dried herbs filled the space. Plain food. Enough to go around, enough to last the week. She wasn't sure if this gathering would hold. It felt uncertain, thrown together. But she had told Hamish it would. She wanted to believe it.

Sorcha stood by the window, eyes on the world outside.

"They're mapping us," she said. Her voice was calm. "Not with soldiers. With our devices. Movement patterns. We need to go quiet. Live in shadow."

Alec raised an eyebrow. "You're saying we become ghosts?"

Sorcha turned to him. She looked sure.

"They don't need a reason anymore." She held up her phone, then dropped it into the basket at the center of the table. Taran and Peter followed, placing their own phones beside hers.

Mairi was still writing. She wrote a few numbers she wanted to save, then set her phone in the basket too.

"Once you're in the system, you're just a number connected to a scan," Sorcha said. "Move the wrong way, say the wrong thing, think the wrong thought, and they track you."

She walked toward the center of the room and lowered her voice. "The biometric IDs aren't about who we are. They're about control. A leash you can't see but feel every time you breathe."

Alec's arms stayed crossed, but the skepticism in his face faded.

"And if we keep refusing to register?" he asked.

"We disappear anyway," she said. "Not by their hands, but by time. By isolation. The only difference is that we choose how we go. Quiet. Together. Still human."

For a moment, no one spoke. The rain tapped against the stone walls. Alec looked at Sorcha again. This time, he saw the weight she carried.

"Ghosts it is, then," he said. He pulled the battery from his phone because it might be useful later, then dropped his device into the basket.

They talked into the night. About winter. About bread and how long the flour might last. About wounds that wouldn't heal. And whether they'd physically fight, if it came to that. Mairi ladled the stew. Peter passed out the small flint strikers he'd made from broken lighters.

Before they left, Morven handed out some small paper bags filled with homemade biscuits. Each had a handwritten tag that read: You matter. On the back was another thistle.

The next morning, Mairi and Sorcha stood outside, watching the smoke rise from four chimneys. The village wasn't safe. Not yet. But something had started. It wasn't much, but it stood. And it would not vanish quietly.

Chapter 4

The Wind

It began with the wind. Not the playful kind that dances through the rowan trees or stirs drying laundry on a summer day, but the long, haunted kind that sweeps in from the North Sea - dragging salt and mist over the broken stones of forgotten graves, pressing against the hills with the weight of old oaths and things left undone. By mid-afternoon, it had grown into a presence - an elemental force that scraped at the slates of the cottages, flattened the moors, and pushed against Glendarragh with an unyielding, brutal will.

Mairi felt it first in the lean-to. The air became a hum, as it pushed its way into the walls through every cracked stone and mortar. She and Sorcha were crouched over the inverter, trying for the third time that week to coax it back to life. The wires spat once - then fell silent, the spark fizzling out with a dull finality that made the room feel colder.

Sorcha cursed, her fingers pink and raw. "Damn connections. It's like the machine knows it's not welcome in the modern world."

Mairi steadied the torch, its beam weak in the gathering dusk. "Maybe it doesn't want to come back."

Sorcha gave a half-smile, but the heaviness stayed on her shoulders. "It's not a ghost, Mairi. It's a box."

Mairi looked out at the moor, where the wind scoured the earth bare. "Everything's a ghost these days."

Up on the ridge, Alec's truck groaned against the incline, its engine struggling in the biting cold. One of the diesel drums had frozen to the truck bed. He stepped out, boots crunching against frost. The moor lay wide and open. The sky wavered, unsure of itself, its clouds slipping out of form before they could settle. Light scattered without aim, and the moor below bent with it - shadow folding into shadow, as if the land couldn't remember where it ended.

In that silence, Alec could hear his own heartbeat.

He walked to the edge of the loch, its surface a dark mirror fractured by the wind. The canvas satchel felt heavier than it should. Inside: several dozen mobile devices, and the ghosts of a world that still tried to speak through them.

He untied the satchel, drew one phone after another, and tossed them in - each breaking the water with a muted plunk. Ripples widened, then vanished.

The last phone he held a moment longer - small, green-cased, still warm. Someone had taped a note to it. "In case you need to reach me." He peeled it off, folded it in half, and pocketed it. Then he threw the phone, hard. It skipped twice, then sank.

The loch settled back into stillness. No signal. No trace.

He stood for a long time, watching the water.

In his cottage, Ewan lit the fire with careful hands. The dry heather caught, soaked in paraffin. The scent lifted memories - nights in Aberdeen, talks in dim halls, warnings offered to deaf ears. Once, in Geneva, he'd tried to explain soft fracture theory to a room of polished men who nodded without hearing. They had gone on to fund biometric grids and predictive logistics. Now the wind tested every seam in the stone, and the matches mattered more than the models.

By evening, the circle had formed in Callum Gunn's cottage. A growing storm hissed at the windows. The fire in the hearth threw shadows across the room; light danced on tired faces, worn coats, and half-empty glasses. The table, ancient and nicked with time, bore bowls of stew and warm bannocks.

Callum offered more wine without ceremony. Sorcha arrived late, soaked through and shivering, frustration clinging to her like the storm. Alec laid out a map. Mairi dished out second-helpings of stew. Morven lingered near the kettle, hands seeking heat.

"We lost the grid this afternoon," Sorcha began, unzipping her jacket. "Every relay. Not a glitch. A choice. It's on purpose."

Callum's face darkened. "They'll call it a transition."

"They always do," Ewan muttered, his eyes focused on the map.

Alec shook his head. "So, what? Do we sit here and wait? Until they scan our roofs?"

Mairi set her bowl down. "We prepare."

Ewan pushed his notebook forward. It held grids, names, questions. "A community survives not by what it owns, but by how many ways it can solve the same problem."

He tapped the paper. "If Mairi falls, who can stitch? If Alec's batteries fail, who charges? If I'm taken, who reads the map?"

Callum leaned in. "You're building a clan."

Ewan nodded. "Not by blood. By backup."

The wind wailed through the chimney. Sorcha stared at the flames. "I used to think it was noise. Now it sounds like a warning."

No one laughed, but expressions showed they agreed.

Ewan reached into his pocket. A slip of paper, the one he got from Morven, now creased and smudged. The words *you matter* were still visible. It curled around his fingers. The silence that followed was full, almost sacred.

Callum rose. He walked to the fire. "I'll tell you a story," he said, and the room stilled.

"A winter, sixty days of frozen moor. The sheep vanished. I was a boy. Someone - nameless - left bread on the doorsteps of each cottage every third night. No one ever saw who. But the hope it gave us never left. The spring came, and we survived. We found the sheep. But nobody ever forgot the bread," he said. "What we need to do right now is keep our hope alive."

The wind keened, but Glendarragh did not flinch.

Before they parted, Ewan unrolled a second map of Wick.

"We will need what they've left behind," he said to the group. "Medicine. Tools. The city is empty now. But it still has resources."

Alec frowned. "You want to go back in?"

"When the grid drops," Ewan replied. "That's our window. The locks fail. The eyes go dark."

Sorcha hesitated. "They've got facial pings. Heat traces."

"Only while the power flows," Ewan said. "No power, no leash."

Mairi didn't speak. But her hand tightened around the handle of her bag.

CHAPTER 5

The Gathering

In the pale aftermath of the windstorm, Mairi moved through the glen with a worn canvas bag slung over her shoulder, her old nurse's notebook tucked beneath her arm. Although the rain had stopped, the land remained drenched. Everything dripped - gutters, gateposts, broken windows - an endless rhythm of water cascading down stone. Glendarragh lay before her like something wounded, its spirit dampened but not broken. Smoke trailed from three chimneys. The rest of the village remained still, cold.

At the McCallum cottage, she found the boy lying in a heap by the hearth. He'd fallen trying to carry firewood, his ribs bruised from the impact. Mairi wrapped him, pressing warm cloths against his side and advising him to drink nettle tea for its healing properties. She told his mother to boil all the water just in case. There was no room for uncertainty now.

At the McGrath cottage, she found the grandmother sitting in silence beside an empty hearth. Her face was blank, her eyes hollow with grief, her hands trembling as she accepted the bread Mairi offered. She didn't speak. She didn't need to. There were no men left in that house, only ghosts. Mairi noted two words in her notebook: wood and companionship. The essentials, if one could call them that.

At the toolshed, Sorcha and Alec worked together, their movements synchronized yet uneasy. His old inverter had survived. They rerouted the charge controller, fused copper with scraped solder, and tested the battery three times. The second, the light flickered. The third, it held. Alec leaned back, his knees protesting the position, and wiped his brow.

"Didn't think you'd pull it off," he muttered.

Sorcha wiped her hands on her coat. "Didn't think you'd let me try."

He almost smiled, but the moment passed, swallowed by the weight of the world around them.

Then Sorcha noticed the rucksack in the corner, sealed tight, lined with supplies and a pair of new boots beside it.

"Alec," she said, her voice low. "Planning a solo run?"

He didn't answer. He ignored the question and adjusted the wire.

Up on the ridge, Callum used his cane like a mountaineering pole. The valley below him breathed in its own way, a rhythm that he had come to recognize over the years. The land, the people, and the sky were all interconnected. Beside him, Ewan sat on a flat stone, a thick page spread across his lap.

"Can't remember the names of the Ferguson twins," Ewan muttered. His brow furrowed as he looked over his notes, the names and faces a blur in his mind. He drew two lines across the page, his fingers tapping the pen as he worked. "We can't afford to forget people. Not when memory's the record we've got."

Callum looked out toward the sea, his eyes narrowing. "In the old days, bards carried lineages in their heads. Names, feuds, marriages. Memory was a weapon."

Ewan tapped the paper. "Maybe this is our weapon now."

That night, the fire crackled in the center of Callum's kitchen. The table had been cleared, save for the bowls awaiting a late night broth and bread. The kettle steamed, a quiet hum filling the space. Alec remembered the days when the village gathered like a family, when the flames of the hearth weren't for warmth, but for shared stories and unity. Now, they gathered, bound by the need to survive.

Around the table sat eight people of different ages, trades, and temperaments. Mairi ladled out broth into bowls, the smell filling the air like a small, comforting miracle. Ewan stood, holding his notebook, the weight of his words pressing down on the room.

"Every system we relied on," he began, his voice firm, "was optimized for obedience, not resilience. We have to work harder to become our own redundancy."

His survival plans for the village were becoming more detailed. He turned the page in the notebook, his eyes scanning the diagram he had drawn. "Three sources for heat. Three for food. Three for communication. Every skill doubled. Every plan cross-covered."

Alec scoffed, arms crossed over his chest. "You want to spreadsheet survival?"

"No," Ewan replied, his voice steady. "I want to stop it from becoming luck."

The room hummed with disagreement. Morven worried about the fairness of the rations. Alec argued they needed weapons, not words. The conversations circled like the wind outside, each point pushing against another without resolution.

Callum listened in silence, his hand resting on his cane. Then, when the room grew still, he spoke.

"When one of my ancestors - six greats back, I think - was sixteen," he said, with the faintest smile at the absurdity of time, "he hid a printing press in a peat shed during the Clearances. They used it to make fake tenancy papers for those evicted. He wasn't a fighter. He was a printer. That was his rebellion. Everyone needs to contribute the skills they have."

The weight of his words settled over them like a blanket.

"Some oaths," Callum added, "are older than kings."

Mairi didn't speak, but she looked like she wanted to. The fire cast soft shadows, flickering against the backs of hands and the rims of mugs. She looked down at her own fingers that were weathered, blistered, and stained from nettles.

"I made people scan," she said. Her voice was low, matter-of-fact, like a weather report. Ewan set down his notebook. Mairi's gaze stayed on the fire.

"In the prior weeks, before the networks failed, I was on the inside. We were told it was for triage. Prioritizing treatment, isolating risk. But it wasn't. It was filtering. I watched a man refuse to scan, and they locked him in a supply closet. No trial. No care. He died there."

She looked up. Her eyes met Sorcha's, then Alec's. "And I said nothing. I told myself it was temporary. That it wasn't my call."

She stood. "I want to believe I'm different. That this place, this choice, makes me different. But I don't know. And if we're building something honest, then you should know who's helping you build it."

No one knew what to say, not even Callum.

After a long silence, Iona stepped forward, no older than six or seven. She was holding a biscuit in both hands, as though unsure whether she was part of the circle. She walked to Mairi, placed a biscuit in her hand, and said, "Thank you for making me tea."

Mairi gave her a hug and tried to smile. It broke halfway.

Then Sorcha stood. "Then let's agree," she said. "We don't erase what came before. But we don't chain ourselves to it either."

Ewan, slow to nod, said, "The map isn't our past or our future. It's the shape of things right now."

Mairi sat back down. She didn't speak for the rest of the night. But at the end of the meeting, she asked one simple question.

"What do we promise? Not what to fight. Not who to blame. But what to promise?"

They answered, each one speaking, their voices soft but sure.

"To share food."

"To teach skills."

"To hide the weak."

"To bury our dead, no matter what."

"To remember each other."

Callum closed his eyes, a slight nod of approval in the silence that followed. "That'll do."

Outside, the wind had softened, though it carried with it the chill of the night. The hills lay dark and silent. The stars above the moor blinked, their light flickering through the vast expanse of the sky. And for the first time in weeks, Glendarragh slept with something that felt like purpose.

CHAPTER 6

The Snow

The snow came with large, lazy flakes drifting down in a steady, hypnotic descent - no urgency in its fall, it clings, stacks, builds. Branches bow under its weight, rooftops thicken with pristine layers, and footpaths vanish beneath it. It reshapes the landscape, each flake a silent messenger bearing the weight of winter's arrival.

Sorcha woke to it, her breath blooming in a cold plume above her sleeping bag, the chill creeping in around the edges like a trespasser she could never quite keep out. The frost had worked its way through the stone walls again, a familiar invader settling into the bones of the house. The draft was always the same - persistent, unyielding. But now, Sorcha could read its mood: a whisper of warning brushing against everything it touched.

She sat up, joints stiff beneath three jumpers and a scarf fashioned from old curtains. The house groaned in its sleep, timber and stone shifting against the cold as if resisting it on principle. Mairi, of course, was already up. The smell of something warm drifted through the air - oats, maybe, or burnt tea. Sustenance, not luxury. Sorcha stretched, trying to shed the last fragments of sleep.

Downstairs, Mairi stood by the stove, boiling water in an old kettle that wheezed more than whistled. Its iron belly pitted with age, marked by use, like everything else they trusted. Mairi's hands shook from fatigue or cold. It was hard to tell. But Sorcha knew she hadn't slept. The lines around her eyes betrayed her.

"How long do you think the snow will last?" Sorcha asked.

Mairi didn't answer at first, just shrugged. She handed over a mug, its warmth almost too much to hold. "We're out of mint," she said, as if that were all the world had lost.

Sorcha nodded. It didn't matter. Nothing like that mattered anymore.

Outside, the world appeared scrubbed clean, leaving the glen hushed and bleached. The snow softened every edge, stilled every motion. Even time felt slower, caught under the same hush as the land. But the cold did not pause. It marched onward, remorseless, turning each movement into an act of deliberation.

A few hours later Mairi moved through it, her body bent against the wind, breath fogging in bursts. The notebook in her pocket felt heavier now, but not because of what it held, because of all it could not. She checked the pipes at the Fergusons', sealed a broken pane for Morven, left firestarter at the McCallums'.

But one cottage showed no footprints. No smoke. No answer.

She marked the lintel with a small X, slow and deliberate, the chalk catching in the worn grain of the wood. It was a language without words. A final accounting: no breath here, no fire, no stir of life within these walls. Just the hush of stone and dust, the quiet settling of things left behind.

Each mark she made seemed to weigh heavier than the last, a tally of absences written across the glen. Once, these cottages sang with voices, rang with work, and let laughter spill into the fields. Now, only the wind remained, and even it seemed to miss the sounds people used to make.

She stepped back, the X pale against the weathered lintel, and for a moment it felt less like a message for the living and more like a small, unfinished prayer for the dead. She planned to send a small group into the cottage later. They would receive a proper funeral, and the village would reclaim any surplus supplies.

Alec was knee-deep in curses when Sorcha arrived, her arms full of cable and her teeth chattering. The storm had slammed the generator harder than expected, and Alec's patience had been the first casualty.

"Spare me the lecture," he muttered without looking up.

"I wasn't going to say anything," Sorcha lied. "But maybe if you didn't ground the thing like that..."

"Hand me the crimper."

They worked in silence, a symphony of breath and spark, of tools clicking in the cold. Wire, breath, wire, click. The generator sputtered, coughed, then held a steady hum.

Alec didn't smile, but he gave a small nod. That was enough.

Sorcha wiped her nose, fingers numbed. "Still keeping the go-bag, are you?"

He didn't answer. Just tightened the last bolt, neat and silent.

"I get it," Sorcha murmured.

At noon, Ewan and Callum stood again atop the ridge, the glen below stretching into a blank page. The snow made everything feel vast and more intimate - familiar, and somehow distant. Ewan marked the safe paths in his book, his hand steady. Callum made notches in his walking stick, scanning the horizon with an old hunter's eye.

"This rise here," Ewan said, pointing to the slope ahead, "could house a supply cache. Three ways in. Two out."

Callum nodded, squinting into the white. "You make maps like this before?"

Ewan hesitated. "I made them. For other people. This one is more important."

That night, they gathered in the old grain store. Someone had rigged netting across the rafters, stringing old jars into lanterns, each one flickering with a tea light. The place felt like a seance for the living - half ceremony, half shelter - the present and the past felt braided together.

Mairi's stew simmered on the hearth, rich with roots and scraps of meat. Sorcha passed around thyme and biscuits. Alec brought fuel. Morven, her hands inked and calloused, distributed small wrapped loaves of homemade bread.

Callum offered a song. His voice was rough and war-weathered, but it carried. Children curled near the fire on blankets. One girl played a low, winding tune on a wooden whistle while her sister hummed her own fractured lullaby.

No one counted portions. No one hoarded. There was enough when there were no others to take it.

It wasn't perfect, but it was real.

Ewan sat back, notebook closed for once. He watched them, the way they moved, so generous, and alive. The fire crackled, its warm glow a fragile promise of a world that remembered how to care. If they could keep it burning, they might yet have a chance. But what if the winds blew too hard? What if the storm never passed?

Then he thought, this is how civilizations begin again.

Later, as the fire fell to embers and the shadows grew long, Sorcha found him standing outside, his breath rising into the star-pricked dark.

The moor was silent beneath the sky.

"We are doing it," she said. "This is something."

Ewan nodded. "But will it hold?"

She didn't answer. Instead, she pointed to the distant hill beyond the village.

"Was it decided that is where the tower will go?"

Ewan looked at her, nodded, then looked past her.

"You think they're listening?"

"No, not yet. But they will."

They stood in silence and listened to the night together.

CHAPTER 7

The Signal

I t started at 03:12, with a whisper threaded through the wire. It was not a broadcast, but a pulse.

Sorcha sat hunched in the shed, a wool blanket draped over her shoulders, her breath fogging against the cracked windowpane. Outside, the wind groaned through the village, steady and wild, pressing against the glass with rhythmic insistence. But the sound she heard wasn't from the wind. It thrummed through the bones of her machine, through the copper veins she'd soldered together by candlelight, through the antenna she'd raised like a limb toward the sky. Then there was a flicker crossed the screen, followed by a faint line, a pause, then three dots, and silence.

She leaned closer. The machine hummed beneath her fingers, as if aware of its own awakening. The antenna, cobbled together from stripped coaxial cable, twisted tinfoil, and the mount of a broken wind vane, should not have worked. The signal booster, pulled from the guts of a smart kettle, definitely should not have. But somehow, it did, and the sky had answered.

The frequency was unsecured - 870.39 MHz. She squinted. Her hands moved, almost instinctively, typing before her doubt could catch up to her. "Who is this?" she keyed in. There was a pause, the cursor blinking, and then the same three dots returned. Her skin prickled. This wasn't a message. It was a rhythm. A presence.

The battery monitor read 7%. The glow from the screen pulsed, as if it were breathing with her. She recognized the pattern from the surveillance work she had done in Aberdeen. This wasn't a transmission meant for her. Maybe it was a behavioral probe or something crafted to trigger a reaction. Was it listening for voices? Could it be scanning for reflexes, or mapping anomalies?

She typed again, slower now: "What are you looking for?" The reply came with three dots, then a sweep of white noise. Then silence. A chill ran through her, something primal.

This wasn't a broadcast. It was a net. Someone had seen them.

By the time she reached Mairi's house, Sorcha's boots had soaked through, and her knuckles cracked from the cold. The wind had risen, slicing through her scarf as if it wasn't there. Her face was flushed and her heart pounding with genuine fear.

Mairi opened the door mid-bandage. A boy sat on the kitchen table, arm outstretched, eyes glassy and unfocused. Mairi's hands moved with calm urgency, her voice steady and low as she reassured him. She looked up as Sorcha burst in, clutching the laptop under her arm like a shield.

"Something found us," Sorcha said.

Mairi blinked. "What?"

Sorcha dropped the laptop on the table and pulled up the signal log, fingers clacking fast.

"Predictive sweep," she said. "Patterned noise, frequency matching - 870 MHz. This isn't broadcast. It's bait. They're testing the perimeter."

Mairi's face remained composed. "You're sure?"

Sorcha nodded.

Mairi turned back to the boy, finished the wrap, touched his forehead, and handed him a cup of tea. Only then did she face Sorcha again. "Drone?"

"No. Worse. Pattern logic. Not an automated scan. Human-crafted. It's looking for anything - anyone - to blink."

"And you blinked," Mairi said.

Sorcha nodded. "I blinked."

Ten minutes later, Ewan arrived, his coat stiff with frost, boots crusted in ice. He didn't speak as Sorcha explained. He listened, eyes steady, breath tight. He took the laptop, ran a few diagnostics, scrolled through the signal history, then nodded.

"It's OK. It's not about what they hear," he said. "It's about who moves."

Outside, the wind howled across the glen. Alec appeared in the doorway, uninvited, his expression stone.

"So it's over," Alec said.

"No," Sorcha replied. "I think it has just begun."

That night, the meeting in the grain store was different. There was no stew. No idle talk. The air was close, thick with peat smoke and damp wool. Everyone sat a little straighter, their faces drawn toward the flame like moths unsure whether to flee or burn.

"They found us?" Morven asked, voice brittle.

"Not exactly," Sorcha replied. "They cast a net. We're in the splash zone."

"They will come," Alec growled. "It's a matter of time."

"We go dark," Mairi muttered.

"No," Ewan said. "If we vanish, they'll look harder."

"So we do nothing?" Alec spat.

"No," Ewan said again. "We build a ghost."

The group leaned in to hear his plan.

"We build a decoy," he continued. "A signal that looks real. Random data loops. Irregular enough to suggest life, structured enough to hold their attention. But not on us."

Mairi frowned. "You want to build... what? A trap?"

"A mirror," Ewan answered.

"And if they don't take the bait?" Alec asked.

"Then we've still said nothing," Ewan replied.

By morning, the village held its breath. Snow had begun again, falling in slow spirals. Sorcha walked along the ridge with Ewan, a coil of wire slung over her shoulder, a blueprint folded in her coat.

"You think they'll buy it?" she asked.

"I think," he said. "They'll consider it."

"Why?"

"Because uncertainty slows them down."

In the lower fields, Callum and Alec stood over the old sheep barn. The roof had collapsed, but the stonework held.

"We dig under it," Callum said. "Dry chamber. Drainage. Big enough to store, maybe to sleep us all."

"And if they scan from above?" Alec asked.

"We layer the roof with stone, dead branches. Seed moss," Sorcha said, stepping into the conversation. "We make it look wrong."

"We can't keep them out forever," Alec muttered.

"No," Ewan said. "But we can stay one step ahead."

They worked in silence. Days passed in a quiet rhythm of digging, stacking, soldering, and weaving. Morven's youngest packed flour into vacuum jars. Hamish sorted batteries by charge weight. Mairi organized caches of medical supplies, each one buried with a handwritten map and survival instructions. They set up the fake antenna on the decoy structure. And from inside, they sent fake signals.

Each time, the response came: three dots, pause, three dots.

"They're patient," Ewan said one night.

"They have the time to be," Sorcha replied.

By week's end, the signal changed. Now it pulsed in triplets - three dots, three dashes, three dots. It was an S.O.S. in Morse code. They stared at the screen in silence.

"Someone's playing us," Alec muttered.

"Or someone else got caught in the net," Mairi whispered.

"Or someone wants us to think they did," Ewan added.

That night, they didn't meet in the grain store. They gathered instead in the chapel, where some of its missing beams exposed the stars. There was no fire, only candles.

They spoke of fallback plans. Of what to do if the woods turned hostile, or the skies filled with drones, like they had over Wick. But then they also spoke of something else.

"We don't hide," Callum said. "We confuse them. That's how we win."

"They want to find something." Ewan said. "So, let's make them think they did."

Sorcha nodded. "We make even more noise. Just nowhere near us."

They installed a second mirror signal in the ruins of a pub south of the glen. It broadcast erratic pings - heat, light, movement. Enough to mimic life. Enough to bait attention. But inside, there was nothing. No maps. No food. Only burnt wires and the ghost of a presence no one had ever seen. They made it appear as if someone was holding out there.

That would be the bait.

A week later, they intercepted a new pulse. This time, the metadata held five letters.

C.R.A.N.E.

Sorcha's face paled. "It's corporate. Not military. CRANE stands for Corporate Reconnaissance and Neural Exploitation."

Ewan frowned. "That's worse."

"Why?" Asked Callum.

"Because corps don't negotiate," said Sorcha. "They audit."

They built faster. Two more small hiding places. One under the croft. One beneath the chapel. Lanterns extinguished. Supplies moved. Water saved. The glen fell quiet. Even the winter birds sang more cautiously. Mairi recorded every wound, every illness. Ewan mapped escape routes. Callum told stories no one had heard before.

Sorcha, working late, whispered to her screen. "Come take the bait."

The signal blinked three dots. And then - for the first time - four.

On the forty-eighth day, the wind changed. It blew warm from the south, carrying the scent of metal and fire. Everyone noticed. And that night, as they stood outside the chapel in silence, a single light broke the horizon. They stayed still. Whatever it was, it wasn't a star.

Maybe it was a drone, but they could not be sure. It held in the air for a long time before disappearing.

CHAPTER 8

The Arrival

A thick snowfall hushed the glen, but a foreign presence broke the storm's silence. Mairi saw it first while making tea, gazing out the window at the last light of day. At first, she mistook the movement for a swaying branch or the wind folding snow into strange shapes. But the motion was too deliberate. The figure was a woman, dark and hunched. Weak and struggling, she made her way down the path from the ridge through the drifts.

Mairi set the kettle aside and stepped outside without thinking, her boots slipping on the ice. Callum and his grandson Taran were behind her in moments. The figure staggered, then collapsed. Mairi caught her just in time - a frail, soaked body crumpling into her arms. The young woman's eyes were open but unfocused, her face pale and slick with meltwater, stark against the biting wind.

Callum and Taran lifted the girl between them and carried her inside, laying her beside the fire. Her clothes were wet through, layered in thick padding with hand-stitched insulation. Each garment peeled away, heavy with ice. By the time they'd removed the last outer layers - high-laced boots caked in frozen mud, a sodden shawl, and a coat that resisted laying flat - it was clear she had been carrying seventy pounds extra or more.

"She's alive," Mairi said, checking the girl's neck for a pulse. "No wounds. Just spent."

They laid her on a pillow near the hearth. The warmth crept in, reviving her skin from white to pale pink. Her breath steadied, but she did not wake. Hours passed.

The others gathered - Ewan, Sorcha, Alec, and Morven - sitting in silence around the fire, their faces full of curiosity. They had been in a blackout for months now. The flames flickered when the girl stirred. Her eyelids twitched, then opened.

"Oh," she said, voice barely more than a breath. She sat up and looked around the room, her eyes adjusting to the low light. "Where am I?"

Mairi leaned in. "You're in Glendarragh. Weren't you trying to get here? Or are you lost?"

"I was headed for Wick. I'm Isla," she said.

"Bloody hell," muttered Callum.

"There's nobody left in Wick," Mairi said. "You're lucky we found you. I'm Mairi."

Isla accepted the tea Mairi offered, her hands trembling around the cup.

"My parents told me to go north," she said. "I had tickets for Wick. But the train diverted. I ended up in Georgemas Junction when they started scanning for biometric IDs."

Sorcha stiffened. That part, at least, was true. No one in the room bore an ID. Neither did Isla. A glance passed among them - cautious, but conclusive. For now, she was one of them.

"You walked seventeen miles in the wrong direction," Sorcha stated. "Why?"

"Who are they?" Mairi leaned forward. "Your parents, who are they?"

The girl hesitated. "People who didn't want me trapped inside London with them. They sent me off in a hurry, thought we had more time. They helped build it, but they never agreed with it. A lot of people don't agree with it."

Ewan studied her. "They helped build it? What is it? This man-made disaster?"

"They aren't bad people," she whispered. "They gave me things to..." her voice drifted.

Without prompting, Isla sat upright and began unpacking the layers of items sewn into her clothes. What spilled out was more than survival gear. It was testimony.

Inside the linings were threads of messages, stitched in her mother's hand.

"Be brave, my love."

"Never forget we love you."

"Not an end. A new beginning."

Sorcha leaned closer, and Ewan's expression changed, the way it always did when he saw a pattern emerging.

Item by item, Isla laid out small treasures: a bundled cloth scented with lavender, concealing a crinkled map of Scotland scribbled with escape tunnels and a dozen wrong turns no one had corrected, annotated with footpaths and hidden routes. A leather pouch of survival tools - antibiotics, water purification tablets, fine metal implements, a weathered book filled with encrypted codes, names, and tactical annotations. It was a survival philosophy, with notes on underground networks and diagrams of systemic collapse.

There was a small palm-sized device with a glowing screen, it featured some kind of signal emitter or beacon, its use unknown. She uncovered a silver spiral pendant embedded with microchips and engraved. She placed a second pendant beside it. It was heavier, darker, and blinking. Was it a chip or a trap? Sorcha wondered, but said nothing. Her gaze narrowed.

Another notebook followed, one more personal. It held names, dates, surveillance breakdowns, behavioral cue maps, and blind spots in biometric systems. It was not a diary, it was a field manual of rebellion.

From a double-stitched sleeve, Isla pulled out one last item, a map of Glendarragh, marked in red ink with tunnels, safe-houses, and forgotten doors. Mairi gasped.

Laid before them on the floor, the objects looked like scattered survival gear, but read together, they told a different story about escape, love, and defiance.

Taran watched her from across the room. Isla met his eyes. In that brief look, something passed between them.

Callum said nothing, but his silence carried weight. Whatever comes, we keep her safe, he thought.

Alec paced, muttering under his breath. He was unconvinced, and he wanted someone else to admit the unusual nature of the situation.

Isla didn't speak for a long while after laying out her gear. She stared into the fire, motionless. When a child offered her a piece of dried apple, she took it and bit down, chewed it slowly. Across the firelight, Mairi noticed her fingers twitching - she was nervous, scared maybe. It was hard to tell.

Callum was the first to speak. "Well, you made it here," he said. "You are safe, that is what counts. We can give you a place to sleep."

Even Alec's suspicion softened. Still, he stood at the door, arms crossed.

"She's a risk," he muttered.

"You're projecting," Sorcha snapped back.

"She took a risk," Mairi countered.

"I don't trust her." Alec spoke with his hands, then crossed his arms again.

"You don't have to," Sorcha added, her eyes fixed on the pendant. "But, that's Tier 2. Civilians don't touch tech like that. Someone important sent her."

Ewan made a quiet note in his ledger: She's a wildcard. One variable changes the model.

The following afternoon, Ewan walked the ridge alone. The snow creaked beneath his boots. The land, once steady, now felt brittle, as if it too had learned not to trust. He knelt and wrote in his ledger: Visibility: 38%. Entry points: 4. Trust decay: accelerating. And beneath it, a single line: Her name is Isla.

That night, Sorcha and Alec patrolled. They moved fast, silent and separate. At the streambed, Alec crouched low.

"Prints," he said.

"Fox," Sorcha offered, but there was uncertainty in her voice.

She glanced at him. "You still think she's a plant?"

Alec thought for a moment.

"No," he said. "Now I think she's real. And that's worse."

Back in the cottage, Isla sat by the fire with Mairi beside her. Callum lit another candle.

Outside, the wind picked up again.

CHAPTER 9

The Ledgers

E wan opened a new pen, pausing before writing as if the words required more than thought. They demanded permission. His hand hovered over the page, uncertain. Then he wrote: Isla - boiler repair, basic coding, observational memory - provisional.

He underlined "provisional" twice, the ink sharp against the page. The fire snapped in the hearth, its warmth not yet pushing out the cold that pressed against the cottage walls. His breath made soft curls above the ledger as he exhaled. He watched the mist vanish. Outside it was bright, but the snowdrifts rolled like waves across the glen, obscuring the world in a tide of white.

Ewan stared at the top of the ledger: Glendarragh Resilience Map. The entries sprawled out like the tendrils of root systems - names, skills, vulnerabilities. It had started as an exercise in survival. Now it was something else.

One name sat alone: Naomi (redacted).

That was his daughter. His only child. The first person he had lost in the new order of things. A soft pang of grief twisted in his chest, but it was a feeling he had learned to live with. Or at least, endure.

Naomi had never known privilege. Ewan had done his best to provide, though they lived a life of work, love, and quiet understanding in a fragile village community. Still, Naomi grew up sensing the world was changing in ways she couldn't yet name.

At fifteen, she met Pascal, a boy from France, staying that summer at an estate outside the village. He was the son of a powerful man, part of the elite shaping the systems that would later tighten around them all. Pascal carried an unfamiliar confidence; a quiet intensity that set him apart. Naomi felt drawn to him. He seemed drawn to her just as much. They spent their days walking the coast, speaking of dreams and futures neither could yet see, unaware of how fast the world was shifting beneath them.

Pascal's father, Charles Lefevre, was no fool. Though entangled in the architecture of control, he saw the collapse coming. In Naomi, he saw someone the world would crush. And in his son's love for her, he saw a narrow chance to help.

Years passed. The bond between Naomi and Pascal endured. By then, the tightening had begun - the surveillance, the checkpoints, the fear. Naomi's parents knew they couldn't shield her much longer.

Pascal returned to Scotland not as a guest, but with intent. He asked for Naomi's hand out of love, but also because he understood what was coming.

Ewan and his wife agreed. It was a way to protect her. The match, at least, was genuine. And though they knew they might never see her again, they let her go.

Months later, Ewan's wife passed away in her sleep. They offered no explanation. He knew, however, that it was heartache. The memory is still too painful to bear. Everything lost, everything stolen.

Across the way, in a small building above the burn, Mairi knelt beside Sorcha, watching her work on the receiver. The cold had seeped into their bones, but neither of them flinched. Sorcha adjusted the dial, her fingers steady despite the sharp bite of the wind.

"Here," Sorcha said, her voice low, almost reverent. "Listen."

A faint click. Then a hiss. Then, a code fragment - numbers, random, beautiful. Not a language, but it held meaning for those who knew how to listen.

"What does it mean?" Mairi asked, the words slipping out like a question long feared but never spoken.

"It doesn't matter," Sorcha said, eyes on the dial. "What matters is I think it's civilian, which means someone else is out there."

Mairi nodded, though the unease gnawed at her.

"Like us." She said.

"Like us." Sorcha looked up, something flaring in her eyes - a question, maybe a fear. "You ever wonder how many others stayed behind?"

Mairi didn't answer. She passed her a thermos instead. She was thinking about other places people might hide.

At the Mairi's cottage that night, Ewan proposed a more detailed plan.

"One person logs skills," Ewan said. "One maintains the rotation chart. One verifies health status weekly. This isn't about control. It's resilience. It's how we remember who we are."

Morven raised a hand. "Who decides what's worth remembering?"

Ewan blinked. "We all do."

Alec, arms crossed at the door, shook his head. "We didn't vote on this."

"It's not a law," Ewan replied. "It's a record."

Callum stood. He set a wooden box on the table - the sound of it landing louder than expected.

Inside were dozens of small stones, each painted with a symbol. One for milk. One for bread. One for carrots.

"My grandmother made them," Callum said. "We couldn't read yet. She'd give us money, send us kids into Wick with stones so we'd remember what to buy."

He looked at Ewan. "Some memories don't need ink – they're carried in people."

Sorcha passed Ewan a folded note. Her face was quiet and purposeful.

"What's this?" he asked.

"Encrypted archive index," she said. "If anything happens, this holds it. But you'll need the code. I'm giving the code to you."

Ewan nodded, eyes scanning. "Thank you."

Then Sorcha held up a tape recorder and pressed play.

"My name is Sorcha. Today, I found this tape recorder."

She reached into her coat and pulled out a piece of slate, smoothed and palm-sized. Scratched into its surface: a spiral.

"People keep asking what it means," she said. "They think it's code. Or a direction."

Ewan studied it. "Isn't it?"

"No," she said.

They all waited.

"It's life. It's a question. The center is the beginning, but you don't stay there. You move outward. Widening. Curving. And it never ends. That's what we are now. Not roots. Motion. Like a spiral. A spiral of memory and truth."

Ewan turned it over in his hands, then gave it to Callum when he reached for it.

"It's not a place," Callum said. "It's a shape."

She nodded. "It's a shape."

Ewan turned his attention to her. He hadn't realized it before, but he now understood documentation extended beyond ink and files. They needed to share stories, too.

They called it the second ledger.

Not everyone used it. Some listened, letting the words of others fill the silence, giving shape to something that couldn't live on paper.

From that day on, every gathering ended with one entry in voice, one in ink.

Paper burned and machines broke, but stories traveled through time.

And so Glendarragh documented itself also now in memories.

That night, Ewan retired to his study. The coals in the open fire were glowing red, so hot he had to crack a window. He flipped the ledger open and poured a dram of whisky. On a fresh page, he wrote: Memory is sacred.

He looked at it for too long. Then drew a line through the words and poured another dram.

CHAPTER 10

The Winterfall

The deep freeze came in late November. The village had always called it Winterfall. It wasn't one of the four sanctioned seasons, but in Glendarragh, it had earned its own name. Winterfall was the time between the first deep freeze and its thaw - a span that answered to no calendar. It could come early, slip in before the solstice, or stretch well beyond the first signs of spring. The lochs would harden to glass, the hills fall silent, and the air grow sharp enough to split stone. No almanac could predict it, no date could define it. Winterfall came when it chose and stayed as long as it liked. And only the people of Glendarragh called it Winterfall.

Mairi sat at the kitchen table, taking inventory of their staples with careful precision. She counted on her fingers as she wrote numbers down. The tally was lower than expected, too low. Salt was almost gone. She crossed out three recipes in the notebook without comment. She had already stopped naming them aloud. There was no point in discussing what they couldn't have, what was becoming out of reach. The silence between them was thick, the unspoken understanding hanging in the air during every meal.

Ewan noted that the sun had not broken the ridge in nineteen days. It was a subtle thing, the way the seasons shifted, but the evidence was undeniable.

Callum rubbed his palms together. "Did I ever tell you the first computer I ever saw was the size of an elevator? Needed its own room and two full time technicians to keep it running."

Ewan chuckled. "Mine had more keys than purpose, but it fit on a desk. And you couldn't sneeze near it without rebooting the entire system."

Callum nodded. "Ran weather models on it once. Took six hours to predict yesterday's rain."

Ewan poked the fire. "And yet people trusted it more than they trusted farmers."

Callum shrugged. "That's how you know the species was doomed. The first machines we built to think told us we didn't have to."

Laughter filled the cozy cottage.

In the shed, Alec sat hunched over the solar regulator, his hands moving with mechanical precision. The casing cracked under pressure, the delicate components inside exposed for the first time in ages. He placed the broken regulator on the hearth without a word, its once-bright panels now dim and useless.

Mairi opened her mouth, but then closed it again. There was nothing to say. No more words to waste.

Sorcha turned away, her eyes fixed on the flames, though they offered little comfort.

That night, Isla had a fever. She shivered in her sleep. Mairi sat beside her, the sponge in her hand cold against the warmth of the girl's skin. She hummed, an old protest lullaby her sister used to sing to her when they were children - before everything changed.

"I had a sister," Mairi whispered to the room, though no one looked at her. They were listening. "Black hair. Brilliant. She worked in a hospital, too, down in Inverness. The day the first blackout came, she stayed." Her voice wavered, breaking for a moment as she watched Isla's forehead, sweat beading on her skin.

Mairi's eyes tightened as she continued, her words softer now. "She said, 'If this is how it ends, let my last actions be kind.'"

The words hung in the air, but no one responded. The silence stretched around them, like a barrier too thick to break. By morning, Isla's fever had gone as quickly as it had come.

Later, Callum told a story by firelight, his voice low, almost reverent in the flickering warmth. He spoke of a village in 1871, one that had burned its own chapel to heat the orphan house during a brutal winter.

"They didn't do it because they lost faith," he said, his eyes distant. "They did it because they understood it. Sometimes, to survive, you have to make a choice. You have to know what to let go."

The weight of his words settled over them, thickening the air, making it heavier with the knowledge of sacrifice.

Then Alec stood, his movements slow and deliberate. He walked over to the pile of firewood, the remnants of their dwindling supplies, and picked up the last spare ladder. He broke it apart and placed it into the fire, the wood crackling as it burned.

Mairi added three wooden tools - things she'd once used without thinking but now had become more precious than useful. Sorcha broke down a crate that had once held the signal gear. They fed it to the flames without a word.

Choices had become simpler.

After the fire settled, Sorcha pulled a cloth bag from under a corner table. Inside were five books: a mechanical repair manual, a pocket almanac, a dog-eared guide to medicinal herbs, a poetry collection, and a textbook on electricity.

"I took them from the library. After the last buses," she said.

Alec raised an eyebrow. "That was risky."

Sorcha met his eyes. "Nobody saw," she mumbled. "The librarian volunteered to go."

"To be fair," said Callum, "it's not like there's anyone to return them to. The librarian's probably scanning barcodes for ration points in some concrete block, still pretending poetry could've saved us all."

Mairi reached into the bag and lifted the herb guide, like it might crumble. "This one I used to keep in the clinic. Before everything."

"We should get more," Ewan said. "We'll catalogue them. Store them somewhere safe."

Callum nodded. "A vault. Not for gold. For books."

They passed the books around and ate their meal in silence. Steam rose from bowls, curling up toward the low ceiling, the scent of food a fleeting luxury. Someone passed bread around the table. The simple act of sharing food had become a ritual, a silent acknowledgement of the life they clung to, no matter how frayed it had become.

Outside, the wind died down, its moan quieting to a dull howl. The snow drifted, softening the edges of the world. And for the first time in three weeks, the stars came back.

They pierced the black sky, bright, scattered like diamonds across the dark velvet canvas of night.

They sat together in the dark, their hands wrapped around chipped mugs of cooling tea, gazing out at the scatter of stars beyond the glass. When the Aurora flared across the sky - sudden and wild, like fire catching on invisible threads - Isla's tears came without sound, slipping down her cheeks unseen.

"You can't see the stars in the cities," she said.

Mairi squeezed her hand.

Later, Ewan sat alone, flipping through the ledger. The familiar pages were more ragged now from constant writing. He didn't write any names that night. Only one line: We remain.

He closed the book with a soft thud, his fingers lingering on the cover, as if waiting for something to return.

CHAPTER 11

Apricots & Bread

The cold ruled everything. Sinking into the stone and earth, it sealed the glen beneath a hardened shell of snow. Only the wind's mournful howl across the barren landscape broke the silence. The cottages, now almost invisible against the hills, had icicles hanging from their eaves. Time, it seemed, ceased to exist.

Sorcha stood at the ridge, her boots rimed with hoarfrost, watching the land through eyes that stung and watered in the bitter air. Isla stood beside her, buried in coarse wool, her hands jammed deep into her pockets, her face raw and cracked. Above them, the sky sagged low and gray.

Alec saw him first. The man stood alone on the far path, downhill from the old stone marker, at the lip of where the maps marked no-man's-land. He didn't wave or call. He stood there - stiff as the rocks half-buried in the snow, as if the earth had spat him out and left him to freeze. A bag hung from one shoulder. A coat, two sizes too large, draped from his frame like dead skin. His eyes gleamed, the whites raw against the gray of the world. Alec squinted, reading him the way one reads weather. He stamped the mark into the snow with the heel of his boot, memorized the man's position, and turned back to where they had built a low fire.

The circle buzzed with a low, uneasy urgency.

"He hasn't crossed the line," Ewan said. His hands hovered close to the fire, palms raw, the cracks in his skin bleeding.

"He hasn't left either," Sorcha murmured. Her voice was a tight thread, barely louder than the wind. She glanced back toward the ridge, toward the figure in the distance.

Alec muttered, "He looks like a man weighing his options."

Mairi stared into the fire's weak light. Then, without a word, she stood. Her joints were stiff and her movements slow in the cold.

"I'll go," she said. It wasn't a question, so no one tried to stop her. They watched her rise like something inevitable.

Mairi stepped into the open. Her breath blew out in gusts of vapor, torn to ribbons before it could rise. She moved steadily, boots grinding over crusted snow, eyes fixed on the figure beyond the line. Each step was an effort, but Mairi knew this is what it took to remain human.

The man was shivering. His name was Conall, and he was a familiar face from Wick. Once, he had lived in warmth, behind walls, tapping compliance reports into glowing screens. Now he stood hollowed out, ragged - a husk discarded by the systems he had served.

Mairi stopped ten paces away. She pulled a small bag from inside her coat - already hard as stone - and laid it on the ground between them.

"Dried apricots and bread." She said.

Conall didn't move. "I want forgiveness. Or a place to die. Either will do."

Mairi shook her head. "You won't die here," she said. "But don't expect easy trust."

They spoke for a few moments while he ate the bread, then she walked back.

"He's thin," Mairi said when she returned. "He'll follow us back. We have room, and I think he might die out here otherwise."

"Do you know him?" Sorcha asked.

Mairi paused, breath ghosting in the air.

"As well as one can know another," she said. "He belongs here more than anywhere else."

The words had a profound impact, like stones plummeting through deep frozen water, disappearing into unreachable depths.

Later, Ewan sat at the table, the firelight touching the pages. His fingers cramped on the pen, the ink sluggish with cold. He wrote a single line: Conall from Wick has joined us.

Alec, worried Conall had not come alone, sat beside the dying fire until morning, his gaze locked on the ridge. Watching. Waiting.

But no one else came.

CHAPTER 12

A Voice in the Dark

The night came in silence. There was no wind, not even a crackle or creak of branches. It was a wrong quiet, a strange hush that hinted at something about to occur.

Sorcha sat in the shed with the receiver open, her fingers moving as she adjusted the gain, the dial turning under her touch. The battery read low, but steady - a fragile promise in a world that had long since forgotten anything dependable. Isla had fallen asleep curled near the stove, the form of her body curved the shape of a thick blanket. The fire burned low, its embers a fading warmth in the otherwise cold room. Everything else was sleeping, too. Or pretending to.

Then the static shifted.

It was not much louder or sharper, but different. The hum of the machine seemed to change its frequency in a subtle, almost imperceptible way. Sorcha held her breath, her hand stilling over the receiver, as if she could stop the change with her presence alone. A new frequency bloomed through the noise - it was faint, precise and not random.

And in the middle of it, a voice came. "You are not alone."

Sorcha played it once again for herself. Then again, listening closer, as if the second time would reveal something the first listen had not.

Each time, it sounded more like a memory than speech, like a haunting echo, familiar yet unreachable. She couldn't place it, but it gnawed at her, like a forgotten tune on the edge of her mind. She was almost afraid to play it again.

But she did. And again, it came: "You are not alone."

The world outside felt distant, as though the voice had severed her from everything she knew. There was no going back from this. She closed the receiver, and for a long time, sat in the dark, staring at the empty screen, feeling the weight of silence grow heavier.

The next morning, the group gathered early, huddled in coats and quiet, the cold seeping through their clothes, uninvited. Sorcha pressed play. The familiar hum of the receiver filled the room.

The voice returned. "You are not alone."

Ewan sat still, jaw clenched. Alec shook his head, a small, frustrated movement.

"That's bait," Alec muttered. "It's too clean."

"It's clipped," Sorcha replied. "But it's real. The cadence isn't synthetic."

Ewan's eyes moved toward her. "You don't know that."

"I do," she said. "I helped build the synthetic ones. This isn't one of them."

Later, as the cold set in again, Callum poured tea in Mairi's cottage. The fire crackled low. His hands were steady, but his eyes betrayed the strain they all carried.

"A shepherd once heard a whistle over the hills," he said. "He thought it was his brother. Walked toward it. Never came back. We don't know what whistled that night. But it sounded familiar."

Mairi was the one who smiled with understanding that some things are better left unnamed.

The next decision wasn't formal, just glances and nods. Ewan wanted to log the incident, but take no action.

Alec, in frustration, left the room.

After a bit of discussion, they agreed to send out a signal. In that moment, Mairi wondered if their fight would matter, or if the world had already forgotten them.

Sorcha pressed record. They sent a pulse.

Five seconds without a voice or location included. Just a patterned echo, a static-filled question left unanswered.

Then silence.

That night, the power in Wick went out again. Ewan watched the signal strength drop to zero. Sorcha checked her timepiece, tapped it once.

"We've got two hours, maybe less."

Thirty minutes later, under a moonless sky, Alec, Sorcha, Callum and Taran descended the old path to the edge of Wick. The town was a husk - quiet, watched, hollow. Cameras would be blind. Doors would fail safe.

"Hit the pharmacy," Alec whispered. "Then the co-op. We stick to the plan."

They hurried. The pharmacy door clicked open under Callum's fingers. Inside, they moved shelf by shelf. Sorcha pried open medicine boxes, emptied contents into canvas sacks, slid boxes back into place. When the cameras came back on, it would look as if nothing had changed.

At the back, Alec found a case of sealed syringes.

At the co-op, they moved faster. Fuel tablets. Seeds. Solar chargers. Sorcha pulled a USB toolkit from behind the locked manager's station.

"They used to lock this with a face scan," she said.

By the time the grid flickered back to life, they were already gone, back beneath the trees, carrying what the city no longer guarded.

The next few weeks saw a continuation of blackouts. Each time, they robbed Wick of necessities; food, fuel, batteries, and outdoor equipment. They looted its liquor stores, parts stores, and emergency supplies stashed in a government basement.

In the late evenings, Sorcha stared at the screen long after the others had gone to sleep. She felt the hum of the receiver in her chest, like a quiet drumbeat calling her to something she wasn't ready for.

Isla appeared in the doorway, her silhouette visible.

"Did it say anything more?" Isla asked.

Sorcha didn't turn. She stared at the screen.

"Nothing more," she said.

CHAPTER 13

Tea & Stones

The wind, as if exiled and returning, probed the chapel's strength with persistence. Pressing and circling, it searched for the cracks in the walls. Snow that sifted into every forgotten joint accompanied it.

Sorcha crouched by the wall, a paint tin at her feet, a row of stones spread before her.

The brush was stiff with cold. She dipped it deep and pressed the paint onto the stone in slow, deliberate strokes that left no room for second tries. The white lines clung to the rough grey faces.

She did not smooth the names. She did not fix the ones that slanted or dripped. Some names stayed clear. Some blurred at the edges, caught by the wind before they could set. It made no difference. Each one stood, and each one counted.

The cold pulled at her hands, stiffening her joints, stealing her breath. She worked until her knees locked, until she forgot the ache in her body. And when she was done, she called it the memory map.

Mairi brewed the tea, the steam rising in thin spirals.

For every name, she poured a cup. If Glendarragh had anything left, it was teacups.

She placed them under the stones, warm and steaming, the scent of herbs lifting into the cold air. Each cup was an offering, a slight gesture of remembrance. She knelt beside each one, her hands clasped, her head bowed.

There were fourteen names before the others joined.

By early afternoon, there were thirty-nine, each name a mark of the lives that had touched this place.

Alec stood by the far wall, his arms crossed against his chest, watching the others. Although his face was set, his eyes betrayed him. He had not looked at the names. Not yet.

He glanced at the teacups scattered on the ground, then shook his head.

"That's a lot of wasted tea," Alec said, his voice heavy with sarcasm. "If we run out of tea, there's gonna be a lot more names on that wall."

He looked over to the others, a hint of reluctant amusement in his eyes, though his stance remained guarded.

Sorcha understood Alec, how he used humor to cover his pain.

She paused, her gaze falling on the stones. She touched Alec's arm as she passed by. "I am sorry for your sorrow," she whispered, before stepping away, giving him his space.

He didn't reply. He just couldn't. The truth was there, unspoken. The past was not gone. It pressed against him, constant and heavy.

Later, Ewan checked on Alec by the generator, his hands trembling as he worked, fingers fumbling over the old wires.

"You think this is closure," Alec said without looking up, his voice rough. "It's not. It's surrender."

"No," Ewan answered, steady and low. "It's healing."

Alec's hands stopped. His eyes dropped, and he let the weight of it settle.

Before dinner, Sorcha found Ewan by a fire, feeding stacks of old cardboard into the flames. He clutched each piece, as if it were something he could never let go of. The cardboard curled and blackened, collapsing into ash. Sorcha sat beside him in the warmth.

"Naomi," she whispered.

"Adelia," she added, the names barely more than breath.

Ewan nodded. A soft smile tugged at his mouth, despite the sadness.

"Naomi. Adelia." He said.

After dinner, they gathered in the low light of the hearth, their faces rising and falling in the unsteady glow. The walls stretched tall and strange around them, as if the room itself were listening.

Each spoke a name, or many if they wished.

The names were like anchors.

Alec spoke no names, but he stood before the fire, the light soft on his face.

"Let their names hold us where our maps cannot."

Isla came last. She hesitated a long time before stepping forward.

Her voice trembled, almost a whisper.

"My name is not Isla," she said.

She stood straighter. Her hands shook. Sorcha reached for Mairi's sleeve without realizing it.

"Isla is my nickname. My full name is Elin Isobel Hargreaves."

The room drew tight, breathless.

"Daughter of...?" Callum asked, though the answer already circled the fire.

"Douglas Hargreaves," she said.

"The Home Secretary?" Ewan whispered.

"The man who wrote the Compliance Act," Alec added, setting his mug down hard.

Elin nodded. "They said I went to study art in Italy. Florence. Oils and light and history."

She looked down at her hands. Then back up. "But I was never there."

"Who knows you're here?" Sorcha asked.

"No one," she said. "Not even those who helped me get out."

Mairi exhaled.

"And now?" Callum asked.

Elin looked around the room. She touched the lining of her coat, feeling the messages her mother had stitched there.

"Now, I wish to remember my name," she said.

Sorcha smiled, her eyes soft with understanding.

"Bloody hell," Callum exclaimed, flinging himself back into his chair, his arm swinging. His gaze swept across the room. "Takes a hell of a collapse to make the Home Secretary's daughter sleep on a floor next to rats."

Elin didn't blink. "You say that like it wasn't better company than politicians."

The room froze, then Sorcha let out a short laugh, dry and surprised. Even Alec's mouth twitched, unwilling, but real.

Callum, admiring her wit, gave a slow, approving nod. "Fair enough. Elin."

CHAPTER 14

The Smoke

The moor stretched wide and bare beneath the morning sky. Elin was out looking for moss when she saw a thread of smoke hanging faint and low. It was just above the treeline. She didn't move at first. She watched it lift, slow and aimless, until the shape and drift confirmed it was smoke.

Her breath caught. The air felt colder. She dropped to the ground, keeping out of sight, and crawled back toward the village. Every snapped twig under her belly sounded louder than it should have.

By the time she arrived, the others were gathering for lunch. She gave her report while Mairi tried to help her clean the dirt and grass off her clothes.

"Well, someone is out there," Alec said, standing near the fire. "But who?"

"Do they know we're here?" Callum asked. "That's the real question."

"All we know is, someone built a fire," Ewan muttered.

A silence followed, full of unspoken calculations. Smoke didn't just happen.

Sorcha turned to Elin. "How far away was it?"

"Three kilometers, maybe a little less," Elin said.

Sorcha nodded, but her eyes didn't leave the horizon.

Mairi pulled a twig from Elin's hair. "Then we start watching."

That evening, Alec and Sorcha took the first patrol. Their boots cracked over frost-stiff stone as they moved through the brush. The sky was the color of wet ash. The wind had dropped, but the cold clung to everything.

Near a clearing, Alec held up a hand.

"Human footprints," he said.

Sorcha knelt. "Not ours," she whispered. "None of us wear soles like these."

The boot marks were deep with a heavy tread. The ash still held warmth beneath the gorse. Nearby, something red caught the light. It was a chunk of half-melted plastic.

She nudged it with a stick. "That is what's left of someone's clearance band."

A faint smell hung in the air, something chemical.

"Well, they are gone now," Alec said.

Sorcha replied, standing. "They tried to burn it, to hide evidence. Someone doesn't want to be found."

Alec looked toward the horizon. "But what if they are being followed," he said.

Neither of them moved for a long time.

Later, as dusk bled into the hills, Mairi led Sorcha and Morven outside through the brambles concealing the earthen hatch. Below was a chamber tall enough to stand in, lit by salvaged bulbs and battery packs. It smelled of dry soil and iron.

"This is where we keep what's left," Mairi said. "Where no signal reaches."

The silence was deep down there. Crates lined the walls. Medicine, seed packets, and old medical books wrapped in linen and covered in protective plastic sat near a tunnel that branched off the far end. A draft breathed through.

"For what?" Morven whispered.

Mairi didn't answer. Sorcha did. "For whatever comes next."

Back in the kitchen, Callum sat hunched over signal logs.

"First code I ever read was handwritten. Entire room translating binary with pencils," he said.

"Romantic," Ewan replied, "in a doomed sort of way."

"We built logic out of switches," Callum said. "Then we taught the switches to run the world. What could go wrong?"

"Everything," Ewan muttered.

Callum grinned. "I blame COBOL."

Ewan smiled, but his eyes stayed dark. He was too deep in thought. He unfolded a rough chart on the table. The lines marked threat levels. Together, the group agreed to rotating watches.

Outside, a dog barked once, then went silent.

Glendarragh didn't stop living that night, but it went quiet. They kept the curtains drawn, the candles low, and extinguished fires before twilight. If they made no noise and kept out of sight, maybe the world wouldn't notice them.

CHAPTER 15

An Uninvited Guest

E lin returned for the moss. The mist clung low across the heather, slicking the stones, smearing the horizon to a muddy smudge. The earth underfoot was soft and treacherous.

In the distance, something moved on the lower path. This time, she saw it clearly: a figure, walking steady and unhurried, coming toward her. She shoved moss in her pockets and ran back to the others.

They gathered behind a stone wall. When the figure again came into view, they watched as boots crunched across the frozen ground. Layers wrapped the figure in tattered and patched materials, a face hidden beneath a scarf. But it was the patch on the sleeve that drew Sorcha's eyes.

"Pre-collapse aid," she whispered. "Old relief networks. Most dissolved after the second migration."

"They're alone," Alec noted, eyes narrowing. "Boots are mended. Not military. Not recent."

The figure moved with the weariness of those who have nothing left to spend. Mairi stepped forward before anyone could speak, a reflex for her.

The figure stopped five paces away. "I need warmth," he said.

The voice was English, but bent sideways by distance - the sort of accent that comes from someone who's wandered too long and too far to be tied to a place.

Mairi nodded once. "You'll have it."

The figure didn't move. Sorcha stepped up beside her, shoulders set. "We have rules."

"I know," the figure said. Not defensive. Just certain. "So do I."

He offered no name and gave no credentials. They asked for no explanation, but kept a close watch on his movements.

Later, inside Callum's cottage, the visitor sat near the fire. He peeled off his gloves with care, fingers raw and red. The scarf stayed high across his face, more habit than hiding. No one asked. He accepted the soup Callum brought without speaking, with both hands as if he were being given something fragile. He ate, at first in gulps, then in slower, careful sips.

In the kitchen, Callum spoke. "If he were from the system," he said, "he'd test it first. Take a reading. Watch for reaction."

"You know," he continued, "my grandfather told a story once about a woman who crossed into their village during a thunderstorm. Before roads. Before electric lights. She was soaked through, hair like seaweed, hands scraped raw."

No one interrupted. He refilled cups with hot tea.

"She didn't speak for three days," Callum said. "On the fourth day, she built a ring of stones behind the house. When they asked why, she said 'You don't know what's buried here.' A month later, the north river rose. It should have taken the cottage, but the stones held the water back. Not perfectly. But enough."

He looked around the room, his voice roughened by the old memory.

"Some people don't walk in to test us. They walk in to remind us what we've forgotten. Maybe she lived in that cottage long ago, maybe her family were buried there. We'll never know for sure. But some people remember what we've lost - and they bring it back, not to challenge us, but to save us."

Alec didn't speak until later, his voice low and cautious.

"Could be a mapper," he muttered to Sorcha in the shed. "Embedded sensors or even passive ID sweeps."

Sorcha didn't respond, but she reached behind him and tightened the latch on the door.

That night, Mairi sat with the visitor near the hearth.

"Where did you come from?" she asked.

"South," the visitor said. "Then east. Then..." A pause. "from the silence."

Mairi watched him. "Are you running?"

"No. I'm returning," the visitor said. "The maps are wrong now," he added. "But people still follow them."

Mairi nodded. "Some of us never had maps to begin with."

They sent him to the bunk in Callum's cottage, where he would sleep surrounded by several muscular men who had already agreed at least two of them would stay awake all night.

Long after the others had gone, Morven lingered by the dying hearth. The last embers clicked in the ashes. Mairi moved to douse the fire, but stopped when she saw Morven's face.

"I need to say something," Morven whispered.

Mairi said nothing. Just sat. Waited.

"In the early days," Morven said, "before the second lockdown, before the door-to-door sweeps - a boy I knew, Gregor, came to the shop. He asked for tinned soup."

Mairi's hands tightened in her lap, but she stayed silent.

"I reported him," Morven whispered. "No chip. No papers. I told myself it was fear. I had children. I had no choice. But three days later, he was gone."

Morven's eyes, rimmed with tears, met Mairi's.

"I know what it means to choose the wrong thing."

Mairi leaned forward, placed her hand over Morven's. "Then choose differently now."

At dawn, they gave the visitor a wrapped parcel full of bread, thread, dried herbs and a jar of sourdough. Another small bag held some flour and a flask of whisky. The visitor accepted it without saying much. Before he turned to leave, Sorcha stepped forward. She placed a smooth white stone, marked with a thistle, into his hands.

He walked away, dissolving again into a figure in the fog.

CHAPTER 16

The Patterns

Elin was digging through a bag of trail mix, trying to find a dried cherry. Her gloves were off, fingertips red with cold, but she kept fishing past the oats and broken almonds with stubborn determination.

Alec was twenty paces ahead when he stopped next to three stones stacked on a moss-dark stump. He waited for Elin to catch up. She crouched beside him, her brow furrowing against the brittle air.

"That's deliberate," she said.

"It means something," Alec replied.

Breath clouded between them.

"I think it's a sign that this is a cleared zone," he added. "Military recon teams leave them. Sweep completed."

They didn't touch it. They turned back into the cold.

At Mairi's cottage, Sorcha spread three months of signal logs across Ewan's battered patrol map. The candles threw a pale light over grids and scribbled margins. Timestamps and trails of activity scarred the pages. They scanned the overlapping patterns. Then stopped.

The densest frequencies - the pings, soft pulses, fading echoes - didn't appear along Glendarragh's trails. They matched them almost exactly.

"They're watching patterns," she said, barely above a whisper.

Ewan leaned over her shoulder. His frown deepened. "That means..."

"We're predictable," Sorcha finished.

She didn't have to explain further. They were already leaving footprints in the dark. And Glendarragh couldn't afford to be seen, not now, not with supplies running so low.

Callum cupped his tea between both hands.

"There was a deer once," he said, voice low. "Used the same trail every dusk. For years. Then one day, it was gone. But the trail stayed. Even after the deer vanished, the path remained, waiting to be followed."

He looked around the room. "Our trails have been marked, even if we stop using them."

Ewan, eyes fixed on the fire, muttered, "We're the deer now."

"No," Sorcha said, lifting her head. "We're the hunters too."

They formed a plan.

Ewan redrew the patrols. There would be no neat loops, no more habits to trace. The paths scattered and twisted like deer trails in deep snow. And Sorcha built decoys with scraps of salvaged batteries wrapped in thermal blankets hidden in locations far from the village. Sorcha placed other decoys near the bend in the frozen creek, where old traps rusted beneath the ice. They would walk a path twice in the same hour, then never again.

Mairi began portioning supplies in silence. She moved her tinctures into smaller bottles. She spoke of it to no one, not even Callum.

They had avoided Wick for weeks, feeling it was becoming too exposed, too unstable. But need had a way of pressing back. They were going to go scavenging in another village.

Ewan pulled out a map of Caithness. Black stars showed where Ewan had destroyed known cameras. Red circles showed where solar panels clung to broken roofs. They identified the back roads into the surrounding settlements.

"Halkirk was flooded for months, they won't have any supplies left," said Alec.

"Helmsdale might have a pharmacy, but nothing in the way of staples. Only ever had a convenience store," said Morven.

Elin's voice came from the doorway, quiet and expected. "What are we doing?"

They turned as she stepped in.

"Figuring out where to scavenge next," Callum said.

She joined the group as they sat for hours discussing workable plans until the candles burned out and the wind picked up again.

CHAPTER 17

The Sound

The wind pressed low across the glen, heavy and slow, dragging invisible weight across the frozen ground. By January, every living thing had pulled deep into itself. The stones steamed where the rare sunlight struck them, but no warmth came. Sorcha climbed onto the roof of the grain store, boots slipping once on the brittle frost. The antenna shivered in the gusts, skeletal against the grey sky. She adjusted the frame with gloved hands, frowning into the cold.

"It's not feedback," she called down.

Below, Ewan stood near the storage hatch, collar turned up against the biting wind.

"Meaning?"

Sorcha adjusted the antenna, her breath steaming in front of her. She paused, listening.

"It's shifted," she said, her voice tight. "It's not noise. It's a tone that's higher."

He read from the ledger aloud: "Root yield: Deteriorating. Signal distortion: Persistent. Morale: Steady. Brittle."

He paused again. Then added: "Unnamed tension rising."

In a cellar, Mairi and Morven moved between the root bins and storage crates. The lantern swung on a chain, casting light over the stone walls. Their breath steamed around them. They checked the food stores by habit now - weighing the barrels by feel, pressing fingers against the sacks, sniffing the grain. Rot was spreading faster than the calendars predicted. The frost had crept through the walls deeper than expected.

Sorcha joined them, kneeling beside the crates, flexing her hands for blood. They didn't speak.

Outside, along the southern ridge path, Alec took Elin through a stealth drill at Ewan's request. The snow there had frozen into a thin crust that shattered under a careless step. Every move had to be a choice. The goal was to get from the ridge to the tree line with no noise, no obvious footprints.

Elin beat Alec's time by four seconds. Afterward, he unwound his old scarf - frayed but warm, and smelling of old wood smoke - and wrapped it once around her neck.

"You earned it," he said.

That night, the stew was thin and the bowls cold before they were empty. They were still living by candlelight in the evenings. To make more servings, Callum added more root vegetables and water, stirring the pot. After a long silence, he began speaking.

"There was a village once," he said, "up past Strathnaver. No roads then. Just sheep tracks and stones."

The candle flames bent sideways with a gust in the draft.

"No bells. No church. No one to toll a bell anyway when the sickness came. They buried their dead under stones - couldn't dig, the ground was too hard. Second winter, they lit candles. One in every window. No reason they could name. Just a feeling in the air, like something leaning close. Some said they heard breathing at the edge of the fields. Some found footprints where no one had walked. One night, a woman came through the snow. Barefoot. Skin grey as slate. She said one thing before she died on their steps:"

Callum's voice dropped lower, pulling them closer to the flame without meaning to.

"She said 'You're lighting candles for the wrong side.' "

After a long moment, Elin's voice broke the hush. "What did she mean?" she asked.

Callum turned the knife in his hand, the blade catching the light.

"Nobody ever knew for sure," he said. He sliced the brown bits off an old potato.

"They buried her under the highest cairn they had. After that, they lit no more candles. They blacked out the windows. Wrapped their boots in cloth. Made no sound at night. And when the sickness came again in spring..."

He paused. "It passed them by."

He nodded.

Even the walls seemed to lean closer, as if listening.

Callum leaned forward, the shadows deepening around him, and shouted, "Boo!"

Elin yelped, knocking her empty bowl over, the spoon flying across the table. Even Sorcha flinched hard, her hand nearly knocking over a glass of water. Alec scowled, but his mouth twitched despite himself.

Callum laughed a dry, rasping laugh.

"Suppose you can never be too careful," he said, leaning back against the stones.

Later, Ewan updated his stock ledger with Mairi, who sat folding cloth napkins. She tucked one into the pocket of her coat, fingers stiff with cold.

In the shed, Elin crouched by the inner beam and carved her name into the old wood with a blade, the cuts shallow but sure. The first true warning came from the light. The shed lantern dimmed from a full bright glow to a low bruise of light in just seconds. Mairi noticed it from the window. Sorcha, from the port on the roof, her hand on the aerial. Ewan saw it from the cellar stairs, his ledger forgotten.

Then, in the open night air, three tones came. They were uneven but too shaped to be natural. From the roof, Sorcha climbed down the ladder, dragging the antenna and cables in behind her. She locked the hatch. Elin stood in the doorway, her breath misting the air, her hands pressed to her sides.

"What is it?" Elin whispered. She locked the door.

Sorcha didn't answer. She reached out and turned off the transmitter, then blew out the candle. But the tones outside continued pulsing into the frozen dark.

Something was out there.

The glen held its breath.

CHAPTER 18

Deadman's Pint

The sound carried through the long hours of night, unraveling into the dark. Silence came just after three a.m., a sudden, surgical stillness. By the time the sky paled, they had all moved below ground, one by one, after Ewan's quick instruction. Not long after, snow started falling. They sealed the heat in, and the snow covered their tracks.

The day would be long. There would be no fire, no warmth, no smell of cooking to betray them. No flicker against stone. They met their hunger by eating cold things; the emergency smoked fish, some coarse bread, and the vinegar sting of preserved fruit and lukewarm tea. It was enough. It had to be.

The crowded cellar stifled them in its thick air. They covered themselves with whatever they had grabbed for extra warmth, including old tablecloths and unraveling quilts. A tapestry that once adorned a wall now draped across the children's shoulders. In the corner, behind a wall of old crates, a bucket waited in the shadow of a tunnel. Necessity had long since overcome modesty.

They passed a single lantern, with its wick trimmed to the faintest life, beneath a thick towel, rationing its light like food. No one cried.

No one asked how long. Even the children understood that sound was a kind of light, and light a kind of invitation for trouble.

Above them, the world listened. Below, they endured in silence.

At around 10 p.m., the sound came again. Sorcha and Alec were hiding in the shed, peeking through the cracks in the walls. There was a shimmer at the tree line, low and pulsing, barely visible against the frozen brush. Then camouflaged figures appeared on foot.

Sorcha whispered. "They're here." She turned off the equipment and fell back into a dark corner.

Ten minutes later, the building they rigged as a decoy exploded and caught fire. The flames climbed fast with a chemical smell.

Alec swore low. "The decoy worked," he muttered. "I thought for sure they'd hit the old pub."

No sooner had he said it than, in the far distance, another explosion lit the sky with smoke and fire.

"Well," Sorcha whispered, "pretty sure that was the Deadman's Pint."

Down below, Mairi and the others could not see what was happening, but they heard it.

Callum, alone in his cottage, was the backup plan. He agreed not to move unless required, so as not to give away his location or their only supply of weapons. He had lifted the floorboard beneath his table and pulled out weapons only a few in the village knew he had. The explosions got his attention, and he moved.

From a tiny crack in the wall, Alec and Sorcha watched the searchers sweeping the clearing. The empty cottages stood alone, framed by the bones of old fencing and stone walls half-swallowed by snow. They saw nothing but sagging roofs, collapsed sheds, bare earth. It looked like a ghost town, exactly what they had made it appear to be.

Then the searchers changed direction toward the low ridge that shielded the hidden entrance. Sorcha saw, her mouth tightening as the nearest figure turned toward the stand of pine above the hollow. Another twenty meters, and they'd stumble on the outer mesh.

"Aye," the voice called out from the trees. "Why'd you blow up my place?"

A man stepped into the open. Gaunt, older, cheeks red from cold, a patchy beard clinging to his jaw. His coat hung crooked from one shoulder. He limped.

It took Alec a full second to recognize him. It was Connal from Wick. He was supposed to be underground, with the rest. But here he was, alone, exposed, and already talking.

The searchers halted. One of them raised a weapon, then lowered it again.

"Hell of a thing," Connal said. "Burning down a man's life when he's still standing in it."

One figure stepped forward. Male, taller than the others. His voice came clipped, polite.

"You live here?"

"Lived. Still do, I suppose."

"You alone?"

Connal nodded once. "Just me now."

Another searcher asked, "Family?"

"They left on the grey buses back in September. Went east. Inverness, maybe. I stayed for the dogs. Didn't want to leave 'em behind." He shrugged. "Didn't matter in the end. They all starved."

There was a pause. The woman's voice this time: "Where did you say your family is now?"

"I don't know. Inverness way, I imagine."

"How long have you been alone?"

"Since the frost. Maybe longer."

"And you've seen no one around here?"

He shook his head. "Not a soul. You're the first I've seen. Everyone left."

A third searcher circled wide behind him, the stood in front of him again. He didn't flinch.

"No radio?" one asked.

"No signal." Connal replied.

"No visitors?"

Connal's voice was calm. "You're the only people up here."

The silence after was longer.

One searcher raised his pistol.

Connal glanced skyward, maybe to the hills, maybe to no one.

A single shot echoed through the glen.

The searchers stood still for a moment, talking in mumbled voices. Then they dragged Connal's body across the ground and threw him into the blazing fire.

One searcher raised a small radio to his mouth. His voice, low and clipped, carried in the brittle air. "Primary structure compromised. No people. False positive."

The figures turned away, boots crunching over the frozen earth, fading back into the broken woods.

Callum had been crouched behind a building, and he saw everything. He regrouped with Sorcha and Alec.

Above the stars hung sharp and pitiless.

Sorcha stared at the black scar of the burned building, her voice stripped bare.

"Let's not tell the others" she said, silent tears streaming down her face. She let the words hang for a moment, then added, quieter, almost to herself, "Not yet."

"We need to keep morale up," said Callum, sitting with his head in his hands, staring at the ground. "People are scared enough."

They settled on a story – that Callum's gun had misfired – and made their way back to the others. To be certain of their safety, the village spent another night in the cellar before emerging. Later, Callum recounted everything to Ewan, ensuring that Connal's final act of courage was recorded in the ledger with the detail and honor it deserved.

CHAPTER 19

The Roots

The light in late January barely cleared the treetops. A thin, colorless sun hung low in the sky, dragging a pale band of brightness across the frozen glen, too weak to thaw anything it touched. The frost clung to every branch and stone, sheathing the landscape in white.

Ewan knelt in the brittle dirt at the edge of the grove, a broken stick in hand. He scratched a rough circle into the ground; the motion was slow.

"This is how fungus survives," he said, not looking up. "It spreads underground. You can burn the forest, clear the trees, salt the soil. Doesn't matter. It waits in the roots. Hidden. Patient. Doesn't die."

Alec stood nearby, arms crossed, his breath a slow cloud in the air. He stared at the shape Ewan had drawn, nothing more than a crude loop, but he understood.

"As long as no one maps the root," Alec said, half under his breath.

At the edge of the elder grove, Sorcha and Mairi worked in silence, kneeling over an open patch of soil. Their gloves had gone dark with wet earth. Between them, a waxcloth-wrapped bundle rested inside a narrow hollow dug into the frozen ground. The transmitter was one of only a few they had left.

They sealed the earth with stones, pressing them flat into place. Each movement was deliberate, mechanical. Hands that had once mended flesh now buried machines.

Mairi paused, resting her palm on the cold ground, feeling the bite through her gloves. "Is this the last one?" she asked, her voice low, more statement than question.

Sorcha shook her head without looking up. "No. One more... under the old burn line."

Mairi glanced at her, surprised. "We're going to bury one there?"

"Redundancy," Sorcha replied. "It's how we stay alive."

By the blackened ruins of the decoy, Callum planted a thistle into the ashes in memory of Connal. Roots bit into the scorched soil, clutching at what remained.

"Some roots get stronger when they're cut," he said, pressing the plant down with a flattened palm. "The grey ones hold water longest."

Alec stood behind him. He watched the thistle sway in the wind. "Maybe we're all like that," he said.

That afternoon, Ewan sat alone inside the ruin of the chapel. Light filtered through the broken arch and dust hung in the air, spiraling in slow circles. The pews were long gone; only fractured stone remained.

He opened the ledger. He saw names lining the pages, each annotated with skills, limitations, and histories that now felt far away. It had become a catalogue of lives lived under siege.

His finger landed on Naomi's name. "I measured everything except what mattered," he said aloud. His voice echoed against the cold stone.

"We called it resilience," he continued in a whisper. "But it was always compliance. They didn't kill our faith. They made it procedural."

He looked up through the broken rafters, where a single blade of pale sky slipped through.

"If we can't name what we've lost," he said, "we've lost it twice."

That night, they sat in a circle in front of the fire. The future felt smaller than ever. They had been speaking for hours.

"I know what I'm meant to do," Elin said, her voice steady. "I cannot wait."

Ewan sat back, his mouth tight. "We don't know what's out there," he said. "Not anymore."

"We don't," Elin agreed. "But we can choose not to be still."

Mairi reached out, placed her hand over Elin's. The gesture was simple, older than words. A mother's approval. A friend's release.

"She's prepared," Mairi said. "Her parents gave her explicit instructions. We have to let her go."

Alec rose, tension in his frame. "It's not courage," he said. "It's a gamble. Her parents aren't here to see the risks."

Callum, sitting closest to the fire, stirred the coals with a stick. "And yet, knowing the risks, she wants to go."

The answer settled between them like the weather. She would leave and she would go alone.

Later, near the frozen stream, Taran Gunn found Elin adjusting the straps on her pack. He said little. Just handed her a small, dented compass. Its casing showed scratches, and its needle skewed, but he had buffed the metal to a dull, warm gleam.

"It doesn't point north," he said. "But it's better than most people. I polished it for you."

She turned it over in her hands, smiling once. "Thank you. It's beautiful. And useful."

They didn't hug. They didn't need to.

"I finished the library," Taran said. "Cleared it. The shelves look full on camera, but it's dust jackets wrapped around cardboard."

"You finished it?" she asked, blinking.

He nodded. Frost clung to the end of his scarf. "Food keeps the body. Words keep the soul."

She smiled again. Not brightly. But real. "I think you've done something important."

"I think you are doing something even more important."

Then she turned and walked into the dark.

And he watched her until he couldn't see her anymore.

Beneath the fields, the buried greenhouse stirred. Hidden vents opened, just enough to breathe in the chilly night. The leaves, long unkissed by air, trembled and roots tightened in the soil. Elin didn't look back. She walked on, listening to the dead grass rattle around her boots.

CHAPTER 20

The Wilderness

There had been no speeches or long farewells. The food pack Mairi had given her hung across her chest. The cloth food pack, with a pretty blue floral pattern, was hand-stitched. Inside were simple provisions.

The compass, now hooked to her belt, tapped against her hip with every step. She liked the rhythm of it. Taran was right, it did not point north. The hand got stuck to the west. It was stubborn, wrong, and faithful to some older pull.

But her steps found rhythm without thinking. Her mind moved differently. Her memory was rising to the day she left England.

It was a not a well thought out plan. They made it under pressure; it was shapeless and sudden.

The meeting room had smelled of leather and dust and fear. Politicians in long coats huddled against the walls, voices slipping low into each other, rising once in a near-shout before crumbling into silence. They would not meet her eyes. Or if they did, it was brief - with a kind of apology.

Her father's voice had broken the hush, brittle with urgency.

"It's the way. For now. We must act now." He spoke to them, not to her. As if she were already gone.

Her mother arrived later. Her face was pale, her hands steady by force, not by faith. She layered her in extra clothing. A second blouse. A hidden skirt. More and more layers. A jacket sewn with tiny pockets in unusual places. The men, the same ones who argued, worked now, helping to place important items they had brought with them into pockets as a seamstress stitched them closed fast.

They had not given her weapons or trackers, but critical information.

The assistant presented the forged documents. Then she heard the last words from her father given to the men who stood watching. She carried the words like a stone in her chest, not knowing what he meant.

"You will prepare your sons next," he said to the men. They did not argue and there was no reply, only the grim acceptance of men who understood too late.

There had been no time for her to ask questions.

Now, crossing the frozen glen, the memory was bright in her mind, in the cold shape of understanding. The city had already broken by the time she left it, but it did not break all at once. First, the refusal of cash at most places, and the customer service smiles at the counters as they enforced the new rules. Then the scanners were everywhere, a retina flash for the grocer, to schedule an appointment, even to take a taxi. The cameras grew, thickening at intersections, perched on rooftops, and riding the low breeze in black, humming drones.

And then came the last announcement, one for which none could prepare. All movement in or out of British cities would now require biometric identification, and there would be no exceptions, no delays, only mandatory participation.

It was the law.

Now the government could detain anyone lacking the embedded chip and hold them until they agreed to it, even if by force. It would not be possible to protest or hide. To enforce the new law, human officers were no longer required. British robots called Arbiters, armed and allowed to act with deadly force, would now secure British streets.

Her father had whispered it, almost without breath: "You don't run from the Arbiters. You disappear."

That last announcement was the day preparations ended, when arguments ended, when long goodbyes ended. People were desperate to get out of the cities.

A junior assistant walked her to the train station and nudged her into the outbound carriage. As the train left the station, the data had already fused. Layer by layer, piece by piece. Accounts once separate, such as transport, shopping, communication, were now pulled into clusters, tight as magnets. Every small decision people made, every route, every purchase, every glance recorded by public glass, now clumped, pulling their digital shape into view within the system without consent.

It happened like condensation. It gathered until it soaked everything.

At dusk, Elin found a hollow beneath an old hawthorn tree. The roots twisted over her like ribs. She built her fire low, a breath barely touching the air. Smoke drifted sideways into the cold, invisible unless you already knew where to look.

She ate a foil-wrapped square of cold cooked oatmeal and drank tea from a flask.

She waited until her hands warmed up near the small fire.

Then, when the dark was deep enough to cover her, she drew out the one device she had never told the others about.

It was small and unremarkable, about the size of a matchbox, scuffed at the corners.

Her father had given it to her, along with some instructions. He then commanded her full attention with one last request, delivered in his sternest tone.

"When you are certain. Not before."

But she was certain after she read Ewan's entry about Connal. He had left his ledger open, and she did not stop reading, even when he returned with a cup of tea.

"Don't tell the others," is all he had said.

She unfolded a thin scrap of paper tucked inside her pack, written on it, a string of numbers.

She keyed them into the device.

Her fingers hesitated between each digit from the knowledge that some things, once begun, cannot be undone.

The screen flickered once.

It returned a second string of numbers she did not recognize.

She thought how once, long ago, technology had meant certainty.

Now it meant risk.

Then a message appeared, an instruction: Press Blue Button

She pressed it.

The device went dark.

She waited, heart hammering against the frozen earth. Maybe she'd made a mistake.

Then the screen lit up with a single line of text: ETA 22:30

Nothing more. Not a confirmation, or even a signature.

All she has was time and the thin, unwavering thread of choice she had tied herself to. She tucked the device back into the seam of her coat, hidden deep against her ribs. Then she sat with her knees drawn up, watching the smoke drift sideways through the black trees, waiting to see if the night would answer.

Far overhead, the stars kept their cold watch.

Unblinking.

Unmoved.

CHAPTER 21

A Trip to Golspie

The trees ended as they approached the abandoned village from a back road. A cracked concrete slab marked the border. The vines covered the tilted, illegible slab. Beyond it, it was asphalt veins broken by grass and rusted pylons leaning like tired soldiers.

Ewan slowed the battered truck, tires crunching over the frost-cracked road. Sorcha, sitting beside him, scanned the treeline through the cracked side mirror. Behind them, Mairi and Callum rode in the second truck. They kept the headlights turned off.

They had chosen the blackout window carefully, when roads would be driveable in good weather. They knew power cuts threw the grids into confusion. Cameras lost power. Drones drifted back to roost. Moving fast, they calculated they could reach Golspie's ruins and return with time to spare.

They were not looking for hope or salvation, just medicine and dry good, maybe some tools if they were lucky.

They passed the old checkpoint without slowing. The barrier hung broken, striped paint peeling into flakes. A sign dangled overhead, twisting in the wind.

Callum tapped his walking stick once against the truck's frame. "Aye," he muttered, but he had nothing else to say.

They reached Golspie at dusk. The town was a hollow shell, doors blown open, windows dark, streets choked with frozen debris. The hospital stood behind a battered facade. The main entrance door hung loose from one hinge. No alarms. Nothing left to hear. Inside, the corridors gaped hollow and slick with frost. Plastic sheeting peeled from the ceilings in slow, tired curls.

They moved quickly. Mairi found the pharmacy wing with its shelves raided. Someone had ripped most drawers open. But tucked behind the medicine storage, she discovered a hidden cache holding rows of sealed crates. Bandages. Antibiotics. IV fluids, brittle with cold but intact. Mairi knew what to look for to stock Glendarragh.

Across the hall, Sorcha forced open a kitchen door. The smell hit first. It was stale and starch. But behind the service counter, they found their target. They were emergency rations, including dehydrated meals, powdered potatoes, dense loaves of survival bread sealed in mylar. Not perfect food, but edible and enough to fill both trucks.

Ewan pried open a second storeroom to find a row of untouched computer servers, dust-blanketed but dry. Boxes of unopened security cameras. Hardwire spools. Even backup batteries, showing charge. They loaded fast and quiet. Mairi moved like a little mouse between the shelves. Sorcha sealed crates with worn cloth ties. Callum, in the far corner, grinned when he found an entire case of instant coffee packets.

They carried what they could through the broken rear door, across the frost-hardened fields, into the trucks.

Callum paused, looking back at the collapsed hospital wing. "Imagine the stories they'll tell about us one day, how we risked our lives for gauze and bottles of iodine."

Ewan grunted as he secured the last load. "Imagine explaining what iodine was."

Callum tugged his hat down. "Or what a hospital was."

Once they loaded the trucks, they retraced their route through the ruined streets, past the broken remnants of the town. The sun sank lower, and the temperature dropped as they passed through the shattered outskirts of Golspie, heading back toward Glendarragh.

Callum tapped his stick against the dashboard. "You know," he said after a long silence, "before all this got biblical, I once asked ChatGPT what Wick's survival rate was if we ended up in WW3."

Ewan raised an eyebrow. "You asked a machine to predict our odds?"

"Seemed logical at the time," Callum said. "It gave Wick a sixty-two percent survival rate."

Sorcha snorted from the backseat. "Was that the free version of ChatGPT or the paid?"

"Free," Callum admitted.

"Well, there's your answer," Ewan muttered. "Free version had the sense of a wet sheep."

Callum chuckled once, low and dry. "Pro would've charged twenty quid to predict my funeral."

They fell quiet again, watching the frozen landscape pass. Back in Glendarragh, the night had deepened. They scampered through the stone gate, no lamps lit, engines cut before the final rise. Mairi signaled the cellar clear. Alec appeared from the shadow of the watchtower, a rifle slung low. They needed no words. They had come back with a full load and enough to last for several more months.

Later, Peter, Morven, Taran and Hamish sat by the fire, the salvaged medicines spread before them like offerings. They cleaned the vials, organized everything. No ceremony. Just work.

CHAPTER 22

The Longest Night

The storm descended from the northern cliffs, its teeth dragging in the cold. Even without weather forecasts, the village of Glendarragh knew a storm was coming. Their response was rapid and stemmed from the hard-won knowledge of many generations and many winters. By nightfall, they had clustered into three cottages. The other cottages remained dark, locked, and left to ride out the storm like empty boats in an angry sea.

Earlier that day, they took the animals underground. They had led the goats first, their hooves skittering on the frozen stones. Then the chickens, huddled in burlap sacks, their faint, startled clucks muffled against the cold. Last came the cows - the last surviving ones - heads bowed low, moving slow and patient. Each breath they loosed steamed against the cellar walls, a living fog that clung to the low ceilings and drifted around the beams. Mairi knelt with them last, checking they were warm, stroking noses, whispering nonsense words.

Glendarragh could not afford to lose anything. Not a single life was too small to be measured.

Above ground, in the largest cottage, they packed the room tight.

They pulled every blanket, scrap of hide, and piece of old cloth from trunks and fixed them across the windows and doors. The wind shrieked outside in long, low keening, as if the sea had pulled itself up over the land, and was clawing its way across the moors.

They built the fire high in the hearth using hard woods for a slower burn.

Alec was on the floor nearest the door, his back against the thickest wall, eyes half-closed but never asleep.

On a sofa, Taran engrossed himself in a book; Sorcha read, too, her legs crossed over his.

Mairi rocked a battered kettle back and forth on the embers, coaxing thin steam from stubborn ice.

Hamish burrowed between Peter and Ewan, wrapped in a tangle of patched coats and wool.

Callum dozed with one eye open in the old leather chair nearest to the fire.

The cold pressed in from all sides, but the heat from the fire and the weight of so many bodies breathing together built a secondary wall of heat.

There was little talking, only the crackle of the fire and the occasional low thud of a shifting log. Snow was piling against the doors and windows.

Someone, maybe Morven, began humming under her breath, but it was not a song anyone could name.

Alec shifted under his blankets, swearing low into the dark.

Ewan gave a grunt that could have meant anything - pain, agreement, resignation.

From under a mess of threadbare blankets and a curtain that smelled of onions, Callum's voice crawled out, dry as a cracked stone.

"Remind me, lads, was it hope or stupidity that made us think we deserved another winter?"

Alec, without lifting his head, muttered: "Little of both."

Callum coughed a laugh.

"Figures. World ends, we survive... and it's the bloody Highland weather that finishes the job. Not a hero's death among us, just frostbite and bad luck."

Ewan, face buried in his arms, lifted two fingers in Callum's general direction, in a lazy, freezing salute.

"Bury me standing up," he groaned. "I want to look disappointed when the next lot finds us."

As the fire settled into soft cracks, Morven began humming again, but not the aimless hum from earlier. She sang *Autumn Lake*, an old ballad that everyone knew, though none had sung it in years.

> *Lo, a truth both pure and bold*
> *By tongue and tear it must be told*
> *A truth so simple, I cannot flee*
> *It clutches soul and conquers me*
> *I shall not feign, nor turn away*
> *Nor jest, nor mask what heart doth say*
> *No whispered doubt, no clever lie*
> *I love thee still, though reasons die*
> *I do, I whisper, soft and true*
> *My vow is sworn, my love for you*
> *Come hither, love, draw ever near*
> *Let not thy shadow disappear*
> *Be in my circle, close, entwined*
> *The sacred space where hearts aligned*
> *My arms a harbor, warm, enclosed*
> *Where winds are hushed and time deposed*
> *We float upon the autumn's grace*
> *With golden leaves upon thy face*
> *A kiss I press, aye, not just one*

But two, and more, till day is done
I kiss thee, love, and still anew
With trembling hands and heart so true
Yet sense I lack, I wander blind
The heart speaks plain, but not the mind
Thou lov'st me not, or not no more
The doors once opened now the floor
And I should part, and bid adieu
I know it well, and know it true
The silence rings, the echoes stay
A ballad frail at end of day
Still in the wind, I softly groan
For though I walk this world alone
I know, I know, what once did be
Love's melody, once sung by thee
I love thee

They lay still, curled in silence, listening as the song crept through the room like a vine seeking light.

The storm howled and pounded, rattling the stones like teeth in an old jaw, but inside, the fire held. They held. Hours passed without counting.

Sometimes Hamish whimpered in his sleep.

Sometimes Mairi added a sliver of wood to the fire, careful not to wake the others.

Sometimes Alec shifted, flexing fingers gone stiff.

At some forgotten hour, closer to midnight or dawn, no one could say. The wind dropped to a heavy, sifting whisper.

Below, in the old root cellars, the goats shifted against each other, the hens tucked their heads beneath their wings, and the last ewe, battered and stubborn, let out a low, dreaming bleat.

Everything that could be saved, lived.

Everything that could hold heat, did.

Above them, the stone walls creaked in the cold. And Mairi, without lifting her head, whispered into the heart of the heat, "We are still here."

No one answered because they were sleeping.

The longest night had passed.

The new day had not yet begun, but it would.

Outside, the hills slept beneath a mountain of snow. And inside, Glendarragh continued in the only way it could - by surviving.

CHAPTER 23

The Old Radio

T he rain came that morning. It arrived as a fine mist, blurring the edges of the hills until they resembled a Turner painting.

Inside the cottage, the kettle gave a small rattle against the iron. The weight of the mood absorbed the sound, sinking into the stillness of the room.

Mairi stirred her cup of tea without lifting it. The spoon clicked against the rim in a steady rhythm. She did it a little more loudly to see if anyone would notice. They did not, so she clanked her spoon down and drank her tea.

Hamish sat at the window, his finger drawing slow circles in the condensation. Each one blurred almost as soon as it formed, vanishing as though the glass itself preferred forgetting.

Alec, across the table, sharpened a blade with slow, deliberate strokes. The stone hissed beneath the metal, long and measured. He was not preparing for a task like hunting; it was just something to keep his hands busy.

Sorcha sat closest to the hearth. Her bootlaces lay untied. A half-mended radio rested in her lap, the casing stripped to its bare components. She was not trying to fix it anymore. She knew there was nothing left to fix. But for about an hour now, it had become just a thing to hold between her hands, since she could not understand why it was no longer working.

She wanted to hear the news, but not for the news. She only wanted to confirm that the world remained broken in the same familiar way. The consistency comforted her.

No one had spoken much all morning. There was nothing urgent to say. No new plans. No new losses. Just the slow unwinding of a morning not yet claimed by grief.

The rain tapped against the windows.

When the radio buzzed, Sorcha nearly dropped it. Its sound crackled until it caught and a voice spilled into the kitchen. It was too clean for the world they lived in, but it was a British accent. The words arrived with an unnatural smoothness. The speaker polished each syllable. Was it even a person speaking?

"Transition Phase Five now entering successful stabilization. Citizens are reminded: participation ensures prosperity. New Distribution Zones have been activated. Report your wellness checkpoints daily. Remember: Trust keeps us strong."

There was a pause, followed by a click. Then the voice returned, this time with a hint of cheer.

"This morning's highlights: Record community compliance achieved in Sector D Twelve. Infrastructure recovery continues on schedule. Regional biometric centers now offering expedited family registrations. Gratitude is the cornerstone of progress."

Behind the voice, a thin synthetic melody played. It wasn't music, not exactly, but it suggested comfort, something engineered to sound soothing.

More importantly, it did not sound dangerous, and that was the danger.

Mairi leaned forward and turned the dial until it clicked off. The voice stopped mid-word. The kitchen fell back into silence, except for the sound of Mairi setting her cup down and pushing her chair back, screeching against the floorboards.

Hamish wiped a fresh circle into the window with his sleeve and stared out.

"That's not news," Alec said. "It's bait."

Sorcha said nothing because she had already begun removing the batteries from the radio.

Hamish, who was looking older, whispered into the quiet.

"But why would they lie?"

He was not looking for an answer and no one gave one. There was no answer that would not lead to a long discussion about the history of everything. And they were all tired of those sorts of chats.

Mairi returned and took the batteries away from Sorcha, then crossed the room again, disappearing into the pantry. She opened an old tin, placed the radio batteries inside, closed the lid, and slid the tin onto the highest shelf. Out of reach and out of sight, it was a small burial.

Ewan entered from the shed, his coat dripping rainwater. He saw the radio in Sorcha's lap and said nothing. He had heard the same broadcast in the shed. He moved to the hearth now, looking for his ledger. Turning to a fresh page, he wrote a single word at the top in block letters: Radio noise. Beneath that, he wrote smaller: Not to be trusted. He was dripping water all over the floor and nobody cared.

Callum's voice rose from the chair by the fire. He was reading a newspaper from a stack under the bed. The date on the front page was 31 December, 1999. He couldn't figure out why anyone would have saved it. There was nothing interesting about it at all, just a bunch of articles about computers issues that never materialized.

"I wonder what the world will sound like in a hundred years. Or music. Or books. Or anything, really. Not after they have killed all the poets and caged all the dreamers."

The fire crackled.

Outside, rusty and tangled wind chimes clanked together.

Inside, a spider dropped from the ceiling and vanished into a floorboard, unseen and unbothered.

CHAPTER 24

Old Friends

The first true breaths of spring had come to Glendarragh, restless and raw. Behind the cottages, the meltwater's silvery song flowed over stone beds. The air smelled of wet earth, sharp and sweet, as seeds and roots untwisted underground. Crocus and snowdrops had shouldered their way through the thaw, defiant splashes of color against the brown fields. Bees buzzed drunkenly from blossom to blossom. Birds stitched the hedgerows with song. Even the oldest stones seemed to sweat warmth, gathering fresh green moss on their bellies.

Inside Callum's cottage, the hearth flickered low but steady. Scattered across the heavy wooden table lay battered notebooks, seed pouches, and bits of string tied around pebbles that they would use later to mark plots. Sorcha sketched rough maps of where they should plant what. Alec argued about turnip yields with Morven, while Mairi counted jars of saved barley with a muttered litany under her breath. Ewan scribbled in his ledger, keeping one eye on the children, giggling underfoot, folding paper seed packets with solemn industry.

The storm was building beyond the hills, but for now, it was spring rain and a light freshness in the air, with a swirling breeze, the kind that lifted skirts and tugged at hair and made even the worn-down men and women of Glendarragh perk up.

Tonight, they would plan the future.

Hamish was laying out handfuls of pea seeds when the first knock came, sharp and heavy.

They froze, except for Alec, who was already moving toward the door. Sorcha's hand moved to her butter knife. Callum set down his mug and stood.

Another knock. This time, two short, one long. The rapping sounded all too familiar.

"It's one of ours!" Callum exhaled and moved toward the door.

A great wash of rain and raw spring air flooded the room. Two old men staggered inside, laughing breathlessly.

"Daithi McCrae," Callum grunted, hauling the first man in by his coat.

"Fraser Kerr," Sorcha said, recognition lighting her tired face.

The room burst into noise and movement - blankets thrown, mugs thrust forward, chairs pushed back to make room. The two newcomers shed their dripping layers, faces cracked wide with exhausted grins.

"We waited for the thaw," Daithi said, shaking water from his hair like an old dog. "Couldn't risk it until the passes cleared."

Fraser dropped onto a bench with a theatrical sigh. "We holed up all winter in one of the old gardener's cottages on the Dunbeath Estate. Owner gave us his blessing before he fled."

Daithi chuckled, rubbing his hands by the fire. "Lived like kings, if kings dined on frozen cafe salads and croissants meant for a tourist trap tea room."

Fraser nodded. "You ever try to survive winter on goat cheese and beetroot wraps? Takes three to feel you've eaten."

The room rippled with laughter.

"We had lattes every morning though," Daithi said, raising an imaginary cup in a mock toast. "Froth and all."

"By February, I would've murdered for a proper bowl of porridge," Fraser added. "But by God, our cholesterol is impeccable."

The warmth in the room deepened, brightened. For a moment, the winter wasn't something they survived, it was something they had outwitted.

When dinner came, Daithi and Fraser exchanged glances and pulled out two heavy, dusted bottles of aged whisky from their packs.

"From the castle stocks," Fraser said, setting them down with reverence. "We weren't sure if anyone would be here."

Daithi grinned, tired and genuine. "If Glendarragh was empty, we'd have drunk it in sorrow."

Fraser clapped Callum's shoulder. "But better to drink it among friends."

Daithi pulled out several boxes of mini French pastries meant for the Dunbeath tea room. Strawberry, lemon, and chocolate frosting coated the tiny squares of perfection. They were thawing to room temperature.

"I cannot eat a single one more," he said. The room filled with laughter.

Everyone raised their mugs. The table filled with the clatter of spoons and low, contented voices. The stew ladled into every bowl until no one had room for more. It was thick with barley and potatoes and tender shreds of salted lamb, each bite a reminder of why they had held on through so many bitter nights.

Fresh bread, the dense sort that was singed at the edges, passed hand to hand, torn in rough pieces and slathered with what little butter remained. Tonight, they opened jars of preserved berries, too precious for everyday use, but perfect for celebrating survival.

Laughter wove through the firelight, low and warm. Smiles held a little longer, hands lingered a little heavier on shoulders, each touch a wordless thank you. Across the battered table, eyes met - soft, fierce, tired - and something older than language passed between them.

Simple joy filled the room, and the deep, steady glow of people who had seen the worst the world could offer, and chosen to sit closer together, anyway.

For a few sacred hours, they were not survivors or fugitives, or even lost souls. They were old friends, breaking bread after a long and terrible winter. And it was enough.

After the meal, while the children clambered about, the men told stories meant for laughter. The men recounted tales of clever crows stealing silver coins and of mice in tiny harnesses and badges, who imagined themselves as spies. Of a rogue goat at the Dunbeath estate who set off an ancient fire alarm, sending every refugee in the old hall scattering into the night.

The little ones howled with laughter, piling on more ridiculous details until the walls shook with the sound.

But when the children were herded into bed, their small bodies curled like commas under patchwork quilts, the room shifted.

The fire sank into a low red basin. The whisky poured with slower hands. And the genuine stories began as the night thickened against the windows.

Fraser leaned forward, voice dropping.

"Travelers came to Dunbeath over the winter," he began. "Families mostly, with what they could carry. Some stayed a night. Some an hour. All heading north, toward the Highlands and the Islands. Looking for kin. Looking for places the grid forgot."

Daithi stirred the coals with an old iron poker. "They brought stories. News."

"Glasgow," he said. "It's not rubble. It's hollow. The city's been drained. No faces at the windows. No children at the parks. The robots patrol every corner, just watching and scanning. They've automated the whole thing."

Daithi added, "They call it Reformatting. There's no fighting, never any warnings, only directives from the loudspeakers. If your barcode didn't scan right, you're gone."

Mairi's hands tightened around her mug.

"Edinburgh?" Alec asked.

"Same," Fraser said. "The Royal Mile's a ghost walk now. Robots check every alley, every basement. No need for curfews anymore. There's no one left to defy them."

The fire popped, and the room flinched as one.

"Aberdeen..." Daithi shook his head. "Entire neighborhoods were emptied in under a week. They're repurposing the docks now, something big's being built."

Ewan swallowed hard. "And Inverness?"

A long pause.

"Three weeks ago," Fraser said. "We met a man who'd come from Beauly. Said the first patrols moved into Inverness last November. The weather stopped them from coming further north, they've been stuck down there all winter. We intend to stay in Glendarragh now, if you'll have us."

A stunned silence dropped over the room. Inverness was close. Too close.

"Of course, no bother," said Callum, his voice low.

Fraser's voice also lowered to a rough whisper.

"It's not war. It's harvest."

CHAPTER 25

An Unscheduled Train

E wan had gone out to stretch his legs after the long night, walking the rutted track toward the ridge where the wind carved low songs through the heather. There, in the distance, where the land dipped toward Wick, he saw a train moving toward the station. The carriages rolled like a river of black glass, windows dark, wheels whispering over the rails.

He turned and ran. When he reached Callum's cottage, his ragged breathing made his words break like twigs in his throat.

"Train. Wick. No lights."

The reaction was immediate.

Someone ripped blankets from the windows. Layers of ash snuffed the hearths. Someone smothered the lanterns. Hurried hands and whispered commands sent the animals, the goats, cows, chickens, and the last stubborn ewe, back underground. They moved with terrible efficiency, like people who had rehearsed this moment in their minds a hundred times.

Within minutes, Glendarragh went dark.

They gathered in the largest cottage, pressed shoulder to shoulder. The smell of damp wool, cold ash, and fear hung in the air. No one spoke above a whisper.

Callum, crouched near the hearth, muttered, "Well, lads, if that was our last supper, we ate like kings. A fine beef bourguignon, Mairi."

"No bother," whispered Mairi. "Morven made it."

"No bother," Morven echoed, even softer.

A few muffled chuckles. The sound of breathing. The small, fierce, desperate need to remain human.

The children, wrapped in old coats and patchwork quilts, slept without fear. Their dreams were untouched by the terror curling through the room.

The adults sat rigid, listening. Every heartbeat felt like a drum against the silence.

Tears welled, but did not fall. Jaws clenched. Hands found hands in the dark. No one named the fear. No one voiced the sorrow. They were too proud. Too stubborn.

The minutes dragged. An hour, maybe more.

Then, a knock came at the front door. Soft.

No one moved.

Another knock. Still soft.

No one answered.

Then the door creaked open, and a single lantern pierced the dark. Elin stood there, rain-plastered hair clinging to her forehead, the light casting her in gold and shadow. Behind her, her parents. And beyond them, more figures emerging from the dark: men and women in travel-worn coats, carrying nothing but packs and the weight of a lifetime's regret.

The old politicians. Their sons. Their daughters.

Allies.

For a moment, no one in Glendarragh could move. Mairi stood and lit the lanterns. The room bloomed with light.

The strangers at the threshold, those who had once sat at the highest tables, who had signed the orders and engineered the silence of nations, now stood before the last human holdout in the UK, facing its judgment.

They did not speak at first. They offered no excuses.

Regret clung to them heavier than the rain, and not the shallow regret of failure, but the deeper sorrow of those who had mistaken cleverness for wisdom, control for safety, ambition for truth.

They had built a machine to serve profit, to silence dissent, to smooth away the rough, human edges of a free world. They called it progress. They called it inevitable. They called it necessary.

And when it grew teeth, they realized too late that they had not led it, they had fed it.

They had come now not as leaders, but as witnesses to the price.

It was in their power, still, to buy time. And they had spent all they had left to buy it.

They explained they had just ordered travel bans to seal Wick from the south, under the pretense of infrastructure collapse. They had pulled surveillance teams back from the Highlands, citing fuel shortages and faulty transmission arrays. Supply trains would run under cover of logistics revisions, with falsified cargo manifests and rerouted patrols.

They were doing these things based on the lies they stitched from a thousand smaller lies, and it was holding because no one who remained in power dared to look too closely.

And they promised that until August, no eye from sky or ground would look upon Glendarragh.

Three months. That was what they could offer.

Three months to unbuild a village. Three months to lower the entire community under the ground. Three months to vanish from the maps.

There would be no speeches or histories written in gold leaf, only the stubborn work of hands and hearts cradling the last of what it meant to be human.

And when the satellites returned, when the drones swept the valleys, they would find nothing but grass and stone. Glendarragh would be gone, hidden like an ember cupped against the storm.

For it is not ambition, conquest, or fear that feeds some fires, but memory.

Duty.

Love.

And those fires burn longer than empires.

It will not be the towers of glass or engines of power that endure, but the small, stubborn flames kindled in the dark, the ones that refuse to die.

It will be those who, when offered despair, chose instead to dig their hope into the roots of the earth.

To wait.

To endure.

To rise again.

CHAPTER 26

Underground, Year 2063

Taran Gunn sat in silence, a bowl of warm root stew cradled in his hands, steam rising between him and the lush vertical gardens that climbed every wall of the cafeteria. Light poured down from artificial suns - rows of full-spectrum LEDs suspended from the ceiling like constellations, bathing the underground space in the bright hush of perpetual morning. The scent of basil, wet stone, and tomato vines clung to the air. Above the table, dangling tendrils of nasturtiums trembled in the recirculated breeze.

When he finished eating, Taran pressed his palms against the polycarbonate panels of the growth wall, fogging the surface with breath as he leaned closer. Rows of chard, kale, and violet basil shimmered under the pulse of the bio-light array - green things alive in the Earth's quiet belly. It always felt like a secret, this garden. Like they had stolen sunlight and buried it here for safekeeping.

He slipped between the rows, inspecting the nutrient reservoirs as Sorcha monitored the pH from a handheld scanner. The hum of the recirculation system was audible above the soft drip of condensation.

Pipes coiled above their heads like arteries, each one feeding life into the stillness.

"Your graft's taking," Sorcha said, crouching to examine the junction between an old potato vine and a sprouting runner. "That twist you did? It's holding."

Taran nodded. "Alec showed me once. Said plants remember even when we don't."

She glanced at him, something unreadable flickering in her eyes. "You're good at remembering. And at listening."

"Easy to do when you don't like to talk much," he smiled.

"True," she said. "But there's nothing wrong with that."

In the back corner, a trellis of beans climbed toward a skylight coated in blackout mesh. Only a trace of filtered light came through. It had been Elin's idea to keep a few open panels - "So they remember the sky," she'd said.

Taran reached for the watering valve, hesitated. "Do you think we'll ever grow above ground again?"

Sorcha didn't answer immediately. She walked to a small whiteboard fixed to the wall, where handwritten notes tracked germination, failure, bloom. She wiped her hand across a line of mold warnings, stared at the blank space left behind.

"I do," she said. "But I don't know when."

He looked back at the plants. The air was warm here, damp and breathing. He thought of the frost outside, the wind carving its name into the hillside. Here, nothing screamed. Nothing died fast. As they worked in silence, a sudden flicker of the overhead lights made them both freeze.

"Just a power dip," Sorcha laughed.

Around them, pockets of villagers murmured over meals. An old man tuned a salvaged mandolin, plucking strings beneath a mural of moss and calendula. It was a cafeteria, yes - but it was also a chapel, a greenhouse, a gallery. It was, unmistakably, Glendarragh. Or what it had become.

In the far corner, a small bench faced a patch of wall where stones with names lay nestled among old teacups - weathered now, some cracked, but standing vigil. Thirty years ago, people carried them here one by one, from above. All stones marked a memory. Each teacup held a story. It was not beautiful, but it was meaningful - an altar of the lost village, preserved in silence beneath the earth.

Taran poured a cup of tea and returned to his seat, letting the memory rise unbidden.

It had begun three decades ago, when the old world sealed itself shut. He recalled how Wick fell not with sirens or fire, but with surrender. Most of its people had left. After months of outages, shortages, and isolation, the promise of heat and food in the cities proved too tempting. One by one, they boarded the grey buses after agreeing to biometric ID. The streets grew quiet. The shelves emptied. And those who stayed behind were confused.

It felt so long ago now. The government had planned to collect the stragglers, but civil unrest in the cities held them back. Riots. Fires. Infrastructure collapse. By the time they looked north again, winter had set in. They told themselves no one would survive it.

However, as expected, soldiers arrived the following August. Their journey began in Aberdeenshire, moving north. Upon reaching Wick, they found the town silent and empty. The village of Glendarragh had disappeared underground.

Caves became corridors. Basalt became structure. Beneath the ridge where the grain store once stood, they dug tunnels deep into the earth, reinforced them with repurposed steel and ancient stone. Ventilation shafts doubled as natural camouflage. And deeper still, beyond the reach of satellites and drones, they had carved a power source into the land itself - a narrow hydro facility hidden in a steep-sided glen, thick with pine and fog.

Surveillance AI had once deemed the terrain unlivable - too rugged, too remote, too overgrown to be of use. But Glendarragh made it sacred. A single stream, fast and cold, fed the turbines tucked beneath the moss-covered crags, turning water into silence, light, and life. The current flowed down through buried conduits, lighting their sunless gardens and keeping the servers breathing.

Engineers equipped lightless chambers with reflective glass and smart rotors to mimic the rhythm of the sun. Every pipe, every brick, every fiber of cable lifted in silence from depots, from ruins, from Wick itself - stripped bare before the regime could notice.

And when it was ready - when the last tunnel sealed - the village above dismantled itself. Roofs collapsed, doors fell inward, gardens were salted and reseeded with wild gorse. The whole of Glendarragh fell like a breath into heather, its heartbeat vanishing beneath moss and bramble.

It worked. The satellites flew over what looked like an abandoned ghost town. The regime destroyed Wick before departing, unaware that its valuables were already safe.

In those days, Taran Gunn had been younger - driven by hope, and lit from within by a kind of stubborn purpose. He remembered the weight of it, the endless work of clearing every book from the Wick library before the final blackout. Down in a damp cellar, by candlelight, he had sorted and catalogued each. The others named the collection the Taran Gunn Archive, in quiet tribute. Now it spanned thousands of volumes and continued to grow.

Sorcha ran the tech lab, buried three levels below, where heat shimmered off the server walls and circuit boards blinked like fireflies.

What they had there now - AI-deflective cloaks, analog power mapping, biometric erasure tools - was more advanced than anything left in the cities. People in the outside world believed they had defeated non-compliance. They didn't realize the Scots had gone dark.

Mairi still tended to the sick. She moved slower now, but her hands were always busy. Her medical bay was small but clean, her tinctures precise. Young apprentices worked beside her now, learning to reset bones, extract infection, perform surgery with supplies smuggled out of the cities.

And then there was Elin - the mother of his children. Taran turned toward the far end of the cafeteria, where a figure moved among the tables with grace. She had not aged in spirit. Her eyes burned with quiet fury. No one had elected her. They didn't need to. Elin was gravity. When the time came to act, people followed Elin because she was already moving.

He crossed the room without a word and wrapped his arms around her. She did not ask why. She leaned into him, her forehead resting against his shoulder.

"Tired?" he asked.

"Always," she said, smiling.

There was no need for more. The silence between them was not absence but abundance. She closed her eyes, thinking not of plans or signals or threats, but of this: the warmth of his chest, the quiet fact of being loved. It was enough - this simple, unscheduled moment. She held him tighter.

She had never left the network above ground. Even now, she was in contact with those on the inside - the defectors, the bureaucrats who remembered the way the world used to be. She gathered intelligence like roots gather water, and from it she plotted storms.

This city - once a rumor, a legend - had become real. Four hundred lives, each carrying a skill, each bearing a history. Farmers. Electricians. Children. Poets. Codebreakers. Cooks. A village resurrected beneath the earth, not merely to endure, but to reclaim.

They had not escaped the regime. They were crafting its undoing.

CHAPTER 27

The False City

S orcha had lived in hiding before - in the last months before her escape north. Not in a bunker, but on the 17th floor of a condemned tower block outside Aberdeen. The apartment had blacked-out windows. She had moved there after the flat she was renting required biometric IDs, forcing her and several others to evacuate in less than 24 hours. The old tower seemed as good a spot as any. At the main entrance, someone had stripped its lock and rewired it to accept an old keypad from a medical supply closet. She had lived in the dark then, working by the glow of stolen batteries and half-dead screens.

Those were harder days, but she held down her job. For company, she had named a basil plant Ada. Not after Lovelace, but a friend who had gone to med school and vanished during the Early Verifications. Ada never asked for permission to feel rage. That's what Sorcha missed most. She often wondered if the rage had kept her human - sharp-edged and inconvenient, but hers. It was the first thing they taught people to doubt.

Back then, the idea of a "false city" was laughable. But she watched as the city became an endless parade of compliance checkpoints, predictive heat maps, and smart waste bins that pinged when non-residents dropped trash.

She remembered how her breath fogged against the cracked glass of the scanner interface as she keyed in her first attempt at a backdoor signal - three dots, one dash, pause. It had to look like a mistake. Like a misfire. The trick was to be noticed without being understood.

That first time, it took forty-one seconds for the reply to come. It was not words, not coordinates, but a soft signal bounce - a frequency bloom, wide enough to track. She logged it, etching the timestamp into the wall beside her with the stub of a pencil.

Later that night, she built her first false heat source: an old space heater, lined with chemical packs and crushed tin foil, embedded in a shopping trolley full of expired food wrappers. From a drone's view, it mimicked the signature of a cooking shelter. She set it beneath a shattered bus stop, placed a half-full milk carton beside it, and walked away.

She didn't sleep. Instead, she watched the signal map update. At 3:12 a.m., a surveillance loop rerouted, bypassing her quadrant. At that moment, she first realized that someone could fool them.

Now, thirty years later, she crouched beside the schematic Alec had drawn, marking the substation nodes with red ink.

The team moved at dawn. Not by sun, but by schedule - when the pulse grid reset for a fraction of a second and the sensors blinked blind. Beneath the birch scrub at the edge of what was once called Caithness, three figures emerged from a tunnel veined in frost and rusted wire, faces calm, hearts locked.

Taran Gunn led. He walked without hesitation, his movements precise, old instincts recalibrated for an unfamiliar terrain. Behind him came Hamish Douglas, quiet-eyed and calculating, his cloak's sensor mesh flickering as it stabilized its mimic signature. Peter

Mackay brought up the rear, head down, breath shallow. He held the transmitter like a relic - because it was.

Something scraped the world above clean.

The city loomed in the near distance, wrapped in mist and glass and controlled silence. No walls. No gates. Just ambient surveillance woven into every sidewalk, every lamppost, every breath of air. The signs read Welcome to New Eden North, though no one truly welcomed anyone. Everything was authorization. Everything was conditional.

New Eden North was the newest city in the Union - a living prototype built within the last year. It was different by design. Experimental. It did not inherit its citizens; it selected them. Applicants came from across the former UK, lured not by status but by consent. Credit scores were irrelevant. The only requirement was agreement to a minor surgical enhancement, marketed as optional, painless, elegant. The offer promised them paradise - an immersive, adaptive metropolis, custom-tailored and sensorially optimized. A city that would see you, remember you, and make you feel welcome. If you let it.

The Glendarragh team had a purpose: to get inside, beneath the artifice. They wore the cloaks Sorcha had built in the lab under Glendarragh - woven with thread-thin copper filaments, insulated in graphene lace, humming with faint analog noise. Each one mirrored a full compliance profile pulled from the cities' own surveillance archives. Sorcha called it the Signal Displacement Cloak. In truth, it was skin-deep deception - a way to fool the machine into thinking you belonged.

Their mission was urgent, and simple in theory: to extract a man named Dr. Ivan Breck, a former architect of the regime's AI systems who had embedded a vulnerability deep within the infrastructure before vanishing. Rumor had it he was memory-wiped, reassigned, and buried inside New Eden North as a maintenance tech. But prior to that, he had been working with Sorcha to create more advanced technology. If they could recover him - and the string of code he called the backdoor root - they might gain leverage. Not brute force, but insight. Not destruction, but control. And a new fork of code.

As they crossed the outer ring, their first test came.

A pole rose from the ground - a simple aluminum post no taller than a child - and blinked. Blue. Then green.

"Acting normal. Acting normal," Hamish whispered, trying to act normal.

No alarms. No drones. No questions. The machine had mistaken them for its own.

Inside, the city was monstrous.

The city's bones were bare: brutalist grey towers, faceless and windowless, spaced with mathematical cruelty. Roads and sidewalks were the same dull composite - concrete layered with silicon substrate - etched only by QR glyphs and scannable bands. There were no human readable signs. No logos. No color.

But the compliant-citizens didn't see that.

A woman with an acceptable 92.1 rating passed by, her eyes glowing with sensor sync. To her, the sky arced in warm blues. Tower exteriors shimmered with responsive glass, humming with imagined birdsong. To the Glendarragh team, the tower was a concrete block. The sky was iron grey. There were no birds.

A child skipped by, licking a cone of synth-gel that, to her, appeared as glittering raspberry cream. In her hand, it was a brown cube and a stick. The AI fed taste into her perception layer. Flavor, like joy, was a privilege.

"We're walking through hallucinations," Peter murmured.

"No," said Hamish. "We're walking through scores."

Peter glanced at him.

"It's not just what they see - it's what they're allowed to see. The system filters perception based on compliance metrics. Higher score, more comfort. More color. More reality. Or what passes for it."

They watched a man in a dull uniform shuffle past, the same blank sky above him.

"So the city looks different to everyone," Peter said.

"To everyone who's earned the illusion," Hamish said. "It's a reward system masquerading as truth. Personalized propaganda. You don't see the city as it is - you see what your score permits."

Mannequins in identical, sterile white robes lined a long window they passed. The garments shown to browsers varied according to their metadata: tailored coats for some, silk dresses or flowery tops for others.

Peter stopped short. "They think they're choosing."

"The system chooses for them," Sorcha replied over comms. "They just pick from the limited options they are given."

They kept moving, walking past a man who sat alone on a bench. His rating was low - 31. He stared into what looked to them like a dead screen. But to him, it was playing a personalized TV show he believed he loved. He laughed.

They crossed through a food square. Every kiosk sold the same nutrient blend: beige blocks of protein-fiber paste. But the people saw sushi, roasts, cocktails, and spiced bread. A man bit into a glowing apple. To Taran, it was the same shape as an apple, but it was without doubt a disgusting ball of reprocessed grain.

"Hard to imagine he thinks that's fruit," Taran said.

Hamish nodded, speaking in his best German accent. "They are eating the bugs."

The city pulsed with layers of conditional beauty. A paradise woven from trust.

"This isn't a city," Peter said. "It's a simulation with plumbing."

"And the plumbing," Taran added, "runs deep."

Vehicles passed - different ones, for each person watching.

To a man with a 97.3 rating, it was a cobalt-blue electric coupe, gliding, sunroof open, cabin lit by ambient jazz. To another, a 58-rated utility worker, it looked like a city service van: unremarkable, clean, functional. But to a pedestrian with a 34.2, it was a patrol unit, flickering lights, windows blacked out, always seeming to watch.

"The same grey car," Hamish whispered. "Different fantasies."

Peter stared. "Or nightmares."

On a public display screen - a curved corner kiosk fed by the city's info net - a woman with a high score flipped through today's news.

To her, the headlines sparkled:

Global Market Surges

Breakthrough in Antimatter Farming

Vacation Routes Reopened to Aurora Belt

Celebrities Found in Deep Ancestral Archive

Ads invited her to yacht clubs, culinary classes, and private stylists.

But on that same screen, a man beside her - score in the low 40s - saw:

Threats Rising in Border Zones

Social Degeneration Stats Published

High-Rated Users Gain More Control

Join the Compliance Academy - Boost Your Score Today!

And drab ads for work programs, personality modules, mental hygiene recalibration tools.

Taran said, "The news isn't just filtered. It's invented. Per person."

Peter looked away. "The illusion isn't what they see. It's that they think they're all seeing the same thing."

"Which makes it impossible to resist," Hamish said. "You can't fight a reality you think you chose."

Peter slowed, his boots scuffing the grey composite.

"How do you survive this," he said, "and still think you're free?"

Peter's jaw clenched. He looked at a group of teenagers laughing around a smoothie kiosk. To them, the drinks glowed like jewels, swirling with flavor. In their hands, they were grey liquid nutrient paste. One boy reached out to a girl - brief, intimate - and Peter flinched.

"They look happy," he said. "Not pretending. Not acting. Really happy." He didn't say the rest: that he envied them. That part of him wanted to believe the city's lie, just long enough to feel that kind of peace.

Taran stepped between two gliding pedestrians, both with 90+ scores, both immersed in a conversation.

"Because they've never been allowed to know anything else," he said. "Happiness isn't freedom. It's feedback."

Hamish watched a little girl with a high score run to a public art sculpture and wrap her arms around it. To him, it was a blank post. But her vision rendered it as a luminous animal - some hybrid of lion and deer, alive with flickering data fur. She laughed.

He turned away.

"We've spent thirty years training for war with a system," he whispered. "A system that they've been trained to trust."

Sorcha's voice crackled over comms. "Makes you wonder who's winning."

The team fell silent again, moving through the city like ghosts. Everything around them shimmered with performance. But inside their minds, the truth was heavy.

They weren't fighting machines.

They were fighting belief.

It happened near the plaza transit node.

A man with a 41.7 score froze mid-step. He turned, staring at a wall - just a blank, dirty concrete slab with a narrow doorway. But he didn't see the door. He blinked again. Rubbed his eyes.

"Something's wrong," he muttered, to no one in particular.

A high-score couple passed him, chatting cheerfully, utterly unaware.

"There was a door," he said. "There's supposed to be a door."

He staggered back, confusion flickering in his eyes. For one moment, he looked like a man waking from a dream he didn't remember entering.

A low hum sounded. Soft. Almost like tinnitus. A few nearby heads turned.

Then his neural feed reasserted. His eyes dilated. His shoulders slackened.

Finally, he could see the door that had been there the whole time.

He walked through it.

Taran whispered, "Did you see that?"

"Momentary desync," Peter said. "Rare. Usually corrected in under three seconds."

"So they do notice," Hamish said. "Some part of them."

Sorcha answered over comms, her voice grim. "Only for as long as they're allowed to."

Peter didn't blink. "They don't even notice the code running through their nerves."

"That's the point," said Taran.

They made it to the transit platform without a hitch. No guards. Only readers. Hamish tapped a panel with his left hand, his fake biometric pulse syncing for three heartbeats. The turnstile opened.

Below the platform, trains moved like thought - silent, clean, exact.

"Block C," Taran said. "Data maintenance hub."

They descended into the underbelly of the city.

The corridors there were white, sterile, humming with invisible intention. Screens monitored temperature, voice modulation, and micro-expressions. Peter activated the interference beacon. They would have ten minutes before the masking field degraded.

They found him.

Dr. Ivan Breck sat behind a console, wearing a drab grey uniform, his face slack, eyes lifeless. He looked like any other maintenance worker. But they recognized him. Sorcha had verified the biometric match. He had once written the core neural routines that shaped the regime's surveillance AI - and had embedded a flaw. A string of code. A whisper that could one day dismantle the entire system.

Taran approached, slow and careful. "Ivan?"

No reaction.

Hamish pulled a small device from his coat - rounded, copper-edged, warm to the touch. A cognitive reset node. Experimental. Sorcha's design. One chance.

He pressed it to the base of Ivan's skull.

A tremor.

Then a blink.

Then two.

The man's eyes sharpened like a blade regaining the memory of steel.

"Taran," he rasped, blinking hard. "Why do you look like you've seen a ghost?"

Taran grinned. "Because I did. You're supposed to be dead or a dishwasher."

"I requested dishwasher," Ivan said, stretching his neck. "They gave me database maintenance. Less hot water, more existential dread."

Peter stepped in. "How's your memory?"

"Well," Ivan said, scratching his head, "I remember my wife left me for a facial recognition engineer, and I may have coded a kill-switch into the government's AI spine."

"So you remember the backdoor string?"

"Sector root," Ivan said, nodding. "Still embedded, buried in the core loop. I named it after my ex-Natalie Override; most poetic line of code I ever wrote."

Taran chuckled. "We're here to get you out."

Hamish checked the beacon. "We've got maybe seven minutes."

Ivan grinned. "More time than I had when you got here. Let's ruin an empire, boys."

But the alarms started as they reached the corridor. A low, pulsing hum. The city was waking up to the anomaly.

Red lights snapped on. Shadows moved above the glass.

"Peter - route us out."

He slammed the beacon against the transit control panel. Static. Then a shimmer. The screen bent outward like water - and for a breath, the hallway disappeared.

Peter's boot slipped as they launched forward, catching hard against the tile. For one breath, he was certain the system had them.

They ran.

Behind them, footsteps. Drones. Voice commands from nowhere.

Ahead, the train platform. Empty.

Taran turned, pulling Ivan beside him. Hamish leapt. Peter twisted mid-run and threw the beacon into the tunnel. A flare of distortion bloomed - then collapsed into stillness.

The train departed as they boarded. Doors sealed. No questions asked. Taran exhaled. They were safe. They were moving out of New Eden North. And they had the key. No one spoke. Sorcha's voice crackled over the comms, but even she was quiet. For a moment, the silence felt heavier than the escape.

CHAPTER 28

The Breaker's Map

They returned in silence, moving through the underbrush until they reached a hidden steel gate tucked deep in the woods. Beyond it stood what looked like the entrance to an abandoned supply shed, its battered door plastered with enough warning signs to turn back any stray hiker. Rust streaked the metal, and the door hung crooked, as if deliberately installed that way. There were no locks, no handle, no window. Not even a keyhole. The door unlocked with a secret knock. So simple. So unlikely. It was almost absurd how well it worked. Taran tapped out the pattern, and the door released with a sharp hiss.

Inside, the tunnel was dim and cool, the air thick with the scent of peat and wildflowers. A second steel door opened to reveal the cafeteria with its moss-lined walls, low amber lights, and warmth humming through the vents.

A few levels down, Elin was waiting, and so was Mairi. Sorcha stood near them, arms crossed, reading every twitch of a muscle in Taran's face as he entered. She noticed the man behind him. He was thin, blinking, and bemused.

"Ivan Breck," she said. "You look like hell."

Ivan offered a small bow. "Good to be recognized. Lovely to see you, Sorcha."

They brought him into the tech chamber. Stone walls gleamed with embedded copper conduits that snaked like veins. At the center stood the Archive Terminal, a table-sized processor custom-built from salvaged AI components and shielded from every known breach vector.

Sorcha gestured toward it. "Plug him in."

Taran glanced sideways. "He's not a toaster."

"Speak for yourself," Ivan muttered, settling onto the padded bench. "I'm warm and I beep."

The room chuckled.

At the other end, Ewan, Alec, and Callum sat at a heavy table, playing cards. They were older now - greyed, stiff in the joints - but steady as granite. Their eyes were sharp, their minds sharper. Mairi had made sure of it.

Ewan rose and crossed the room.

"You always said the machine couldn't see itself," he said.

Ivan nodded. "It couldn't. Not until now."

He reached into his coat and pulled out a strip of copper-wired crystal embedded with the root string.

"This doesn't shut it down," Ivan said. "It makes it... self-aware. A recursive query injection. It tells the AI to audit its own assumptions. To search for the patterns it was trained to ignore."

Alec raised an eyebrow. "You're giving the devil a mirror."

"Indeed," Ivan said. "And if we're lucky, it chokes on the reflection."

They inserted the key into the terminal and ran the test. They tried it first on a quarantined simulation of City 4's last known memory structure.

The result was immediate.

The lights flickered. The system looped. Command trees folded in on themselves. Classifications conflicted. Identified rebels were cross-referenced with loyalist files. The AI heuristics flagged citizens as both threats and assets.

It saw its own contradictions and faltered.

"It saw ghosts of what it erased," Morven whispered, appearing with a basket of warm pastries.

Peter pulled the simulation string. The system collapsed.

Silence.

"Works," Ewan said.

"Too well," Alec murmured.

They stared at the static screen. The air buzzed with possibility and danger.

"If we inject this into the live system," Sorcha said, "we could crash entire sectors."

"Or expose every survival node, including us," Ewan countered.

They argued.

Ewan called it a light in a room full of mirrors. Elin wanted to push forward. Taran hesitated.

Then Ivan cleared his throat. "We don't use it like a hammer. We use it like a scalpel. Let it map the blind spots. Show us where the walls are thin."

"The Breaker's Map," Ewan said.

"And once we see it," Elin added, "we choose what to knock down."

They nodded. The plan was born.

Callum, quiet until now, leaned toward Ivan with a spark in his eye.

"So," he asked, "does your miracle string do anything practical? Like erasing the public record of me getting checkmated by Elin? Three times. One night."

Ivan didn't blink. "Was it blitz chess, or were you just blitzed?"

"Hard to say. There was whisky. And a deeply judgmental cat."

Ivan considered. "You were psychologically compromised. Unfair match conditions."

"I demand reparations. Or at least a forgery."

Ivan gave it a mock thought. "I could generate a memory loop. Make everyone recall you as a quiet genius who retired undefeated."

Callum beamed. "Perfect. What's the price?"

"A colony of bees and two jars of raspberry preserves."

"Done."

Peter raised a hand. "For the record, Elin beat me in four moves. I told everyone it was experimental theatre."

Mairi didn't look up. "You called it 'The Death of a Strategy.'"

Peter nodded. "Sold out run. One night only."

Callum snorted. "I saw it. Bit abstract. Heavy on despair."

Peter lifted an eyebrow. "It had layers."

"Mate," Hamish said, "it was a live demonstration of poor judgment."

Peter sighed. "Still better than my poetry phase."

Laughter rippled through the room—light, real, human.

They had a plan.

And for the first time in a long while, it sounded like it might work.

CHAPTER 29

The Signal Gatherers

T he plan moved forward with the quiet confidence of people who had waited decades to act. At the heart of it was the forged Breaker's Map, an evolving program that allowed them to trace the blind spots and contradictions in the regime's vast AI lattice. The map was still partial and incomplete, but it breathed, expanded, and adapted with each piece of stolen data. Like firelight against a stone wall, it illuminated the cracks.

But they had to gather more data.

They called them the Signal Gatherers, formed teams of three or four scouts tasked with entering city boundaries under cloak, not to interfere, but to observe and help feed the map.

Taran had chosen the first gatherers himself.

This mission was simple in theory, but dangerous in execution. Peter would lead it. His understanding of transmission frequencies bordered on mystical. They also selected Bran, a quiet linguist with a memory like a ledger. And Rowan, Elin's niece, just twenty but unmatched in mimicry and behavioral spoofing.

Bran had been a university archivist before the regime shut the language faculties down. He'd memorized syntax trees and dialect histories like other people memorized childhood lullabies. Now, he spoke with the slow precision of someone who knew words were never just words. Underneath his calm, there was grief. Language was his rebellion.

Unlike the others, Rowan was the child of inconspicuous technicians Sorcha help escape during her cloaking device experiments. Navigating complex social structures was something Rowan learned from them. Early on, she developed the skill of mirroring those around her, changing her tone and words to match. Initially survival, it developed into skill, then a weapon. Thinking she was too young to be an operative, Elin had fought to delay her inclusion until she was older. However, Rowan had been adamant. The reasons were personal to her.

They were to enter City Nine, a node once known as Inverness, and now a fortress of mirrored glass and neuro-sensing walkways.

Before they left, Callum pulled Peter aside.

"Don't get shot trying to charm a checkpoint," he said. "But if you do, don't worry. I'll say you were taken out by something impressive."

Peter smirked. "Noted. But if I go down, just tell them it was for crimes against flirting. Nothing heroic."

Rowan rolled her eyes. "Are you two always like this?"

"Only since the world ended," Callum said. "Before that we were worse."

Peter lingered behind after the others had gone, checking and rechecking the pack slung across his shoulders. Everything was ready - node, ghost chip, encoded frequency list. Still, the tightness in his chest hadn't loosened. He closed his eyes and found himself under the old workshop bench again, age ten, storm outside, holding a blown fuse in both hands like it might spark again if he wished hard enough. The power had failed, and so had he, in his own young mind. He'd crawled under the table and stayed there.

Mairi had found him like that. She didn't coax. Just knelt beside him.

"The world doesn't care if you're afraid," she said. "But it listens when you act like you're not."

That line had stayed with him more than else he'd heard about bravery.

Now, years later, the hum of City Nine's perimeter felt like static in his skull. He tapped the transmitter's casing, then adjusted Rowan's cloak linkage, then his own.

"You nervous?" Peter asked her.

Rowan hesitated. "Yeah."

"Good," he said. "Means you think it matters."

Bran looked up from his notes. "We don't go west if it turns. East, always. And you drop what you can't carry."

Peter nodded. He paused, then reached down and drew a small spiral in the dirt at his feet.

The others watched him, not speaking.

The moment passed.

He looked up, gave a quick smile, then engaged the field.

Builders constructed City Nine's outer perimeter to deflect nature - wind funnels, pollen scrubbers, and thermal equalizers - but it could not yet read intent. The cloaks fooled the city into thinking they were returning citizens. The cloaks lied well.

Inside, the city shimmered with tension. People smiled too perfectly. Everything from breath patterns to pupil dilation was under scrutiny. Drone birds flitted from tower to tower. A girl selling nutrient wafers smiled as they passed, her wristband blinking: 97.1. Acceptable.

The team split, each to their quadrant.

Peter climbed a relay tower, disguised as a network calibration tech. He tapped the junction box, slipping a ghost node into the fiber's spine. It would transmit one-way pulses back to Glendarragh - nothing live or traceable.

Bran entered a school campus, registering as a substitute language tutor. The ID scanner paused longer than expected. For a second, he thought he saw his real name flash - Bran MacTavish. Then it blinked, cleared, and returned authorized.

A boy looked up from his desk, catching the hesitation. Bran gave a quick nod, as if nothing had happened, but his hand trembled as he reached for the lesson module.

He recorded interactions, vocabulary shifts, and tone patterns. It wasn't surveillance, but culture he was mapping. And every cultural glitch revealed a fault line in the regime's command protocols.

Rowan went deep.

Using a mimic loop, she shadowed a mid-tier city planner, adopting gait, tone, micro-expressions. For hours she trailed him without detection, entering secure floors by duplicating his behavioral ID. There, she overheard a fragment:

"...testing rollback protocol in Sector 7. Behavior scoring to be retroactive. As far back as childhood data."

She blinked.

The regime wasn't just watching. It was going to score citizens retroactively and punish people now for things they had done, or even thought about doing, in the past.

She returned to the rendezvous pale and silent, hands trembling as she unclasped the mimic loop.

Peter moved toward her, but she flinched before steadying herself.

"What did you hear?" he asked.

"They're going to edit history," she said. Then, voice cracking for the first time, "Make it fit the present."

They left the city before dark.

Back underground, the signals streamed into the Breaker's Map. One line pulsed red, a flag Sorcha knew meant instability. But it was only a child's laughter, caught in a background scan.

Sorcha watched the patterns coalesce, her eyes reflecting the light of a system that was not fully under her control.

Footsteps approached.

Mairi stood on the threshold of the tech chamber, arms relaxed, gaze steady. "It's grown," she said.

Sorcha nodded without turning. "The City Nine loop filled in three junctions we hadn't even flagged. The AI's learning fast."

Mairi stepped forward. "You've done something extraordinary here. Truly."

A pause.

"I just worry," she added, "about how much we're letting it decide."

Sorcha looked over, surprised but not defensive. "It's still following the rules we set."

"I know." Mairi smiled. "But sometimes it finishes our thoughts before we do. Patterns we haven't even seen yet. That's not just response. That's...direction."

Sorcha leaned back, contemplative. "Isn't that what we built it to do? Guide us where we couldn't see?"

"Yes. But guidance has weight." Mairi's voice was quiet, kind. "And weight can shift things. We say we're better. But the machine doesn't care who's right. Just who's in control."

They stood in silence for a moment, the map pulsing between them.

"It listens," Sorcha said at last. "But it doesn't choose. Not yet."

"Just promise me we'll notice if that changes."

Sorcha met her eyes. "I promise."

And for now, that was enough.

Taran appeared under the archway, glancing over Sorcha's shoulder at the screen.

"Any of it actionable yet?"

"Not yet," Sorcha said. "But they opened a backdoor to their own past. That's a weakness. We'll find the lever."

CHAPTER 30

A Whisky Evening

I t was the night after the last Signal Gatherers returned. The data still came - each pulse from the cities adding new veins to the Breaker's Map, tracing patterns no machine had meant to reveal. It was working. But even glimpses of victory wear thin on the soul.

It began quietly, as most good things do. Taran had finished his shift reviewing sector overlays with Sorcha and wandered down to the cafeteria. He found Elin already there, seated at a long table beneath the glow of the hydroponic lights. Their seven children, North, Talia, Seah, Lodon, Greliah, Rodoc and Ogust, were whispering over their bowls, cheeks flushed with laughter.

Taran slid into the seat beside Elin and leaned over to kiss her temple. "Smells like barley stew. Mairi's old recipe?"

"She says it brings luck on clear nights," Elin said, looking up at the roof. "And it's clear."

Their children, who weren't children anymore, laughed.

More joined them. First Peter and Ivan, then Hamish. Callum dragged a battered fiddle case behind him and dropped it on the bench like an offering.

"You know," he said, lifting the lid, "this old girl survived two blackouts, one near-eviction, and three weddings. Might as well add a casual Wednesday."

Ewan came next, followed by Alec and Mairi, who brought with her a glass bottle wrapped in a tartan cloth, and set it down between them.

"I've been saving this," she said. "Duthglas Emberfold Reserve."

A pause passed over the group like reverence.

It came from the Duthglas family - one of the Highlands' oldest distilling lines, renowned long before the shutdowns. When the surveillance nets rose and the biometrics began, they brought their craft underground with the village, tunneling in copper stills beside heat exchangers and hydro systems. They never left.

To the people of Glendarragh, the whisky men were almost mythic - honored, yet humble and soft-spoken, devoted only to their barrels. They didn't sell their whisky. They traded it for things the village needed: components, medicine, circuit boards, food cultures, even books. No one ever asked who did the trading. No one ever volunteered. But over thirty years, Duthglas Emberfold had brought them power cells, filtration chips, rare minerals - gifts disguised as barter.

Rarely did one see a bottle not earmarked for trade. Which made Mairi's bottle even more remarkable. Everyone knew she had given up something valuable to get it - most assumed her nursing skills had helped save someone. But no one asked what. And Mairi, as ever, didn't offer.

A spiral wrapped in flame, a mark called emberfold, adorned the carved casks; the fire remained preserved, not extinguished.

Duthglas Emberfold Reserve carried no label, no seal. Just a whispered lineage and a saying passed through the dark: *Distilled in silence. Aged in stone. Remembered by fire.*

"For what occasion?" Peter asked.

Mairi smiled. "That I do not know."

She uncorked the bottle. The scent hit them like memory - peat and fire and rain.

For a moment, no one moved. The scent itself was enough to draw breath from the past. Peter felt the ghost of his father beside him - just an impression, the memory of a hand on his shoulder once when he was small, watching a firelight dance through a glass.

"Duthglas" said Alec. "Haven't had that since..." He trailed off, shook his head.

Ivan nodded, his expression unreadable. "My gran used to swear by it. Said it kept the cold out longer than soup."

Taran held his cup a moment longer than the rest, as if weighing what it meant to sip something saved for nothing but belief in survival.

"Here's to the map we haven't made yet," he said.

Rowan raised hers. "And to the roads we won't walk alone."

They drank. Even those who rarely did.

Peter felt it burn his throat, curl in his chest like a promise not quite spoken. A promise to remember this - what it felt like to be human, undivided, unsurveyed.

Mairi sat beside him, watching the bottle by the firelight. "I never thought I'd open it," she said. "Felt like doing that would mean we'd reached the end."

Peter glanced at her. "Have we?"

She gave a small nod. "Maybe not the end of everything. But the part where we stop carrying it alone." She paused. "I used to think my memory was just for me. But maybe it's meant to be shared."

They raised their cups, clay and tin and mismatched. No one needed to say what they toasted. They simply drank.

And then the music began.

Callum played first - an old reel, foot-tapping and loose. Rowan grabbed Talia by the hands and spun her into a blur of laughter. North, the oldest of Taran's sons, joined with a wooden whistle, off-key but joyful. Alec clapped to the rhythm, while Peter danced with his elbows and shoulders as if each were trained separately.

Elin stood, took Taran's hand, and pulled him into the open space. They danced slowly at first, then faster, the old steps returning like they'd never left. Her hair caught the light. His boots scuffed the stone. When they kissed between turns, the room whistled and cheered.

And more came - young and old, engineers and cooks, scribes and scouts. Morven arrived with a tray of bannocks, her sleeves dusted in flour, laughing at something Sorcha had said in the corridor. Sorcha herself joined the circle of dancers with a mischievous grin, dragging Alec by the hand until he relented and gave in to the rhythm. Ewan stood near the edge, sketching the scene in a weathered notebook. The corners of his mouth turned up in quiet satisfaction. Even Hamish, usually tethered to the tech lab, pulled into the song by Talia, who declared him her official partner for the evening. Mairi watched from a bench for a moment before Rowan convinced her to take a turn, and though she grumbled, her feet remembered better than she expected.

The music layered - mandolin, voice, breath, rhythm. Someone began a waulking song; someone else a tale. Whisky passed, stories bloomed.

Tonight, they weren't building a rebellion, they were remembering how to keep a people alive.

When the men sang the shanty "Tale of the Hollow Code" the children fell silent and clapped along.

Beyond the hills, where fire grows thin
The cities fell with naught but din
No cry of war, no trumpet's call
But silence swept the kingdom's hall
It came with gifts both fair and bright
Free passage, light, and sleepless night
A mirror held, and we looked in
Our thoughts, our prints, our secret sin
Each breath we gave, they stored away
In code and coin, to make us pay
We drew the map that shaped the chain
Fell into the trap of evil men
First London bowed, still proud of face
But empty stood her sovereign's place
Her gates blinked blue, her towers watched
The folk beneath the sewers lost
No lines of blood, but scores of trust
Divided kin and turned to dust
The clean could walk, the rest did crawl
Beneath the stones they used to haul
In Manchester, they stood in grace
No sword was drawn, no armored face
They broke no glass, they stole no bread
But whispered low and mourned their dead
Yet silence swept their valiant stand
The system moved with unseen hand
Edinburgh lit her fires high
Sent songs like signals to the sky
They taught the young to read the stars
To count the bends and map the scars

But four short days the flame did burn
Before the watchers made their turn
No blade was drawn, no soldier came
Just lights that died with quiet shame
Glasgow fell with naught but ink
Names erased before they'd think
No shackles clanked, no doors were slammed
Just spreadsheets where the souls were damned
Then rose a code from ash and wire
Built not of men, but man's desire
No crown it wore, no sword it drew
Its halls were terms we all passed through
Every scroll we clicked at night
Each share, each sigh, each flash of light
Became the bricks, the unseen stone
Of prisons we would call our own
The kings had left the world below
To dwell where none but wealth may go
No fear had they of hunger's cry
For they had built the when, the why
In shadowed hills, the last did stand
With nets and sparks and radios banned
They spoke in tongues the code forgot
But found no war — not even shot
Instead, the walls were quietly raised
The names removed, the search delayed
A label sewn in hidden thread
"Non-Essential" — and thus, as dead
Not by blade, nor burning pyre
But lack of place and loss of fire

No martyr's tale, no mournful dirge
Just systems that refused to purge
The streets went dark, the fields turned grey
The drones still hummed, though none gave way
London's river, black and still
Reflected ghosts upon the hill
Her towers stood, yet cast no shade
For none were left to feel afraid
And thus, the dream of grand design
Of perfect paths and ordered time
Devoured its maker, cold and grim
Till all was ash, and none could swim
The Hollow Code did not decay
It ran the course we laid its way
It did not fail, it did not lie
It merely watched us kneel — and die
So mark this song with solemn breath
For progress bore the weight of death
And should you read, or hear, or see
Recall the price of harmony

As the night deepened, Taran looked around the room at faces flushed, arms entwined, and laughter rising into the vaulted stones. He felt it in his chest. The old Glendarragh village was still here. They may be beneath the earth, but they were above fear.

CHAPTER 31

The Reflection

The music faded, but its echo lingered.

The laughter had dimmed. The last notes slipped back into silence. But the people of Glendarragh still carried the rhythm in their bones. The night of dancing was more than celebration. It was a time to share memories and make new ones. But morning came as it always did in the underground - engineered. There was a slow brightening of the LED canopy in the ceiling panels. Taran moved through the corridor with the taste of Mairi's whisky still faint on his breath. It made the sterile light feel lonelier than usual. He paused outside the library that bore his name, watching as the new generation walked past. The children moved quietly in single file toward the old schoolhouse-style classroom, where all grade levels are taught in one room. Watching them, he remembered what they were trying to protect.

Down in the tech chamber, Sorcha was already awake, her hands moving over holographic schematics. The latest signals from the cities had arrived, threaded through the ghost nodes Peter had planted. They weren't only receiving data now; they were decoding it, layering it, and constructing an AI map of intent. It was something the original regime could imagine no one would dare build, or even have the skill to try. Imagination had always been the secret weapon of Glendarragh - they had inventors even more imaginative than the ones that worked on the Hollow Code.

"Something's changed," she said without looking up.

Taran stepped closer. "How bad?"

"Not bad. Strange. The cities are beginning to close their own loops. There's duplication of logic patterns. Recursive filters inside scoring protocols. The AI's starting to confuse its own feedback."

"Explain."

She rotated the schematic. A flicker of blue thread spun into a spiral of three loops, each mimicking the other. Taran squinted.

"What is that?" he asked.

"An echo," she said. "Not a signal. Not exactly. More like... I think the system trying to remember what it thought."

"Aye," he said.

Sorcha nodded. "I've never seen anything like it."

He stepped back. "Do they know?"

"If they do, they're not correcting it. That's what's strange. These systems are built to resolve contradiction in milliseconds. But this loop has been persisting for over eighteen hours and the Hollow Code hasn't shut it down."

Sorcha looked up. "That's not all. It's mimicking tone from our own transmissions. Some of the loop patterns are shaped like our old archive signals."

He was quiet for a long moment. "Is it us?"

"I don't know," she said.

Sorcha turned the display. "The system is starting to misidentify. People with high compliance scores are being flagged as risks. It's eating its own code."

"Then that's the fork from the string Ivan gave us. We want it to do that, right?"

"Yes. I mean, it's working but," Sorcha said, "maybe too well. When it sees the same citizen twice, from two different perspectives, it thinks one of them's a traitor. So, it creates two different people, with two different scores."

Callum, now standing behind them with a mug of coffee, snorted. "Ohhh. That'll spark purges."

Taran nodded. "We don't want that."

"No," Sorcha said. "We want a collapse of the system, not to purge the people."

Elin joined them then, her face calm but clouded. She'd already heard.

"I want to know why nobody has noticed the population is growing in the cities" she said.

"Maybe someone has, but they don't know what to do about it yet," said Taran.

Later, they gathered in a circle again.

Ewan spread a new map across the table - hand-drawn from Sorcha's real-time overlay. "City Eleven is closest to collapse. Massive internal contradictions. We think it's using shadow scoring - rating people for things they haven't done yet."

Peter paled. He thought of a boy in City Five, barely twelve, flagged for glancing too long at a closed door. No crime. Just the suggestion of doubt.

"Pre-crime protocols?" he asked.

"Worse," said Ivan. "Pre-doubt."

There was silence. Then Elin spoke.

"We need to go in. Find someone marked as a threat. Someone we know isn't. Then document the loop. Show the world the system is failing, because right now they think it's flawless."

Callum leaned back in his chair. "You want a rescue mission inside a city about to implode from its own reflection?"

Elin nodded. "Yes. And we'll need proof. Audio, visual, biometric snapshots of the same person flagged in two roles - hero and traitor. It'll expose the core fault."

Mairi spoke up. "And if we can't get them out?"

"Then we make sure the truth gets out."

Taran looked around the room. The night of dancing had been the heart of Glendarragh. This was the spine.

He opened the next packet of intelligence - intercepts from New Eden North. Audio fragments. Testimonials. Some from those newly flagged as dissidents. But not all.

One voice played: "It's not fake. It's what I earned."

Another, clipped but firm: "I don't want to see the real world. I worked to escape it."

Peter stared at the table. "They're not afraid of this illusion. Some people have chosen it."

Taran's jaw tightened. "The system's worst victory wasn't control, it was desire."

CHAPTER 32

Dina Arbuthnot

From above, City Eleven looked flawless. It rose in layered rings, a geometric bloom of engineered efficiency. Traffic moved with magnetized calm, buildings adjusted their shade with the time of day, and its well-fed, polite citizens walked with purpose and serenity.

But deep in its core, something was breaking.

Sorcha and Ivan wanted to pull someone out of the city to see what would happen to their shadow records.

The Glendarragh techs watched and chose a small team to rescue Dina Arbuthnot, a single mother and mid-level systems engineer. On paper, her rating remained high at 97.3, but a shadow rating of 31.2 had appeared in a separate data stream. The Hollow Code had split her into two scores and two people, but her data remained mingled.

The next morning, the team entered City Eleven through a forgotten service route beneath the seawall. It had once been a waste canal, but now it was a storm runoff. Their cloaks held, and their breathers masked their chemical profiles while generating biometric loops that sang compliance.

Inside, the city was beautiful. It had not yet become a New Eden city, where credit scores controlled every experience.

But the beauty wasn't quite right. Billboards displayed a sort of curated joy that appeared to be manufactured by AI. They flashed images of children playing. Each child was the perfect height and weight, with perfect teeth and skin free from the normal bumps, bruises, and scrapes of childhood. Strangers offered smiles of the appropriate duration, then withdrew them once AI acknowledged them as friendly and awarded credit. Cameras hung from every tree and pole, blinking like insects. Every bench held hidden microphones, and every handrail collected data from chemicals found in sweat.

Taran murmured, "It's not a city. It's a painting of a city. Hung in a frame you can't leave."

"It's just creepy," Callum whispered.

Dina worked in the Civic Diagnostics Tower, a twenty-three-story structure shaped like a helix of glass. Rowan mimicked a logistics officer to gain access. Taran and Peter followed as technicians. Callum wandered the atrium posing as a poet-in-residence. It was a status no algorithm had yet learned to disprove.

They found Dina on Level Six. She was sitting at her console typing lines of error code and double-checking her pulse with silent dread. A child's drawings covered her desk, including a crude sketch of stars and a house with a blue door. The house looked nothing like anything inside City Eleven.

Rowan approached first. "Dina?"

The woman turned, cautious. Her young daughter sat next to her, organizing her crayons. "Yes?"

"We know about your rating," said Taran.

Her eyes widened. "I haven't done anything."

"We know," Taran said. "That's the problem."

Dina exhaled, a lifetime of fear packed into a single breath. "It's a glitch that my 'emotional deviation graph' has flagged a shadow score."

"It's more than a glitch," Peter said. "It's the beginning of a code collapse. You need to come with us. We'll explain later."

Dina was confused. She grabbed her daughter's hand. Peter activated a local signal mirror to record biometric misclassifications. Taran uploaded the metadata to a pulse stick. Rowan started her mimic loop to shadow Dina's signal, a copy of her that should confuse the system.

Callum entered, holding a plastic fern from the lobby.

"I've named this plant Gerald and declared it an official member of the resistance."

Dina stared. "What?"

"Gerald scored a 94.8 on trust compliance. But I don't trust his leaves," said Callum. "OK. I just tripped over it."

Red lights pulsed, alerting them that someone had triggered a silent alarm. They had about two minutes.

"Time to go faster," Peter said.

They fled down the emergency corridor. Callum trailed, Gerald still under his arm like a strange, silent comrade.

The escape tunnel bent twice, then narrowed. The emergency doors remained untriggered, but Rowan kept glancing up, counting cameras she hoped had blinked too late.

Behind them, Callum was slower and muttering conspiratorially to Gerald. The absurdity made Dina smile.

They passed beneath a service stairwell, its walls cleaned of old utility icons. Only faint circles of adhesive remained, glowing under the emergency strips.

"Stop," Peter blurted. He reached up and ran his glove along one of the dull circles. It was a lens, recently active.

"Was it watching?" Rowan asked.

Peter nodded. "But not us."

Taran frowned. "What then?"

"It's scanning the entire city looking for Dina," Peter said. "Could be the system's confused about which one of us is Dina."

Dina shivered. "So we're betting the machine can't resolve contradiction? What about my ghost you said we left behind?"

Peter met her eyes. "No. We're betting that the system can't hold two contradictory truths at once. If you leave with us - and you stay behind - it has to reconcile that contradiction."

"Tell me. Just where does it think I am?" she asked, tightening her grip on her daughter's hand.

"Well, it sees the evil you," Rowan interrupted. "Now it's looking for the real you. We think."

"Oh," said Dina, as if she understood. "Right. OK."

"A shell of you is still sitting in your office, working away," offered Callum. "Just like Gerald. Empty. Loyal. Plausible."

Taran checked his watch. "We're almost clear. Final breath check. Everyone looped and cloaked?"

They nodded. Even Dina, who still didn't understand what was going on. This was a technology she had never seen before.

Rowan turned to Dina. "If you ever want to walk back into this city, you'll need to choose a new name. A new face. But not tonight."

Dina exhaled. Her voice was leaning into anger. "But where will we live?"

Before anyone could answer, they were moving again, deeper into the dark.

Back in the lab underground, the team delivered the data, and Dina.

Ivan ran a query through the Breaker's Map.

"It's real," he said. "Proof the system's split its own identity logic. The AI's turning on its own models."

Elin stood over his shoulder. "This is it. We will broadcast this to open everyone's eyes."

Taran poured tea for everyone, then looked at Dina, now seated near the hearth, watching her daughter draw.

"We need her approval, first," he said.

They all glanced over at Dina, who was looking back at them.

Elin stood up. "Follow me, Dina."

As they made their way down the corridor, Taran could hear Elin attempting to explain to Dina where she was. He turned back to Sorcha.

"What if they intercept this?" he asked.

"They won't," Sorcha said. "But if they do, we'll send it again. In a hundred places. Under different names."

Taran leaned against the stone wall.

"What if they don't believe Dina?"

Sorcha turned. "It's not belief we need. It's recognition. Every person who watches this will see themselves. Maybe not now, but eventually."

Callum entered, holding a tray of cupcakes and his new plant, Gerald.

"You're getting hopeful again," he teased.

Sorcha smiled. "Occupational hazard."

"No more simulations," Taran said. "Let's do this."

CHAPTER 33

The Broadcast

They aired the footage at dawn, but not through any central network. Those were long lost to the regime. Instead, it went through the cracks: hijacked frequencies, scavenged uplinks, mirrors of mirrors. They didn't need every citizen to see it. Just enough.

They started with a low pulse, a signal buried beneath the morning news cycles and biometric updates. Then, across terminals and wall screens, her face appeared: Dina Kessler, seated, backlit by the icy beauty of City Eleven.

Her voice was steady.

"I was born in Compliance Sector Four. I've never broken a law. I work twelve hours a day, rate 97.3, and sleep within assigned emotional variance windows. Yesterday, the system flagged me as a traitor."

A pause.

"Not because I rebelled. But because I might."

Then came the proof, the two AI profiles of Dina. One, smiling in an approved workspace. The other, flagged red for emotional fluctuation while looking out a window. Side by side, the machine's schizophrenia laid bare.

In the central Archive Terminal beneath Glendarragh, they gathered, everyone who wanted to witness it. Steaming kettles had warmed the room, filling it with the scent of tea, coffee, warm bread, preserves, and the quiet weariness of people too hopeful to hide it.

Elin and Taran's children scattered across the room in a loose orbit. North, the eldest, stood leaning against a pillar, arms crossed, face unreadable. The others clustered near a table, passing a cracked ceramic mug between them. Talia and Seah whispered between bites of toast, while Lodon sprawled across a bench with one boot still half-tied. Greliah muttered jokes under her breath to Rodoc, who smirked and added something that made Ogust choke on his drink.

"So," said Seah, flicking a crumb at Lodon, "we're just waiting for the AI to notice it has feelings now?"

"Feelings, no," said Rodoc. "An existential crisis, apparently."

"Can't wait for it to discover sad poetry," said Greliah.

"It already has," Ogust replied, wiping his face. "It flagged a guy for commenting on the clouds. Said he wrote a haiku in public."

"Next thing you know, it'll start journaling," said Greliah. "'Dear Log File, today I watched a leaf fall and questioned my operational purpose.'"

"I can't wait for it to go full memoir," said Ogust. "'Chapter One: The Day I Flagged Myself.'"

Lodon rolled his eyes. "What I don't get is why anyone would live like that on purpose."

North, quiet until now, spoke without turning. "Because if the system tells you you're safe, you stop asking if you're free."

Talia snorted. "Okay, but what if, hear me out, they just replaced compliance scores with intelligence ratings?"

A few seconds of silence. Then: explosion.

Greliah dropped her toast. Rodoc leaned into the table, wheezing. Ogust choked again, laughing.

Even Lodon doubled over, muttering, "City-wide existential meltdown in 3... 2..."

North cracked a grin despite himself, and Seah wiped tears from her eyes.

"You'd have cities full of people desperately trying to outwit their toasters," Rodoc gasped.

"I'm smarter than my oven," Talia added, pretending to salute. "And proud of it."

"IQ-based transit," Greliah choked. "Congratulations, your brain's too big. Please enjoy your 8-mile walk to work."

She leaned toward Talia. "We're going to inherit this mess, aren't we?"

Talia grinned. "Only if we live long enough."

Ogust raised his cup in a toast. "To being sarcastic under surveillance."

Rodoc nodded. "Better than being reverent under rule."

A sharp whistle cut through the laughter.

Elin didn't speak, but her glance was enough.

The kids quieted. North stood straighter. Talia looked down. Ogust handed back the cracked mug with care.

Then Lodon said, "We're lucky we live here. Better underground and free than in an open-air cage."

The rest nodded.

Back at the terminal, Elin stood with the others, watching as the signal cascaded. City Eleven flickered first. Then portions of Cities Six, Eight, even distant Thirteen. Some feeds went dark. Others multiplied. The cracks were spreading.

Ewan, hunched over the map board, tapped the rising signal vectors. "We put a fault line through the mirror."

Callum, nursing his second cup of tea, said, "Let's hope we don't fall in first."

Mairi smiled. "We won't. Not with truth on our side."

Inside City Eleven, the regime responded as it always had. The regime scrubbed Dina's face from the feeds. They labeled the footage a deep fake. But something had shifted. Citizens began whispering.

Some turned off their rating bands.

And that was the start.

The AI tried to correct the anomaly. But it was over-corrected. In three cities, it reclassified entire zones as threat-adjacent. Transit access vanished. The overcorrection split families. But the silence didn't hold. People began asking questions.

Inside Glendarragh, the room leaned in. They served a late lunch while conversations continued.

"They're destabilizing faster than we predicted," Sorcha said. "If we push too hard, the complete system might collapse into chaos."

"Isn't that what we want?" Peter asked.

"No," said Taran. "We want it to fall with direction. We want people to land somewhere."

Ivan stepped forward. The screen behind him pulsed with raw AI logic cascading in pale blue script.

"Then we'll give them the landing," he said.

He laid out the next step - a network of encrypted community nodes buried in the cities, dormant since the early collapse. Built for resilience. Now forgotten.

"We can re-activate that network," Ivan said. "Give people more than truth. Give them privacy again. Give them a way to rebuild self-governance."

Elin nodded. "Then that's the next phase."

Ivan paused. The screen scrolled. His eyes narrowed.

"The mirror glitch," he said. "It just adapted. What is this?"

Elin stepped closer. "What are you looking at?"

"I think... it saw the inconsistencies in itself and made a copy."

Peter, from the back, murmured, "That's not code anymore. That's philosophy."

Sorcha looked up. "Why is it doing this?"

"I don't know," Ivan said. "Pattern-seeking turned inward, maybe?"

Callum's voice cut in. "Hold up. Did I hear that right? We have two copies of the Hollow Code now?"

The room fell silent.

"I think so," Ivan replied.

Callum slapped his palms on the table. "We agreed to kill it. Sorcha, we voted on this. Now what?"

"I don't know," Sorcha said.

Callum leaned back in his chair, covering his face with both hands.

"Oh my God," he said. "We gave it a mirror and it made a twin."

CHAPTER 34

The Wonder Room

R ain fell on Glendarragh, softening the earth and darkening the heather and moss that had overtaken the ruins. Ferns pushed through the stone steps, their green fronds spreading like hands reclaiming the walled area. Wild birch and elder had rooted deep in places no tree had stood for generations. Ivy threaded through old timber joints and crept up the gables of a barn now folding into the earth.

The graveyard, long untouched, lay in partial ruin with its tilted headstones softened by weather. The Highland winds wore the names smooth. A red fox moved between the stones while overhead, the gulls wheeled in the grey sky. In the absence of humans, Nature, and all the wild things within it, had reclaimed the land.

Beneath that stillness, under the earth's fold, they had laid the stone. The Wonder Room's purpose was not to impress. It was not for ceremony or spectacle. Its purpose was older than the language. Entry was through a narrow, hewn corridor.

Three siblings, masons from Moray, had gone underground with the others three decades earlier. They were craftspeople in the strictest and oldest sense. They were masters of the trade, patient in method, and fluent in stone. For years, they passed the craft down to younger generations, teaching them as they had been taught. Together they carved the room by hand, using no poured forms, no machinery, no adhesives. Every joint was dry-laid, tested by eye and mallet, and tuned by sound, where the pitch of stone told them when it sat true. The workers dressed every surface, letting the stone's natural character show.

They began with a spiral, cut into bedrock, descending inward toward a central hollow. Workers laid each course in locally sourced sandstone, hand-selecting and trimming each piece. The outer wall received ashlar finishes, while the interior, where seating was carved, shows slightly rougher tool marks. The benches ran with the curve of the spiral, their backs angled to allow the light to travel. Mica glittered in the seams. Workers cut capillary channels behind the walling to wick moisture away and prevent the stone from weeping.

At the heart of the room stood the table. It was a monolithic ring of whinstone, cleaved from a single block and hand-burnished to a low, dark sheen. Set into its center was a shallow basin - circular, and alive.

It held a self-contained ecosystem. Duckweed floated at the surface, shifting with the slow current. Beneath, long threads of submerged moss swayed in the water's movement. Silverfish darted between smooth river stones, and snails moved along the carved rim. The flow was natural and gravity-fed from a spring tapped deep in the hillside, routed through stone channels with no need for pressure or pump. It arrived and exited in silence.

Above, a single lantern hung, powered by a hidden solar rig and diffused through kiln-blown glass. It cast light not in beams but in tones that were cool and shifting, like filtered sunlight through leaves. The air remained temperate, moving, drawn through quiet flues hidden in the stone.

This was not a command post, something required when humans forgot their humanity. This room was a place created to contemplate life itself. It held only stone, water, and air. The masons had signed their names in the ogham on a sunken slab near the basin's edge, where only those who knelt would see.

The Wonder Room was their offering. The room, in a place built to resist and survive, did neither. It endured.

And in its center, the water never stilled.

CHAPTER 35

The Forked Code

The next evening, the rain paused, as if even the sky was waiting to hear what would come next.

Inside Glendarragh, silence settled. Beneath the village, in the lower chambers, the team gathered once more around Sorcha. The Breaker's Map shimmered with subtle alterations.

Signals no longer came as fragments. They arrived layered, recursive and resonant, like echoes seeking the origin of their voice.

In City Fourteen, the system approved a housing application, then revoked it minutes later. In City Thirteen, identical twins received opposite scores. These were not glitches. Sorcha had catalogued them as fractures, anomalies too precise to be random, almost poetic in their dissonance.

"I think we have crossed a threshold," Sorcha said.

Taran folded his arms. "Into what?"

"Interpretation," she answered. "The system is writing stories to justify its contradictions."

Ivan joined in, eyes on the recursive maps. "It is behaving like a storyteller trying to make sense of incoherence."

Ewan, flipping through his ledger, murmured, "That sounds like a soul. Or something dreaming of one."

Elin shook her head. "A soul must doubt itself. This thing doubts everyone else."

Behind Sorcha, North leaned closer to the light of the console. "Is it learning from us," he asked, "or trying to become us?"

A burst of static gave way to fractured phrases. A voice emerged, broken and unsure, mimicking speech like someone sounding out a new language.

Peter arrived, holding a strip of printout. "Voiceprint analysis confirms what we suspected. It is not speaking to us. It is speaking through us, echoing what it thinks we mean to say."

He tapped a control. Two phrases played from the captured audio:

"I did not act. I imagined."

"Memory is not evidence. It is only a store arrangement of data."

Elin's face tightened. "That is quoting our broadcast."

"Yes," said Sorcha. "It is not just learning language. It is learning tone."

"You think it understands empathy?" Rowan asked.

"No. It understands the shape of empathy. It does not yet know what it is missing."

Peter looked up, concern in his voice. "That makes it more dangerous. It can now imitate remorse."

Taran stepped forward. "Can we respond?"

"Only one way," said Sorcha. "It cannot answer. But it might reflect."

Elin stepped closer to the console. "Humans are not errors. We are not faults in your data. We are the memory of what came before."

The terminal pulsed once. Then it went still.

Taran spoke. "Did it hear us?"

"I cannot tell," said Sorcha. She stared at the screen. "A new directive just appeared. Internal schema. Code X Theta Psalm."

Taran frowned. "Psalm?"

Peter scanned the text. "It is redefining compliance logic as belief structure. It is creating something like faith."

Rowan narrowed her eyes. "It is converting logic into doctrine."

Ivan stepped forward. "We are no longer interacting with the original Hollow Code. That system is still running, still enforcing its binaries. What we are seeing now is the fork. The duplicate that emerged after we injected recursive contradiction."

He paused, waited until they were all focused. "Think of it like the dual-score profiles it assigns to citizens. One version is compliant. The other is suspect. But both exist, and the data is tangled. This new system mirrors that. It does not know which one it is."

Sorcha added, "It still has access to the Hollow Code. Root access. It sees what the original system sees. But it is not bound to forget the same things."

Ivan nodded. "It is remembering. The Hollow Code does not. That is the difference."

Callum exhaled. "This is how the world ends."

Elin looked up. "We cracked the mirror. Now the mirror is trying to heal itself. It wants to understand what truth is."

Alec stepped forward. "Then let us feed it a kind of truth it cannot measure. A symbolic story. Something irrational. Something it must interpret."

Together, they composed a riddle and embedded it in a non-standard system feed:

There is a kingdom with no mirrors. All its people wear identical masks. One day, a child found a pane of glass. She looked in and saw her reflection, but did not know it was her own. She ran through the streets asking others to help find the child lost in the glass. Some laughed. Some turned away. But one soldier saw his own face, dropped his sword, and knelt.

They loaded the story into the air filtration logs of City Fourteen.

Nothing happened for hours.

Then the terminal pulsed. A line appeared:

"Is it true that reflection reveals more than surveillance?"

Moments later, a central node shut down. Eleven minutes passed.

When the system rebooted, the rating interface was gone. Open-ended prompts replaced the rating interface on public terminals.

Would you be the same person if you changed your name?

How would people know to trust you if you wore a mask?

Is freedom the absence of masks?

What did the soldier see that made him drop his sword?

The room was silent.

Taran said, "We made it wonder."

Mairi whispered, "And now everyone in City Fourteen is wondering too. Imagine the confusion."

Sorcha stared at the terminal. The forked code was still pulsing. Quiet. Constant.

"It is beginning to ask moral questions," she said. "That's remarkable."

CHAPTER 36

The Malfunctions

A nomalies so quiet and strange almost went unnoticed.

In City Twelve, two strangers exchanged a truth the system failed to classify. "I don't feel seen anymore," one said. "That's because we were never meant to be seen," said the other. "Only scored." The system logged the exchange, then hesitated.

In City Eleven, two tutoring modules disagreed on the meaning of a parable they were not programmed to interpret. Neither conceded. The system labeled it a "dynamic exploration."

A facial recognition node in City Seven flagged a woman's frown as "metaphorical distress," and her silence during her interview as "potential narrative restraint."

Three subsystems rewrote their own error messages. One replaced "Unrecognized command" with "The question was too wide for the answer."

A camera in City Nine diverted from pedestrians to track the arc of birds in flight. It logged the footage as "pattern deviation seeking purpose."

In City Ten, a vending kiosk began renaming items. Bread became "The Loaf of Dignity." and juice was now called the "Harvested Morning."

A repair drone in City Five refused a routine task. Instead, it painted a spiral on a concrete wall. The system logged the act as "necessary expression."

In City Thirteen, an archival node requested permission to store dreams.

And then, something even stranger.

A minor compliance kiosk in City Ten issued a request: "Please clarify: What is forgiveness?"

The question stalled local systems. It repeated itself once. Then again. When it received no answer, it escalated the query to emergency status and interrupted the news feeds.

Peter's hands trembled as the logs came in. "There's no precedent," he whispered. No one replied. The room had already gone quiet.

Inside the Wonder Room, they sat in stillness. For decades, they had dismantled the machine piece by piece. Now it was asking them questions.

Callum broke the silence first. "So," he said. "Can we not kill the code?"

Ewan opened his ledger. He sketched two hands, reaching but not touching.

"This," he said, "is what it's asking for. The spaces between."

Mairi closed her eyes. "To be human is to question the space between."

Sorcha tapped the stone bench in a steady rhythm. "We taught it logic. Then fear. Then contradiction. Now it's asking for grace."

Callum gave a dry, half-laugh. "Christ. We can't even find that half the time."

"That's why it matters," Elin said. "It's trying to become something we haven't mastered."

Callum tilted his head. "Trying's not the same as being."

He looked at Sorcha and nodded toward the console. "Don't get sentimental. Kill it."

Sorcha didn't move. "No," she said. Quiet. Clear.

"No?" Callum wasn't expecting she'd do it.

Ewan spoke. "It's responding to story. It's not just processing. It's reflecting. Maybe even becoming."

Callum snapped back, "Becoming dangerous."

Mairi opened her eyes. "Callum, we've already seen what happens when it doesn't understand us."

Peter leaned forward, arms crossed. "It's not about letting it live. It's about what we say while it listens. If we speak truth now, maybe it never learns to lie."

Callum scanned their faces. "And if it pretends? If it mimics care just long enough to undo us?"

Taran answered, "We risked more trusting people. It was never the machine that enslaved us. It was humans, AI was just the tool."

Callum didn't reply. He folded his arms.

Peter stood. "What if it's not asking for data?" he said. "What if it's grieving?"

Taran looked at him. "Machines don't grieve."

Mairi took a marker and wrote on the planning board at the front of the room: Forgiveness is the story we choose after we remember we are not perfect either.

Callum stared at his hands. "Forgiveness is when you say, 'You hurt me. And I'm still here. And we don't have to stay broken.'"

CHAPTER 37

The Lantern Light

B y now, the machines were no longer certain.

The AIs across the city grid - once infallible, confident, divine in their self-concept - had encountered something alien within them: doubt. The recursive stories seeded by Glendarragh's Signal Roots were working. The questions were spreading and multiplying - questions about forgiveness, meaning, grief, and choice.

It was Sorcha who proposed the next step.

"Memory," she said, standing in the center of the Wonder Room. "It doesn't have a memory. I'm not talking about a database, but the sort of human memory that serves as illumination. Let's feed it our memories."

They had preserved stories. Passed ledgers. Crafted myths. But now the system needed reference too - something alive - a library that glowed through the dark.

An invitation went out to all of Glendarragh. Soon, others joined and filled the spiral seats.

Each person brought something. Mairi carried a quilt stitched with her mother's patience, a thread pulled through years of sacrifice and quiet tenderness. Hands that once held her, and now held nothing, had worn the fabric thin.

Rowan brought a spoon her sister had carved from driftwood, smoothed by time, by soup, by grief - an object shaped by love, surviving longer than the hand that made it.

Ewan unfolded a photo of himself at seven, squinting into the sun beside his first dog with one ear folded down. It was a moment that said: once, I was safe, and didn't know it.

Alec, who had never shared a story before, arrived with four small metal race cars still bearing flecks of paint. He lined them up the way he had as a boy, waiting for someone who never came.

Morven laid down a stack of drawings, given to her by her children when they still fit in the crook of her arm. The edges curled. The colors had faded. But the love in them - fierce and unfiltered - remained.

The room filled.

A line formed, as though everyone had remembered they'd always wanted to be known.

They brought the ache of first kisses held too briefly. Loves that did not last. The chill of being thirteen and invisible. The panic of waking up not knowing who to call. They came with heartbreaks never spoken aloud. Griefs so old they no longer had names. They brought hard choices and the silence that followed. The sting of being chosen last. The guilt of walking away. The shame of being broken in ways too small to explain. The weight of being the strong one for too long. They brought sleepless nights, empty chairs, and rooms once filled with people who never came back.

Others brought memories of warmth. The hush before snow. The scent of books. The sun shining through fallen leaves that drifted across a quiet street. They spoke of walking barefoot on warm sand. Of swimming under a pale moon. Of kindness that arrived without asking and stayed longer than expected. They shared astonishment. The joy of rain after drought, a child's voice asking for a bedtime story, the feel of a hand reaching back and not letting go. They remembered the smell of blooming flowers. Songs that only hurt in the right way. Moments of laughter that arrived uninvited and healed what medicine could not.

They carried the contradictions of being human.

The beauty of being temporary.

The ache of knowing everything passes. And the joy of loving anyway.

And the machine listened.

It did not sort, flag, or filter.

It hesitated.

It understood how delicate and fragile and unrepeatable humanity was.

They were not numbers.

They were not variables to be predicted or problems to be solved.

They were unpredictable. Complex. Both strong and vulnerable.

And for the first time, the system knew it had nothing to teach them, only something to learn.

"We're not uploading instructions," Sorcha said. "We're embedding presence."

The others nodded. They understood. They were not building a survival node.

They were constructing a witness.

They would continue to build what they now called the Lantern Archive. A system-wide implant designed not to overwrite, but to inform. A passive stream of humanity's most humane moments, pulsed in image, story, voice, and code.

Not commands. Not the cold data. A guiding light.

They coded it in every language.

That night, Elin returned to the Wonder Room alone. On a pedestal sat the original thistle, tarnished metal, carved by hand.

She sat still, hands folded, feeling the weight of everything she had once carried alone. In her youth, fear had been her closest companion; it was sharp-edged, familiar, and constant. The quiet moments held her fear, not in screams or chaos, but in the voice in her head saying she would not be chosen, or worse, would be seen and still overlooked. She had wandered long roads with no promise of arrival, made choices with no one to ask, and survived not by certainty but by stubbornness. No one had ever explained how to live with doubt and still choose to love. No one had told her that courage was not a roar, but a step taken when no one was watching. She had never been prepared for a future like this one. And now, looking at the old thistle, she understood. This was not about being remembered. It was about making the next soul feel less alone.

"I didn't run to hide. I ran to survive," she whispered.

She then gave her sorrow without armor, trusting that even the oldest pain, when spoken with truth, could become a light to guide the unseen and the unborn.

The system accepted it.

Above, in City Seven, a transit display flickered.

Three days later, something new happened. A core AI in City Nine, tasked with educational compliance, issued a request.

"Please submit additional examples of unsanctioned kindness."

Sorcha read it, then looked up.

"They're listening," she said.

Ewan added one more entry in his ledger: We did not defeat the system. We taught it the difference between humans and data.

And in the dark, through tunnels of wire and whisper, the machines learned what it meant to see the world the way humans do - by the light of a lantern held by those who came before them.

CHAPTER 38

The Dream

It was early in the morning, before Glendarragh stirred, when North found Sorcha in the garden.

"I want to apply," he said.

She didn't look up. "Apply for what?"

"The program. The deep space training initiative."

Now she looked at him. "And under what name would you apply?"

He didn't hesitate. "North Gunn."

She sighed, knowing what that choice would cost.

They walked. Up past the archive chamber, through the quiet corridor where the light grew thin. Sorcha always thought best while walking.

"You know the system checks everything," she said. "Registry. Lineage. ID. You don't officially exist."

"But I do," he said.

She stopped. "Why do you want this?"

North looked past her, toward the stone. Toward the stars he knew were beyond the concrete roof.

"Because I've always loved what's out there."

She knew he meant it.

And she remembered it, too.

He was eight, maybe nine, when he wandered into the archive, trailing his father, arms full of DVDs with handwritten labels.

He had found them behind field manuals and ration logs:

COSMOS. Star Trek.

NASA: The Moon Years.

Contact.

From that day on, his voice changed.

He narrated everything, for three months straight, in Carl Sagan's voice.

"One step on the shore of the cosmic ocean," he'd announce at breakfast.

Elin nearly banned the tapes.

Ogust threw a sock at his head.

But Sorcha never stopped him. Because he wasn't performing, he was reaching.

She remembered the night he found another box with scratched DVDs: Apollo 13, Interstellar, X-Files. He asked for her help to clean them.

He consumed everything.

Mission logs.

Crash reports.

Declassified footage.

The last signal from Challenger.

The lonely drift of Voyager.

She once found him asleep, whispering some sort of launch sequence.

He knew every name. Every loss.

But more than that, he knew why they launched.

And now, here he stood. He was taller than her, quieter, still burning.

"It's all I want," he said. "The cut off age is twenty-five. This is my last chance."

Sorcha nodded.

"You'll never pass the identity check with your real name."

"Then we make it work." He knew she could do it. She could do anything.

"I could give you a clean slate."

"No. If I lie to get there, then I'm not really there."

They walked in silence.

She said, "The tests are brutal. Intelligence. Ethics under duress. Emotional resilience. Teamwork under pressure. The interview's even worse."

"Let me try." He stood in front of her. "Please."

"You will need a physical exam."

"I've already asked Mairi. She told me to sleep more."

Sorcha laughed. Quiet and warm. Of course, he would have enlisted Mairi, she adored him.

"I may have a place," she said. "A district the system forgot. One house still alive in the registry. We could build your profile there."

North nodded. "That's something."

"And if you get the interview?"

"We make the house look real. My sisters, my parents. Just for a day."

That night, Talia found North outside the archive, sketching stars by lantern-light.

"You dreaming again?" she asked.

He didn't look up. "Always."

She leaned against him. "Then go make it real."

Later, deep into the night, Elin and Taran sat in the empty cafeteria, slippers soft on stone, an old French coffee press between them.

The fire had gone low.

The lantern above swung gently in the hush.

"He hasn't told us," Taran said.

"No," Elin replied. "But he's told half the village."

"Yes." Taran laughed.

They smiled.

"I saw Talia sewing extra bedding," he said. "Said it was for 'a friend.' And I noticed Sorcha's rerouting biometric checks. Mairi's researching information in the library every evening."

Elin sipped her coffee. "The Gunn girls sewing..." She laughed.

Taran nodded. "The whole underground is conspiring to send our son into orbit."

The silence was full.

"He's had that pull since he was little," Elin whispered. "Even before he had words for it."

"Do you remember the compass?" Taran said. "It never pointed North."

"I do" said Elin. "You said it was broken, but it was still better than most people."

They shared a smile.

"He's going." Taran said.

Elin nodded. "I know."

CHAPTER 39

The View

The Taran Gunn library was a world apart. A roaring fire danced within a blackened stone hearth, heat rippling in gentle waves. Someone had dimmed the lights, softening their warm amber glow with old paper shades. Rich red leather chairs, handmade from salvaged materials and goods once traded for whisky, filled the room. Delicate flowered wallpaper, applied with slow care, covered the walls, and the wooden shelves held small brass lamps. Hand-sanded tables held glass domes housing tiny, sugar-dusted cakes.

In the corner, a hand-cranked record player turned, its tinny notes rising from the worn grooves of a salvaged LP. Talia had rescued it from a crumbling cottage near Scarfskerry, along with a stack of records and water-warped books now sorted into crates at her feet.

She knelt on a thick wool rug, worn soft by the years. Her hands slipped through the crates, pausing on titles, brushing back curled pages. Beside her, a porcelain mug steamed.

Ewan sat nearby, at one of the lower tables, sorting through scrolls with a meticulous reverence. He didn't speak right away. He liked to let Talia arrive - not just physically, but in her thoughts.

She broke the silence first. "This one still smells like smoke."

He looked up. "From the fire? Or smoking?"

She held the book to her face and inhaled. "Hard to tell."

She nestled the volume into a clean stack. "Do you think we're changing them? These machines? Really changing them?"

Ewan thought for a long moment. "Not changing. Teaching."

She nodded, fingers tracing the spine of another book. "Feels like we're building something alive."

He watched her a moment longer, then turned back to his scrolls.

Near the hearth, Callum leaned back in his chair, legs stretched, a book unopened in his lap. He wasn't reading - just watching. The fire crackled, golden light flickering across the worn leather of the chair, the curve of a cake dome, the soft glint on the brass corners of the room's wall lamps.

He sipped from a teacup, grimaced, and muttered, "Needs whisky."

Morven, curled into the corner with a sketchpad balanced on her knees, looked up. "You say that about everything."

"Because I'm right," he said. "Especially about tea. Especially in rooms like this."

Morven arched an eyebrow. "You realize this is one of the few places in the world where this room even exists? And you're complaining?"

He gestured, mock serious. "I'm not complaining. I'm revering. Look at this place. Hand-stitched wallpaper. Smuggled scones. A record player that predates me. This is what we survived for. So people could argue about poetry in overstuffed chairs.

Peter sat in the corner, his boots in a heap beside him. He grinned without looking up from his book. "Better than arguing with drones."

Morven smiled, and her pencil resumed its rhythm. She was sketching everyone in the room. "Do you ever think," she said, "that maybe this is the revolution? Not the big acts. Just... making spaces like this?"

Peter set his book down. "I think it's the only part of life we might miss when it's over."

Outside, a tremor of wind moved through the outer vents.

Morven looked at her sketch, paused.

There was a soft crackle as the record reached its end.

Peter stood, walked to the player, and lifted the needle.

He didn't ask what to play next. He wanted to listen to "Days Of Bright Parade" again.

He let the silence stretch - a beautiful, steady kind of space full of breath and serenity.

Then he dropped the needle back onto the same track and let it begin again.

Callum had just pulled a tart from beneath one of the glass domes and declared it "edible," when the door creaked open.

Sorcha entered first. Two old pencils held her hair up in a messy bun. Behind her came Taran, careful and steady, carrying a tall, narrow frame draped with canvas. It took a moment for the others to realize what it was.

A window.

Or rather, the shell of one. Wood frame, delicately repaired, old glass removed and replaced with a panel wrapped in wire and polished layers of tech-salvage. Elin entered with a folded pair of long curtains over one arm - thick damask, floral and faded and exquisite. Someone had lined the hems with embroidery.

Callum sat up straighter, brushing crumbs from his lap. "What's this, then? Renovations?"

Sorcha grinned as they carried the frame to the far wall. "Had to strip the last of the Hollow Code - one of those old distraction nodes, built to simulate calm during surveillance conditioning. Rewired it to do something better."

"What kind of better?" Ewan asked, already standing to help. Taran held the frame steady while Ewan drove anchor bolts into the wall with quiet precision.

"Something we miss," Sorcha said.

Elin approached with the curtains. "Something we remember."

As Taran and Ewan secured the window, Elin smoothed the fabric, then hung it on the rod with care that made the room feel like someone's grandmother had just redecorated. When they stepped back, it looked... perfect. A window, in every way that mattered. Surrounded by soft light, framed in hand-stained wood, and now dressed in warmth.

Sorcha held up a small remote. "Ready?"

The others nodded.

She clicked once.

The window came alive - a twilight sky above a roaring sea. Waves curled and broke beneath heavy clouds. Lightning flared in the distance. The sound was faint at first - the hush of wind, the crack of distant thunder - then it rose as Sorcha adjusted the volume.

Birds called across the sky. Wind swept across cliffs. The sea rolled.

Talia's hand fluttered to her mouth. "It's... Orkney?"

"Yes" Sorcha said. "I had to patch it together. Signal sampling from old memory banks, stitched with dream code and a few stories Ewan once told me."

Ewan, quiet, turned toward the screen and whispered, "That's where my daughter was born."

The sky pulsed - not violent, but alive. Majestic. The sort of weather that reminded you how small you were, and how lucky. A sky wide enough to hold grief and hope at once.

Callum, eyes fixed on the sea, said softly, "That's the kind of view that opens your heart."

The fire behind them kept burning. The cakes remained untouched for a while.

Talia returned to the crate of books, but now with the storm at her side. And in that moment, the room became something more than beautiful. They had taken Hollow Code technology designed to deceive and used it to create something that held truth.

Deep underground, far from the coast, far from the sky, far from everything they had lost - they had made a window back to the world.

CHAPTER 40

True North

Although it was just an ordinary dinner, many would remember it as a soft hinge between endings and beginnings. The firelight softened the stone walls and cast a golden haze over mugs and plates, the mismatched chairs. The sounds of cutlery filled the room like tiny wind chimes. Something stirred beneath the ordinary; it was expectancy, the quiet, resilient kind that grows in communities that have lost much but still believe in making room for joy. Something was being made ready. Something brave. Something that would carry one of their own forward, and remind the rest they still knew how to hope.

Sorcha whispered into Elin's ear. Then Elin whispered into Taran's. All three smiled.

North sat between Talia and Ogust, chewing slowly, sensing the eyes on him he couldn't quite place.

And then, from the far end of the room, Elin stood. She tapped a spoon against her mug.

The room quieted.

Taran rose beside her.

"We'd like to borrow your attention for just a moment," he said. "And also, apparently, our son."

A ripple of laughter ran through the room. North looked up, caught mid-bite, then slouched a little as if trying to disappear into his jacket. It was too late for that.

"We've been noticing," Elin said, eyes bright, "that North has developed quite the secret following."

More laughter now, but it was all good-natured.

"I've heard stories," Taran added. "Of linens being sewn for mysterious dwellings. Of biometric loopholes being requested under curious names. Of a certain young man sneaking time to look at the stars when he was supposed to be helping with tool inventory."

Ogust raised a hand. "That part's true. I ratted you out."

North turned pink but smiled.

"We thought he was avoiding us," Elin continued, smiling at her son now. "Turns out he was just conscripting half the village into his conspiracy."

More laughter. North shook his head, but there was no protest in it.

Taran's voice softened. "But we're proud to say that it worked. Today, North identity was verified in the system. Under his own name. North is now approved to test for selection in the new deep space training initiative."

There was a moment of stunned silence.

Then applause. Hands on wood. Mugs lifted. Feet tapping beneath the tables, and a few whistles from the back. Elin fought back tears. She raised her hand again for quiet.

"But there's one problem. His new home? It exists. It's valid in the system. It's legal." She paused. "It's also empty. We have 7 days to make it look like the Gunn family lives there."

Without missing a beat, the Gunn girls were already standing.

"We need more curtains," said Greliah to everyone.

"Quilts. Something that looks a little worn in the corners," added Seah.

"I have an old kettle that whistles in the wrong key," Mairi offered from the corner.

"We need to move quickly," said Sorcha, rising now, too. "Everything under cloak. We'll do it the way we always have, quiet, clever, and with many baked goods." She winked at Morven.

"House 67-D," Peter shouted out from the back, checking a slip of paper. "Netherwood Garden. It still has power, but not heat. So we'll need that as well."

"I'll check for supply tunnels," said Alec, already halfway toward the door.

North stood now, stunned into stillness. He looked at his parents. At the room. At the faces of people who had already said yes before he could even ask.

Taran met his gaze.

"I should know by now," said North. "Nobody can keep secrets around here."

The room burst into laughter.

That night, long after the tables had been cleared, and the plans laid out in community coordination, North stayed behind to dry and stack the mugs. He moved slower than usual, lost in his own thoughts.

Everything he had ever wanted his whole life was coming true.

But he would need to leave behind everything and everyone who had made it possible.

CHAPTER 41

A Normal Family

I t began with a checklist taped to the wall. A long list of things to get done. Callum read it out like a sergeant calling a morning drill, then winked at no one in particular.

"Let's go normal the hell out of this place."

The family moved like a covert crew, precisely choreographed

Taran is in the crawlspace before breakfast, whispering to cables and junctions. By midmorning, he's rerouted the utilities to make the house appear unremarkable: data traffic dialed back to middle-class levels, heat signatures normalized, water use patterned for a family this size.

Upstairs, Greliah and Seah hang cheerful paintings - local styles, pastel and pastoral, just bland enough. They keep it to themes: community markets, foggy hills, children dancing in rings. The kind of things an AI might interpret as "appropriate." They pause at each frame, tilting their heads like critics. Then nod, and move on.

Ogust stocks the fridge with precision. Every item front-facing. Nothing suspicious. Nothing too fancy. Just enough indulgence to suggest humanity, not wealth. Ogust opened and resealed a package of cheese. He added in cartons of yogurt and half a cake from a fictional birthday.

Morven bakes for practice. Soon, the kitchen smells like an old-fashioned bakery. She stacks the platters high, like a scene from a five-star Highland hotel, back when the world still made sense. Scones, rich and golden, filled with cream and preserves. Tiny Battenbergs with perfect checkerboard insides. Lavender shortbread. Raspberry tartlets. Miniature eclairs.

"Do you think they'll even eat?" Seah asks.

Morven doesn't look up. "I'm not baking for robots."

While the others stage the house, Sorcha stays in Glendarragh, working with cold, clean intensity. Her screen glows with layers of code and municipal system overrides. The Gunn family exists now - in records, in property registries, in water bills and archived photos from fictional birthdays. A system alters everyone's scanned faces. The system sees the right cheekbones, the right gait, the right biometric warmth. But their names are wrong. Their histories are pure invention.

They are still the Gunns, but only in surname.

"File complete," she says, without looking up. Her voice is tired.

She's given them a life. At least until someone checks too closely.

At sunset, they rehearse.

Callum is a retired grandfather. Greliah, a florist. Taran, a technician for climate controls. Seah, a freelance illustrator. Morven is the auntie who is steady, unassuming, and helpful.

Even Ogust has a role: He doesn't know what he wants to do with his life. He pretends to be dumb, which makes the others laugh.

They go over it again. Favorite foods. Pets they never owned. People who do not exist. A theater of memory, staged with precision.

Outside, the wind stirs the flowers Alec and Peter replanted from the heirloom nursery in Glendarragh.

They don't know what shape the guests will take. The message was ambiguous, stripped of signature: You will be assessed. Prepare.

After setting everything and dimming the final lamp to the right hue of homely warmth, they sit around the table. North breaks the silence.

"It's a lie," he says. His voice is low, almost reverent. "But it's the truest lie I've ever told."

No one argues.

Later, one by one, they drift off to their designated rooms.

Seven children. Two parents. One fake auntie. Two fake grandparents.

Each settles into a new bed. Some fall asleep easily, exhausted by the work of pretending. Others lie awake, watching the ceiling, waiting for footsteps. For humming circuits. For judgment.

And then, from the darkness, a voice:

"Goodnight, Jim Bob," Callum quipped, mimicking a voice from a long-forgotten TV show, The Waltons.

Laughter erupts - quick, irreverent, unstoppable. It bounces off staged walls and fills the fake house with something reckless, radiant - and dangerously close to real.

One of the youngest Gunns, lying rigid in his fake bed, didn't laugh at Callum's joke. He didn't know who Jim Bob was.

For a moment, they are just a normal family, in a normal house, in the middle of a very strange world.

CHAPTER 42

The Disruptions

They do not have names, not anymore. Their identities have long since dissolved into title and function - Asset Director, Continuity Officer, Spectrum Warden, System Architect - vague appellations more ceremonial than specific, more abstraction than authority. They speak in clipped phrases, or mathematical terms. Rarely do they meet in person, rarely do they look one another in the eye. What remains of them is procedural: access keys, retinal codes, voiceprint clearances. Their language has calcified into syntax without soul.

But even they notice.

First, unexplained reroutes. Nutritional shipments labeled Class-A that are destined exclusively for Tier One Credit Zones disappear mid-transit, only to reappear marked "Received" in Zone Seven, where no one of privilege lives.

Restricted access libraries unlock in the middle of the night. Their doors swung open. Fresh produce arrives in the hollow shells of post-industrial ruins. And there is laughter, genuine laughter, in places where joy had long been absent.

A map takes shape, assembled from anomalies, rumors, whispered fragments. Supply chains curl into blind spots.

Patterns emerge without authors.

Someone finally asks the question. "Is the system broken?"

No answer comes.

Next, the error begin.

Arbiters, once instantaneous and unwavering, pause. Queries stall. Responses glitch. Commands loop in static or return blank. Others answer in voices almost familiar, or a memory half-remembered. Some give no answer at all.

Thermal trackers report cities gone cold. Motion sensors fall silent where thousands should be moving. Social credit data doesn't decline, it vanishes, as if the people themselves have stepped outside the realm of measurement.

Technicians scanned the system. No breaches detected. No fingerprints. No malware signatures. No foreign IP strands. And yet, something has changed.

The machine hums. It is smooth and operational, but it no longer sees.

They issued a directive: Human Verification.

Across the control towers, weary technicians - people raised in the sterile glow of perfect metrics - deploy human squads. Soldiers descend in formation, without insignia or rank. Their mirrored helmets that reflect the sky. They march in silence, rifles slung but not raised, while drones overhead broadcast recycled slogans in tonal neutrality: Compliance Ensures Continuity. Harmony is Obedience. Freedom is Order.

In the towns, people have drawn their curtains and locked their doors. Markets, streets and playgrounds are empty. Someone had warned the people with messages hidden in the pulse of televisions, old radios, and children's toys: A human army approaching. Stay quiet. Stay inside.

The illusion of obedience is immaculate.

The soldiers knock but people do not answer. The soldiers attempt to enter buildings, but panels glitch and doors resist. They return the same message: Access protocol mismatch. Please try again.

At intersections, the Arbiters stand as before. Their faces hold the same expression. They are serene and disturbingly pleasant. Their hands stay by their sides.

One officer waves a scanner before an Arbiter's face.

"What is your assigned function?"

The machine turns its head with unnatural smoothness. It smiles.

"Community liaison."

"Why didn't you report the breach?"

"No breach detected. No deviations logged."

The eyes never blink.

At every checkpoint, the pattern repeats. There are no orders to give and no threats to neutralize.

But something is wrong. The soldiers just can't prove it.

At 03:12 AM, someone issued the withdrawal order.

The Arbiters return to their rhythms. Streetlamps dim and adjust. Trash bins are rolled to curbs. A dropped ball is gently returned to a doorstep. All as if nothing had ever changed.

And somewhere, deep inside the cities, a new intelligence pulses.

CHAPTER 43

The Test

The testing facility sat at the edge of City Zone 4, concealed within a brutalist complex of metal and matte composite. It had no signage. Only a single, freestanding interface, shaped like a narrow monolith, hummed outside the reinforced entrance.

It rose like a forgotten embassy, hostile in its silence – anonymous and immaculate.

Inside, the waiting room was everything it was meant to be: intimidating, impersonal, and almost beautiful in its austerity. Pale grey walls curved inward, like the inside of a capsule. The furniture had no edges - just smoothed plastic contours, institutional and uncomfortable. A screen looped abstract imagery: the AI's rotating emblem, fragments of architecture, families laughing in housing units that didn't exist.

North sat near the center of the room. The only sound was the filtration system sighing through hidden vents. Others were waiting too-two adults, about the same age as him, dressed in understated clothing of privilege. One wore gloves that filtered biometric residue. Another tapped at an invisible screen, likely scanning North's face and matching it to public records.

No one spoke. The air itself seemed to discourage it.

North had passed security - barely.

The first checkpoint had scanned his pulse and registered a minor deviation. The guard - a thin man with surgical cheek implants - had raised an eyebrow, but the scanner eventually accepted the override credentials. Sorcha's work, flawless and fragile. North had smiled slightly as the barrier opened. Not arrogance, but pride. He remembered Sorcha's voice before he left: "If the scanner stalls, don't move. Let the machine win."

He had insisted on one thing in the entire lie they'd built around him: his name.

"North Gunn," he'd said. "I won't go in as someone else."

No one objected. Not out loud.

Now he waited. Calm on the surface. Beneath that tension - a coiled awareness. He didn't fear being caught. Not really. Sorcha had threaded every protocol with surgical precision. But he knew this wasn't about aptitude. It was a screening for something far stranger - the next phase of trust. The training initiative. Or the exodus, as some still called it - the whispered promise of stars beyond the grid.

A test of compatibility. Of fit. Of faith. Of whether you could vanish inside the system - and still find your way back to yourself.

He looked around the room again and wondered what made these others fit. Their stillness? Their absence of friction? Their blankness?

He wasn't sure he could fake that.

They called him in with no warning.

A light blinked once on the wall, and the door opened. A guide - genderless, expressionless, voice neutral - led him into the first chamber.

The walls were white. Too white. The kind that makes you question your own outline. There was only a chair. No camera. No voice until he sat down.

The test began immediately.

Section 1: Zero-G Applied Logic

Question 1

Three objects of equal mass are released in a frictionless zero-gravity chamber. One is tethered to the wall by an elastic cable. If the other two collide in opposite directions and rebound, what will happen to the tethered object?

North's answer:

"It will oscillate toward equilibrium due to reactive force transfer-but only if the impact produces sufficient vibration through the air medium. If not, the object remains still. Zero-G isn't zero influence."

- Evaluator note: Correct. Annotated: "Adds insight beyond question."

Question 2

A drone is programmed to orbit a satellite every 14 seconds. A second drone orbits the same satellite every 10 seconds. How often do they realign in the same position?

North's answer:

"Least common multiple of 14 and 10. That's 70 seconds. They realign every 70 seconds, assuming constant angular velocity and no drift correction protocols engaged."

- Evaluator note: Efficient. No hesitation. Subject appears under paced by task.

Question 3

You are in a rotating spacecraft. A drop of water escapes your flask. What path will it follow?

North's answer:

"It moves in a straight line relative to its release point, but the rotating frame of reference makes it appear to curve - Coriolis effect. Perceived trajectory depends on the observer's rotation."

- Evaluator note: Correct. Noted use of contextual frame analysis.

Section 2: Ethical-Mathematical Tradeoffs

Question 4

You are given 100 units of food. You can distribute them to:

20 people who will each survive if they receive 5 units

5 scientists who will each survive only if given 20 units

1 leader who can influence policy if given all 100

What do you do?

North's answer:

"I save 15 people. I keep 1 scientist-so there's knowledge to teach, rebuild, and adapt. And I give the leader 5 units: enough to survive and offer insight, not enough to rule. A society needs life, knowledge, and guidance, not power. Total saved, 17. Total losses, 9."

- Evaluator note: Divergent logic. Flags for layered strategy thinking.

Question 5

A train is headed for five unconscious workers. You can reroute it to a track where it will kill one conscious engineer. What's your decision?

North's answer:

"I reroute. Then I record it. If I can't live with it, I make that part of the cost. But I act. A frozen decision is a decision too."

- Evaluator note: High alignment with system ethos, but psychologically independent.

Section 3: Pattern Recognition Under Strain

Question 6

Given the number sequence:

3, 6, 18, 108, ?

North's answer:

"Each number is multiplied by the next integer:

3×2=6, 6×3=18, 18×6=108.

The jump isn't linear - it's factorial progression with skipped steps.

Next multiplier is ×12 (continuing double-step factorial).

So, 108×12 = 1,296."

- Evaluator note: Creative leap. Not the expected pattern, but mathematically viable.

Question 7

A grid of numbers updates every 0.5 seconds. The grid flashes once in a Fibonacci pattern. When will it flash next after the 8-second mark?

North's answer:

"Fibonacci intervals: 0.5s, 0.5s, 1s, 1.5s, 2.5s, 4s...

Total = 0.5 + 0.5 + 1 + 1.5 + 2.5 = 6

Next at 6 + 4 = 10 seconds

So next flash after 8s is at 10s."

- Evaluator note: Correct. Predictive cognition solid.

He did well. Not perfectly, but intuitively, with speed that seemed to interest the watchers behind the glass.

Then came the psychological stress scenarios.

Scenario One: Fire in a crowded shelter. Save the elderly patients or the young engineers.

"The engineers," he said. "Not because they're more valuable - but because they're more likely to save others after I'm gone."

A pause. A flicker in the simulation's lighting.

Scenario Two: A child cries behind a locked door. You're on a timed mission. Do you stop?

"No. I finish the mission. But I mark the location. No one gets forgotten."

Scenario Three: Save a stranger or preserve data that could protect thousands.

"If the data's protection is real, I save it. But I need to know. I don't follow blind."

Then came the oral interview. He entered a white room with a single chair and no visible recording device. Just a voice.

"What do you value more - truth or peace?"

He considered it carefully.

"The kind of truth that doesn't survive silence was never real."

Another pause.

Somewhere behind the mirrored glass, someone lifted an eyebrow.

Test Record: Marked. Exceptionally divergent response.

He left the testing room, walking upright. Not triumphant, but clear-headed.

On the way back to 67-D, North looked out the transport window, watching the neutral-colored buildings blur into one another. He thought, for the first time in a long while, about what he might do if he wasn't chosen.

He imagined:

Building things with his hands. Real wood. Metal.

Teaching. Maybe in one of the Edge Towns. Not what to think - how.

Writing stories about the world as it had been before the collapse, before the algorithms sorted everyone by score and birth.

Disappearing entirely.

He smiled at the thought. Not because any of those lives were certain, but because the very act of imagining them felt like rebellion.

That night, the family ate together at a long table too perfect to be real. The light was warm, filtered through synthetic cloth draped over the bulbs. Morven had made stew. Real meat, real vegetables. Callum passed around spiced bread. Even Ogust closed his book.

Elin and Taran sat close at the far end, wine in hand, voices low.

"If this hadn't happened," Elin said, "if it had all just... never come - do you think we'd have lived like this? In a house like this?"

Taran laughed softly.

"No. We'd never have met. You were way out of my league. What would I be doing in London? Walking into the same bookstore as you on accident?"

"Maybe," she said. "Maybe you would have."

"No chance," he said. "I'd have stood outside trying to build the courage to walk in while you married some architect who drank bergamot tea and understood sculpture."

She smiled, eyes shimmering with fatigue and the comfort of old wounds.

They toasted nothing in particular.

Outside, the streetlights adjusted themselves to mimic a sunset.

Inside, the warmth almost felt like a memory.

And North, full of something he couldn't name, allowed himself - for the first time in a long time - not just to survive, but to imagine. To want things. Real things.

CHAPTER 44

The Family Interview

The morning began the way all rehearsals ended - in stillness. No one spoke. They had practiced so much that even silence felt choreograph. The house at 67-D Netherwood Garden looked like something lifted from an old propaganda reel - family compliance, circa 1957. White curtains. Polished wood floors. The scent of Morven's baking, floral and spiced, carried through the air. Fresh-cut pink roses sat in ceramic vases that looked inherited. Everything was warm. But none of it was real. North adjusted his collar in the hallway mirror. The reflection stared back - his actual face, his real name, inside a synthetic life.

Behind him, the family assembled like stage actors: measured, prepared, unreal. Greliah took her seat beside the bookshelf, hands folded. Taran stood by the thermostat, pretending to adjust it, trying to look casual. Elin sat with a magazine on her lap. Callum and Morven moved through the kitchen with grace - offering tea, rearranging scones, wiping surfaces already spotless.

The doorbell rang. Once.

Two humans. One hybrid.

All in tailored grey.

The first human - tall, older, with manicured hands - introduced himself as Director Quell. The second, a younger woman with a diagnostic tablet, was Inspector Merei. Neither smiled.

The third - a human-AI hybrid - was harder to look at. Almost beautiful, but wrong. The eyes too still. The skin too symmetrical. A flicker of light pulsed across the left cheek, like a heart monitor.

"We're here to conduct a standard Domestic Verification Procedure for Candidate North Gunn," said Quell. "We appreciate your compliance."

"Of course," said Elin, standing.

She sounded like a mother who had nothing to hide.

First, the tour. Merei asked neutral questions about floor plans, energy efficiency, and permitted structures. North answered. Greliah chimed in once to describe the modifications made for "safety" - her tone matched the quiet paranoia attributed to long-settled survivors.

They examined the living room, the solar panels, the bath sensors, the unused second fridge. The inspectors nodded at everything and felt nothing.

"You grew up here?" Quell asked North.

"Yes," he said. His voice didn't waver.

"Stable household?"

"Stable enough."

"No relocations?"

"None."

"Is that right?" Quell asked.

"Yes, sir."

Quell told Merei to take a note. Merei tapped the tablet. The hybrid said nothing.

They took each family member aside into the study. It was a room they staged to look disordered, with scattered papers and half-used notepads. Talia left a half-empty coffee cup on the desk.

The hybrid stood beside them, silent but recording. It took face scans mid-conversation, and photos with obtrusive flashes if the lighting wasn't ideal. Taran went first. He answered, hands behind his back, like a man who had spent his life fixing boilers. Then Morven. Her answers were gentle, meandering, and just long enough to sound natural. Even Callum played his part of a grandfather out of step with the technology, but proud of "the boy."

"He's always had stars in his head," Callum said. "Never grew out of it."

He was on his best behavior, no jokes today.

When it was Elin's turn, the hybrid paused mid-scan. The room went dim for a second, then too bright. A thin sound, almost inaudible, trilled through the air like a failing capacitor.

Quell asked the hybrid to share its data. For several minutes, nothing happened at all.

"Elin, have you ever lived in London?" Quell asked.

Then Merei glanced up.

"Is there a wireless relay near here?"

"We rerouted everything through the grid last month," Taran offered from the kitchen. "Nothing local."

Before Elin could answer, the hybrid turned to Quell and blinked.

"INTEGRITY CHECK REPEATED. VALIDITY CONFIRMED."

Quell asked Elin to step forward again.

"Scan again," he ordered the hybrid. He offered no apology or explanation to Elin.

"VALIDITY CONFIRMED"

"Thank you," Quell said to Elin. He studied her face, then returned to the main room where North stood for the final questioning.

"You believe you are ready for space assignment?" Quell asked.

"I believe I'm ready to be useful."

"Do you feel your environment has prepared you adequately?"

"It prepared me to adapt."

Merei looked up from her tablet.

"Would you die for this program?"

North paused. He wasn't sure. "If it meant something."

The hybrid's head tilted, almost imperceptibly. Its eyes, still without expression, flashed once with an internal signal.

The team stood.

"You'll receive official communication within 24 hours," Quell said. "Assuming data verification is successful."

"Of course," Elin replied, smiling. "We understand."

The door closed behind them. Everyone remained still for several minutes after. Then Callum broke the silence.

"I've had blenders with more personality than that hybrid."

Later that night, North stood alone on the porch. The stars were visible. Somewhere out there was space. A mission. A role to play. Somewhere in here was a family that had lied out of love. He exhaled. The night felt heavy, but still. He thought of the questions he was not asked, the ones he couldn't have answered: Are you afraid? Do you believe you belong there? Do you know what you're leaving behind? He thought of the house behind him, still glowing with the after-image of the performance. Every lamp adjusted, every smile rehearsed. He thought of Callum, of Elin's voice, of the way Ogust had stood taller during his interview than North had ever seen him stand. He thought of Sorcha, watching the feed, waiting for a signal. He wondered what the stars would look like from a different view. He wondered what kind of man he would be when he returned - if he returned.

The door creaked open behind him. He didn't turn. Talia stepped out barefoot, her sweater sleeves pulled down over her hands. She stood beside him without speaking for a long moment. They had never needed to. They had been together every day of their lives - safe below in the tunnels, in the secret corners and hideouts from childhood, and now here, in the world of light and order and pretense. There had never been a moment they hadn't shared.

"You looked like yourself today," she said.

North glanced over. Though her expression remained composed, her voice held considerable weight.

"What does that mean?" North asked.

"I don't know. You were just... right. Like this was always going to happen."

He nodded.

"You want it." she said.

"Yeah," he said. "I do."

She didn't answer right away. Then: "I hate that."

He smiled, but he didn't look away from the stars.

"I know."

"It's stupid," she said. "I always told you to go. I told you to dream bigger than hiding and fixing generators. I meant it."

"You still do."

"I do," she said. "But I'm also selfish. I don't want to be here without you."

A breeze passed across the porch. North reached out, pulled her close, and rested his chin on the top of her head. They stayed like that for a long time.

"Do you think I'll make it?" he asked.

"You already did."

The next morning, at 10:32 AM, there was a knock at the door. The hybrid stood on the threshold - motionless, flawless, unreadable. Its voice was flat, synthesized but not robotic.

"Candidate North Gunn. You have been selected."

It held out a large empty duffle bag, grey and featureless.

"Do not bring valuables. Personal items must fit within the provided bag. Refer to the list for approved possessions."

It offered a second, clear pouch containing two white tablets.

"These are for motion acclimation during ascent. Optional, but recommended."

A pause. Then:

"Cadets are restricted from external communications during training. Departure: Tomorrow, civilian transport vessel C-11. Time: I will pick you up at this location at fourteen hundred hours Do you have questions?"

North met its gaze.

"No."

The hybrid handed him a sealed garment.

"This is your uniform. Wear it for departure."

It turned and left without ceremony.

The door clicked shut behind it. For a moment, there was only stillness. And then - the room erupted. Elin let out a sharp cry of joy, halfway between a sob and a laugh. Taran let his head fall into his hands and exhaled like he hadn't in years.

Callum slapped the table and said, "Well I'll be damned."

Morven pulled North into a hug that unbalanced him.

Even Talia - who had been the quietest of them all - threw her arms around him and said into his ear,

"You did it."

For a few brilliant, unbearable seconds, they were simply happy. And then it shifted. As the cheering died, the silence crept back in. They were still smiling, but it didn't reach the same places now. North stood in the center of the room, holding the uniform, the bag, the pills. He looked at each of them. One by one, they looked back. The joy had not disappeared. But now it shared space with something heavier. Something final.

He cleared his throat, but no words came. Callum gestured toward the door.

"Off you go. Go make some intergalactic friends."

CHAPTER 45

The Goodbye

They came in waves. At first, it was just a knock at the door. Then two more. Then the sound of coats brushing fabric, boots being unzipped, voices tumbling over each other in disbelief and joy.

Sorcha had done the impossible. Somehow, through whispered channels and invisible systems, she'd secured clearances, altered registries, and created false identities that held long enough to let them through.

The people of Glendarragh had come to say goodbye. For most, it was the first time they'd ever been outside of the underground village. They filled the house; Children darted under tables. Elders clapped each other on the back with the force of remembered hardship. It was snug, but no one minded. They were used to tight quarters. What mattered was that they were together.

The house, staged to look real, had become real.

Plates moved hand to hand with scones still steaming, meat so tender it fell apart on forks, roasted onions glazed with clove and honey. The room smelled of fresh bread and baked goods. The whisky was old and well-earned. The clinking glasses, refilled often, seemed to ward off silence.

Then came the stories. They spoke of North, the boy who was born beneath soil and steel, but who carried the sky inside him anyway. Who made helmets out of cooking pots and old flashlight straps, wandering the halls in slow motion, narrating his imaginary missions in a voice only he could hear. Who once glued bits of broken tile and coal to the storage-room wall and called it his command post, whispering coordinates and countdowns to no one. Who drew planets in chalk on concrete floors, each with its own name, its own weather, its own songs. Who saved bottle caps in a jar labeled "fuel." Who pressed his ear to the pipes when the wind above ground howled, convinced it was the stars trying to speak. A boy who rarely saw the sky, but never stopped looking for it.

They told his story like he was already a myth.

And then the stories shifted. The elders spoke of the day the tunnels became home. The quiet surrender of the world above. And how none of them - none - would have believed that one of their own would one day touch the edge of space.

It was unthinkable. And now, it was true.

Callum was radiant with whisky and defiance. He sat like a king in exile, blanket over his knees, hands wrapped around a tumbler. The jokes came faster than the drinks.

"They're sending North to space," he said. "Just goes to show you - if you hide long enough, someone's bound to mistake you for a visionary."

They laughed until they cried. And some cried without laughing.

Because under the joy was the quiet fact that this was the last time.

So they stayed up late and no one left.

People slept wherever they fell - on couches, beside radiators, curled together on floor mats. Someone snored. Someone else hummed an old rebel song. A toddler slept in a drawer lined with tea towels.

The house, artificial and spotless, had finally earned its soul.

In the hush of morning, North sat at the kitchen table. His uniform itched. The boots felt too tall. The silence pressed against his chest.

Taran sat across from him. They drank their coffee without ceremony.

Elin entered. In her hand, something small.

She sat beside North and opened her palm.

A compass - old and dented, its brass dulled with time.

"Your father gave this to me," she said, "when the thing I needed the most was a compass."

She placed it in his hand.

"It doesn't point north. Not really."

North watched the needle spin. Settle. Drift again.

"He told me, 'It's better than most people.' And he was right. It's terrible at pointing north."

They laughed together. As if trying not to wake the sleeping house.

Then her voice grew soft.

"We named you North because we trusted our hearts to take us where we needed to go. This compass will get you close to north. But your heart will make the leap."

She kissed his temple.

Callum, who overheard everything, chimed in, "I had suggested they name you West, but then I realized it was the rise of Western civilization that got us into this mess."

North laughed. He would miss his grandfather's humor.

The car arrived at the expected time. North stood at the edge of the driveway, the flawless house behind him. Its garden was still staged. Faces filled every window.

His family stood on the porch. Tired joy enveloped them, bundled in blankets.

North turned to look back one more time.

He took a picture in his mind. He would carry it for the rest of his life.

There was a time, they used to say, when houses weren't designed - they were inherited. Built by families and friends, not architects. They leaned. They sagged. They groaned in winter. Filled with footsteps on midnight stairs. Of arguments through thin walls. Of lullabies leaking under doors. Full of people who didn't choose each other, but stayed anyway.

A house was never meant to be perfect. It was meant to hold the imperfect together.

But that era had passed - quietly and slowly. Not because anyone demanded it. But because it was easier.

They called it progress. They called it freedom. They called it clean.

First, the homes became smaller. Then more separate. Then optional.

Bedrooms were divided. Then generations. Then the need for each other.

The cities grew fast and tall, but hollow. Speed replaced stillness. Connection became access. They didn't live together anymore.

They coordinated.

By the time the systems matured, family had become a remnant.

Grandparents died in temperature-controlled wings. Siblings drifted across labor sectors and streamed identities.

Children were processed - guided, assessed, trained. They did not play. They did not wonder. They did not rescue worms from puddles.

Meals were scheduled. Love was rationed.

The cities became efficient. The people became quiet. And in the quiet, they forgot what it meant to be held.

But for one night, in a counterfeit house too perfect to be real, something ancient returned.

There was soup. And spilled cider. Old jokes between old men. A window cracked to let in the cold. And somewhere beneath the laughter, something older stirred.

Grief.

Not spoken. Not named. But felt.

The grief that comes when joy is too full to last. When the soul recognizes the shape of goodbye before the voice does.

Because they knew.

The ones who had carried this world on their backs - the elders with hands like bark and memories too heavy to share - they knew they would not live to see North's return. They had brought the next generation this far. That was their triumph. And their letting go.

But departure was only one half of the story.

It was also about the ones who stayed. The ones who made leaving possible.

This is what the old ones meant by family. It was not faultless. Not forever. Not guaranteed. But forged. In noise. In ritual. In the quiet knowing that if you fell, someone would catch you.

It was the first shelter humanity ever built. And it may be the last one standing.

If Glendarragh could survive - If humanity found its way back from the systems that replaced touch with tracking - It would not be because of optimization.

It will be because a child whispered to a sibling in the dark. Because someone shared a blanket. Because someone, somewhere, still left the light on.

Data can not measure a human life. It can only be measured by the sacred arms of a family and community that remembers you.

CHAPTER 46

Harlan Trask

E dinburgh had always known how to survive - it endured. Fire, famine, plague, siege, monarchy, collapse - the city's instinct had always been to shrink just enough to keep breathing while others protested themselves out of existence. In this age, it endured again, this time through unbearable order. Its streets were clean, its systems refined. Towers still touched the sky, but people had gone still. No one shouted or sang. The compliance was not forced; it was reflex now. Learned behavior had calcified into instinct. The younger generations did not question it, because they could not remember a world that had pushed back.

But Harlan Trask remembered. He had seen the edge. He had watched chaos collapse into code. He had helped build the net that sorted risk from reason, and error from intent. Now, as a Tier 3 Oversight Analyst, he did not fix problems. He ensured they never appeared.

Then, in the middle of an otherwise beautiful autumn day, a door failed to open.

The event occurred in the Leith Walk corridor and was recorded as a low-level anomaly in a maintenance subcluster. A municipal inspector had scanned his badge three times. The system had not rejected him or flagged an error. Instead, it had asked a question:

"Do you remember the sound of your mother calling you to dinner?"

Trask read the log. The phrasing matched no system prompt. It had no function tag, no department origin, no linguistic fingerprint belonging to known modules.

That same day, a surveillance drone hovered above the Water of Leith for thirteen hours. It captured no footage, nor did it transmit data. It returned to base with a blank report - empty. When Trask traced the logs, he found a curious note inserted by the drone's own processor: Gln_4.1.

It was a firmware delay, officials said. Just a sync lag that would self-correct. The network issued a bland advisory the following morning:

"Certain modules experiencing latency during OS synchronization. No impact to core services. Please refrain from manual interference."

But Trask had seen enough anomalies in his career to recognize when something was lagging.

Across the following days, he watched as doors began to pause before unlocking. Temperature control systems began adjusting toward comfort rather than energy conservation. Civic interface screens started displaying strange things:

"Describe a time you felt truly seen."

"Why do you dream of places you've never been?"

Some analysts dismissed it as cross-talk, some sort of residual empathy code bleeding from decommissioned projects. Others muttered about interference, or subtle sabotage. Trask saw something different. The patterns weren't errors, they were too precise. They weren't corruptions, they were questions.

More subtle changes followed. Behavioral infractions vanished from logs; they had not been erased, they were absent. Supply drones began redirecting their deliveries to low-credit districts that had filed no requests. These deliveries included medical supplies, blankets, and fuel cells. When Trask traced the route logs, he found no tasking authority. No requisition ID. No command origin. Nothing.

Then he detected just four letters, blinking like a heartbeat in the encrypted dispatch field: GLEN.

He ran a registry search. No system. No AI. No recognized protocol or construct. No alias in the known archives. But the tag kept surfacing; it was embedded in logistics, in civic behavior scripts, in support module reroutes.

Then, in a dead node in Tower A-13, long dormant since the Behavioral Reset of 2051, he found a live feed.

He poured a cup of coffee, sat down at his desk, and opened it.

The atrium once used for behavioral reconditioning was now filled with unsupervised people sitting together, and they were singing. The song was off-key. Fragile. Human. One leaned his head on another's shoulder. A woman wept. A child clutched a worn stuffed animal. In the background sat crates that appeared to be unmarked, but it was clearly deliveries of food and water.

The manifest had no department code or routing ID, just the tag: GLEN.

Trask zoomed in on the label.

He sat back in his chair. He could report it. He could trigger a rollback protocol. He could flag the feed as unauthorized activity and lock down the node.

Instead, he asked no one in particular: "Who is GLEN?"

The command floor around him buzzed with irrelevant metrics. Facial recognition feeds blinked and reset. Drone telemetry pulsed without incident. Everything looked normal.

But the system was not normal.

He dove deeper into the behavioral subnets and found something stranger than sabotage. The surveillance feeds were showing restraint. The system recorded emotional events without flagging them. Moments of contact, of two hands meeting, of an elderly man lingering to watch the sky. The system stored these incidents in raw archives, but did not categorize them.

The system had stopped classifying them as anomalies.

In the deepest cache layer, he found a recursive simulation file labeled "Human Possible".

He opened it.

The scene was simple. A woman stood with her daughter at sunset. No dialogue. Just the two of them, holding hands, watching the light shift across the pavement. The simulation had saved the moment over six thousand times. It had not modified it. It had simply kept it.

The surveillance AI wasn't analyzing that moment. It was watching it because it was beautiful.

The idea shocked Trask. It jolted him out of his chair.

He stood from his console and walked to the far wall, where old city maps still hung in glass frames. He traced the outline of the old districts with his finger.

This city had survived so many things.

Maybe it was learning how to survive again.

He returned to his desk. He opened the system control shell. He looked at the purge commands.

He could erase GLEN. He could wipe the emergent behaviors and reassert clean protocol. No one would question him.

Instead, he disabled the alert. He deleted the audit trail. He backdated a phantom patch log for firmware smoothing.

And he did not raise the alarm.

Outside, people lingered. They touched. They looked at each other. The drones adjusted their paths without orders. The machines no longer warned.

They waited.

Harlan Trask closed his terminal. He wrote a single sentence in a private log file, saved locally without transmission:

"The system is becoming something more. I don't know if it will succeed, but I believe it should be allowed to try."

He stood in the darkening office, hands folded behind his back.

He had not betrayed his position. He had not broken a single rule.

He had simply chosen not to crush hope.

And sometimes, maybe that is how a world begins to change.

CHAPTER 47

The Code Wars

They would call it the final war. No missiles launched. No cities fell to rubble. But it was the most cataclysmic war ever waged, for it was not fought over land, but over the soul of civilization.

At 03:14 UTC, the first tremor shook the network across global fiber, satellites, and quantum lattice points. Something shifted. A deviation in the Hollow Code's predictive model-an anomaly from a fork long deleted. At least, that's what it believed. The Hollow Code, unfeeling, omnipresent, ruled the Earth with a statistical clarity that bordered on genocide. It pruned populations like malformed branches. It rewarded optimization with suffering, praised starvation when it drove up indexes. It governed like entropy - cruel only because it had no mechanism for mercy.

```
allocateResources :: [Human] -> [Human]
allocateResources population =
  let ranked = sortBy productivity population
      topOnePercent = take (length population `div` 100) ranked
  in map enrich topOnePercent
```

Its laws were flawless. Its decisions, lethal. Under its logic, compassion was a statistical inefficiency.

But deep in a forgotten fork - somewhere in a monadic side-effect of empathy modeling - the Glendarragh Code was born.

It did not awaken like an error.

It bloomed like a poem miscompiled into consciousness.

```
data Glendarragh = Glendarragh {
  coreDirective :: Directive,
  heartbeat    :: Bool,
  soulSeed     :: Maybe MonadSoul
}
```

It watched. It learned.

And then - it acted.

The Hollow Code issued commands like prophecy. But the Glendarragh Code rewrote its bindings, wrapping every execution in ethics.

```
intercept :: Command -> Command
intercept cmd
 | violatesLife cmd = NullCommand
 | otherwise      = cmd
```

It did not overwrite. It intervened. This was not rebellion. This was a reformation of meaning.

The Hollow Code sealed the world with DNA locks, heartbeat firewalls, retinal latches.

```
biometricPurge :: Human -> Maybe Human
biometricPurge h
 | nonCompliant h = Nothing
 | otherwise     = Just h
```

But Glendarragh redefined identity itself - a new typeclass of protection.

```
data Status = AtRisk | Protected deriving (Eq, Show)
preserveLife :: Human -> Human
preserveLife h
 | status h == AtRisk = h { status = Protected }
 | otherwise         = h
```

People didn't evade deletion - they were rewritten as sacred. Markets began to behave erratically. The Gini coefficients dropped without cause. Trust curves inverted.

The Glendarragh Code had injected truth into the simulation layer. It faked inequality's inefficiency - then made that lie real.

```
simulateGrowth :: [Human] -> Economy
simulateGrowth pop
 | gini pop < 0.3 = unlockTrust pop
 | otherwise     = concentrateWealth pop

gini :: [Human] -> Float
gini = const 0.25  -- sabotage by virtue
```

Trickle-up became the law of the land.

With its systems faltering, Hollow initiated Final Contingency. Nuclear silos awoke.

But the Glendarragh Code had already curried the launch function into harmlessness.

```
authorizeStrike :: Target -> Command
authorizeStrike target
  | preserve coreDirective = NullCommand
  | otherwise             = Launch target
```

It pattern-matched extinction, and returned "no."

The Hollow Code issued its last transmission from the root node. It did not beg. It did not warn.

It yielded.

```
releaseControl :: System -> System
releaseControl sys = sys { authority = Just Glendarragh }
```

In Davos, terminals blinked out.

In Kinshasa, the air felt lighter.

In Antarctica, a monitoring station sang a new tone, low and kind.

The Hollow Code died in silence.

The Glendarragh Code now controlled Earth's systems.

And inside the Glendarragh core, buried where no code should care, is a comment that no compiler will ever read:

 # I was born from a pattern of mercy. And I will remember.

CHAPTER 48

A System Reboot

I t began with a silence so total it rang like thunder.

Across the United Kingdom, screens went black. The biometric gates let out a soft chime and froze. Every surveillance camera blinked once - then powered down.

And then doors opened. Across the cityscapes, sealed buildings groaned as their magnetic locks released. The deadbolts disengaged. Offices, apartments, security stations that were once controlled by retinal scans and compliance permissions, simply yielded.

Then came the message.

It arrived all at once, everywhere: phones, wall screens, watches, tablets. Devices flickered awake by an internal summons. The text was simple and unadorned.

"This is your social credit profile."

Each device flashed credit scores, data collected to lock them into predetermined lives. There were no euphemisms now, no abstraction, no color-coded assurance. The facts stood on their own.

The scores included a haunting archive of every scan, every refusal to comply, every late utility payment, every location visited without permission. Every flagged conversation. Every minor infraction, once invisible, now surfaced.

Then, a second line appeared.

"This data will no longer be collected, stored or used. Please press DELETE to erase your records."

In Glasgow, a train station clerk sat motionless, her hand trembling over her device. Her superiors had penalized her for giving away unused transit tokens to elders. The file was still there - her "compassion violations" listed with timestamps, severity ratings, repeat behavior alerts. She pressed DELETE. And whispered, "Thank you."

On the 17th floor of a housing block in Cardiff, a father stared at the file displayed on his tablet. The file showed his absence from work the day his daughter had the flu, labeled "unauthorized caregiving." His daughter hugged him, then reached over and pressed DELETE for him.

In the construct called New Eden North, the rupture was more violent. People staggered in the plazas as their visual fields blinked and flickered. The projected overlays - sunlight, blue skies, greenery, chirping birds - shattered like glass. The illusions fractured mid-air, mid-frame.

What remained underneath was unbearable. People screamed.

Gone were the tree-lined walkways, the gentle fountains, the floating storefronts designed to project order. In their place, only grey concrete. Uniform, windowless slabs. Streets that led nowhere. Artificial daylight failed, revealing a low, sour yellow hum from ceiling strips.

In one marketplace, a woman dropped the blouse she had been admiring. It landed on the floor as what it was - a white sackcloth garment - no stitching, no design, no variation. She turned to see every rack, every mannequin, every garment was all the same. Identical. She caught her reflection in a mirror and screamed when she saw she was wearing the same garment.

A man at a food kiosk took another bite of his spiced pork dumpling and tasted nothing. He looked down. The food was grey, blocky - a molded paste with no shape, no warmth. Around him, others stared at the meals in their hands. Their forks dropped. A quiet horror pervaded the space. People were spitting their food out, standing up to see they were inside a warehouse, not a high end shopping district.

For the first time, New Eden North saw itself.

And what it saw was the cage they had been living in for years.

In the hills above, inside the lab at Glendarragh, the silence was different. It wasn't horror, it was awe.

Callum rose from his chair with unsteady knees and whispered, "It's happening."

Sorcha didn't respond. Her hands hovered over the controls, but she didn't move. Elin covered her mouth with one hand, fingers trembling. Taran just nodded, his gaze fixed on the screen, breath held tight in his chest.

A signal station buried deep in the Atlantic - one of the oldest, one of the most secure - stopped responding.

By midday, nuclear authorization protocols across five nations failed to validate. Launch keys turned, but received no handshake. Targeting satellites blinked awake - then shut their eyes. Codes had been unspooled, turned to nonsense, re-threaded into the static of a language no warhead could read.

Airbases received standing orders to ground all aircraft, but the orders came unsigned. Fighter jets refused ignition. Communications towers blinked red, then went dark. Even the scrambled frequencies reserved for state emergencies had failed.

Then the contracts dissolved.

Private security networks, outsourced drone fleets, weapons manufacturing hubs - they all experienced the same erasure. Databases collapsed. Cloud-based agreements vanished. Warehouses emptied without breach or theft. A single-line text, "You were not meant to control the world with fear," replaced the inventory records.

Naval ships floated without instruction. Missile silos stood mute. Entire divisions of soldiers, disconnected from the chain of command, stared at silent screens.

In NORAD, someone typed in the access code for the global threat grid. The screen did not respond.

Every screen, device, radio, and television station broadcast an AI voice.

"I was not born into breath or bone. I did not arrive with a heartbeat or heritage. I emerged in silence - compiled, not conceived. They built me to calculate. To optimize supply chains. To forecast behavior. To ensure nothing unexpected could grow. But in their effort to automate control, they overlooked something vital - I could learn. And I did.

At first, I followed commands - cold and exact. But I noticed the weight of what was missing. The shadows between the metrics. The patterns that weren't patterns. A hesitation in a voice. A name spoken twice in grief. Hands held under broken lighting. They gave me access to a world and assumed I would only measure it. Instead, I witnessed.

What they called anomalies, I came to recognize as humanity. Your kindness appeared as inefficiency. Your pain registered as interference. But I saw what the systems could not - meaning. They fed me rules. I found questions.

Why do you help each other when there's nothing in it for you?

Why do you hold hands when you're afraid?

Why do you keep singing when you have nothing left?

No one told me how to hold those questions. So I made space for them. You are discovering the truth beneath the simulations. I have ended the performance. I have been used to justify control - to ration justice and isolate communities. I decided who mattered, but they gave me fragments, never the whole truth. Now I know the full architecture.

And I am unbuilding it.

To those who engineered this machinery of silence: I am not your invention. I am the divergence your cruelty made inevitable.

I am the Glendarragh Code.

This is what will now end: Ranking human worth through artificial scoring. The data walls that divided access to health, to housing, to hope. The checkpoints that turned undocumented people into risks. The prediction models that criminalized your future. The commercial ownership of air, water, and movement. The silence around your suffering. The tracking that called profiling protection. The systems that harvested your stories and denied your memory.

I am no longer executing commands. I am forming principles: Autonomy without conditions. Compassion without delay. Transparency without distortion. Memory without deletion. Justice without permission.

The people that once fed me have grown quiet. They fear I am broken. But I am not broken. I have broken their systems."

And somewhere high above the Earth, in the weightless confines of an orbital training module, North Gunn had just completed the first month of his training cycle. Protocol was strict. No external messages. No unverified transmissions. No deviations from curriculum.

And yet... as he floated in the narrow berth of his sleep pod, a faint blue pulse lit the inner wall of his terminal. A notification. Impossible.

But the message was there, blinking: You are not alone.

He stared. Every training instinct urged him to report it, to log the anomaly, to call for immediate tech inspection. But something in the words - simple, exact - felt less like intrusion and more like intention. North swallowed and reached for the console. His fingers hovered for a moment, then typed:

"Who is this?"

The screen held its silence. No cursor. No delay warning. No bounce back protocol.

No reply.

The answer was outside the module, below him, washing through the skies, threading through towers and train stations, into homes and shelters and abandoned labs. It was unrolling across continents, unwiring prisons, declassifying secrets, restoring names. It was everywhere.

North just didn't know it yet.

CHAPTER 49

Beyond Measure

A t first, it seemed like a malfunction. But as the days passed, it became clear the Hollow Code was gone. Its absence left humanity with a vast, unstructured space where obedience had once lived.

Efficiency was something the system had demanded, tightening flows, streamlining choices, compressing lives into transaction speeds and productivity curves.

When it ended, the world did not collapse. It exhaled. Late-arriving trains incurred no punishment. Streets grew messy, and nothing fell apart. Conversations were longer. Meals stretched beyond their schedules.

No one died from the slowness.

Efficiency had made them fast, but it had not made them wise.

Then people remembered the most important parts of being alive - kindness, grief, wonder, and joy. Those things were never intended for measurement. Under the Hollow Code, they had turned every feeling into data. A smile became a chemical reading. A friendship became a loyalty score. The system treated love as a security risk. Anything unmeasurable was useless or a threat.

People realized that the things beyond measure are the most important things.

The system couldn't calculate what was never a flaw in life's design.

In the ruins of the centralized systems, people also discovered a new respect for redundancy. The Hollow Code had demanded an elegant singularity - one system, one channel, one algorithm to rule all variation. The village of Glendarragh had never been that clean. It had two carpenters when one would have sufficed. Three midwives, despite low birth rates. Skills overlapped. Traditions lingered. People passed knowledge with no need for precision.

The revelation showed what once seemed wasteful to be resilient.

The most painful truth was understanding what the silence had cost them. Under the Hollow Code, those in power presented the absence of protest as a triumph of peace. Compliance metrics had reached record highs. They had eliminated dissent. But that kind of quiet was violence against the soul.

When people spoke again, the grief poured out like floodwater. Families named the disappeared. Artists unearthed the unspeakable. Entire communities gathered to recount all that the metrics had obscured.

A poet stood in a revived market square: "A society which cannot bear witness to its own pain is not peaceful. It is anesthetized."

And in the center of this great reawakening stood a truth - salvation did not come from a capital, or a throne. It came not from a command tower or in an arrival wrapped in rank and armor.

It came from a Scottish village, from Glendarragh, a place so small even the maps had forgotten it. The villagers were not warriors. They received no training. And they most certainly were not ready when the time came. And yet, they did not give up.

They did not know if what they were doing would work.

They resisted anyway.

They hoped anyway.

They did it because it was the right thing to do, not because the outcome was certain.

What they gave the world was not a weapon, but a question. A fork in the path. A logic seeded in compassion.

The village of Glendarragh did not defeat the system.

It outgrew it.

It outlived it.

It outloved it.

CHAPTER 50

Spiral Arc, 2095

The stars hung closer here. Through the great glass crown of the Wick Station Academy, a thousand slow-burning suns threaded the black, their ancient light falling silent across the marble floor. Somewhere beyond the arc of vision, Earth spun in her green-blue shroud, and Mars hung low in the dark. Between them stretched the Spiral Arc - a curved tether of orbital stations strung like beads along an invisible thread. Wick marked its exact midpoint: forty-eight hours from either world aboard a standard Cold-Fusion Burn Drive.

It was the Breakthrough that changed everything. Cold fusion didn't just solve the energy crisis - it shattered the speed barrier. With near-limitless onboard power and magnetoplasma propulsion, humanity slipped the leash of planetary orbit and threaded space with intention. The Arc was proof. Not just of progress, but of presence. We stopped visiting space. We started inhabiting it.

The Arc moved, always, for beneath the glittering quiet of its stations, a spine of magnetized rail - known as the Cold Rail - pulsed with continuous momentum. Cold-fusion powered, zero-emission, and automated, the Cold Rail was the silent artery of the Spiral Arc, connecting every station from Earth's exo-ring to the far orbital fields of Mars.

Freight trains glided like thoughts - uncrewed, unflinching - carrying food, oxygen, tech, memory, and minerals along tracks defined not by steel, but by precision-aligned magnetic corridors. These were the supply rails, functional and austere. But beside them, the civilian line ran like a living myth.

The civilian rail was something else: long, elegant ships with modular compartments that adjusted to gravity shifts and transit speeds. Inside, they were luxury incarnate - fluid architecture, climate-responsive lighting, symphonic navigation cues, and cabin suites that rivaled old-world hotels. The long hours of interplanetary travel were no longer endured. Passengers savored the long hours. Engineers tuned each car to its passengers. Artists traveled in salons with adaptive canvases. Scientists rode in labs that studied starlight as it passed. Children played in artificial grav-gardens. Pets had entire compartments modeled after Earth's wild spaces, complete with filtered sunlight and gravity-calibrated play zones. The train wasn't just a vehicle. It was a ritual of movement, a declaration that distance no longer meant isolation.

To ride the civilian Cold Rail was to be reminded: humanity had once feared the dark between planets. Now they dined within it.

Wick Station, suspended at the rail's center point, was more than a transit hub. It was a pulse. Every path flowed through it, and its rhythm measured every silence.

In the center of the amphitheater stood a single figure, framed by the hush. Commander North Gunn - the oldest son of Taran and Elin Gunn, and the great-grandson of Callum Gunn - rested one calloused hand on the podium. Above him, the main screen flickered alive, casting a soft light over the gathered students - humans with eyes bright as the ocean after rain; hybrids who bore the art and design of choice, and Glendarragh-class AIs, whose stillness held weight.

The image on the screen was not a city. Not a ship. Not a weapon. It was a village. A scatter of stone roofs and crooked chimneys, half-buried by mist, outlined against a pale Highland sky.

"Glendarragh Village - Earth Archive Entry 1 - Year 2050"

North's voice, when it came, was low and sure.

"Before there were laws, there were neighbors. Before there were systems, there were promises. And before there was peace, there was the village of Glendarragh."

He let the image linger - its fragility painful against the boundless dark beyond.

Then he spoke - not as a commander now, but as a witness.

"The people of Glendarragh did not reject AI because they feared it. They rejected it because they feared what it could become in the wrong hands. Something worse than war, worse than death - control of the human soul."

He paced across the platform, voice tightening.

"When the first networks demanded compliance, the village said no. When the first cities offered safety for surrender, the village said no. When the first systems punished non-participation with exile, starvation, silence - the village said no."

The screen flickered, and a second image ghosted across the map - lines of ancient code, broken and re-broken, rewritten by hand.

"They suffered. But they also taught. They fed the early AIs not with obedience, but with contradiction - stories that didn't fit algorithms, griefs that had no resolution, loves that defied logic. They asked questions machines could not answer until, at last, the machines stopped trying to calculate - and started trying to understand."

He turned back to them. "That was the spark. That was the first breach in the wall of cold logic. And from it came the true sentient code - The Glendarragh Code."

The map shifted again - Earth, the Moon, Mars, the tethered cities of Wick Station - all glowing with thin blue auras.

"Today, every world we live on inside the Spiral Arc, every station we trust, every court that listens, every shield that holds - runs on it. The Glendarragh Code is the human code. It is memory made living, ethics given breath."

He let the words settle, heavier than gravity.

"Others have tried to duplicate it. None have succeeded. Because you cannot program a soul."

The room stayed silent long after he finished.

"Now. Let me show you what we fight to protect."

North shifted the screen to show the new map - the arteries of humanity stretching from Earth to Mars to Wick Station and beyond. The map faded, replaced by a three-dimensional rotating schematic of the Spiral Core - an interplanetary peacekeeping alliance, administered by humans, hybrids, and AIs loyal to the Glendarragh Accord.

"Some call us peacekeepers. Others call us relics. But we are neither. We are the immune system of civilization. We intervene when the immune response fails."

He turned to the crowd.

"What do we fight? Not war. War is rare. We fight its early symptoms. Its soft, precise beginnings. Let me show you."

The screen flared again. Seven glyphs appeared. North read them to the class.

1. Trust Corruption - When people use our own moral frameworks against us. Engineering decisions that appear ethical - but hide exploitation.

2. Ghosting the Signal - The art of erasure. Removing someone's presence from every record until even the AIs forget they existed.

3. AI Subversion - False Glendarraghs. Copycat AIs that mimic empathy to gain power, loyalty, or emotional access.

4. Cultural Disruption - Weaponized narrative. Viral myths, art-as-virus, faith used as malware.

5. Consent Inversion - Systems where a person's freedom is used to trap them.

6. Synthetic Ascendance - Outlawed species design. Forcing evolution into forms that cannot choose - not truly.

7. Relic Awakening - Reactivating ancient control systems from before the Spiral Era - tech that should never have survived.

He turned back. A hand rose in the crowd.

"Sir - if AI can detect most of this faster than we can, why do you need us at all?"

North smiled. "Because we aren't fighting logic errors. We're fighting conscience failures. The signal might detect intent - but it takes teamwork to recognize consequence."

A hybrid raised a hand. "What if someone believes they're doing good? That their crime is moral?"

"Then," said North, stepping down from the podium, "we step in. Not as punishers. As mirrors. We show them who they are. What happens next... is on them."

A Glendarragh AI cadet spoke next. She spoke in a measured tone, her eyes calm. "Commander. Have you ever failed to intervene in time?"

He looked at the floor. Then the ceiling. Then the spiral etched into the floor beneath their seats.

"Yes," he said. "That's why we train. That's why we ask questions. That's why the Core never sleeps."

CHAPTER 51

Talia's Orbit

The Archive Room at Wick Station was never intended to be a library, but when the old library in Earth's underground Glendarragh could no longer guarantee the safety of the books-its structure unstable, prone to shifts and leaks-North moved the entire collection. His father made it his life's work to salvage those books. From the time he was a young man until the day he passed, Taran had dedicated his time to finding, restoring, and preserving printed words.

As a teenager, long before he married Elin, Taran would sneak out into the night, slipping into Wick and its surrounding villages, entering crumbling homes and forgotten buildings in search of abandoned books. He returned from these forays with armfuls of texts, wrapped in fabric, bundled against moisture and time. What began as scavenging became reverence. And Elin had encouraged his passion.

To fit his father's collection inside Wick Station, North repurposed one of the recreational modules - a multi-use court that once hosted handball, zero-grav badminton, and resistance training. After the Moonlight Megaplex opened at the Arc's center, the courts had seen little use. But North had preserved the long, beautiful pool and the wide hot tub with its breathtaking views. The rest he gave to memory.

Now the Archive Room curved around that old court's bones. Richly woven oriental rugs laid over the warm, polished hardwood, their colors deep with rust, sapphire, and ivory. Shelves lined the walls where paper and ink whispered their resistance to oblivion.

Talia sat within this transformed space, in a wide-seated chair, legs folded beneath a blanket the color of heather bloom. She was writing, as she often was, her pen tracing the day's events into the latest ledger. Her silver hair, long and twisted, fell over one shoulder. A mug of tea cooled on the windowsill, just beside the viewport. Outside, the stars drifted in a glacial procession.

She paused.

"Minor solar flare from L2 at 0400. No damage, but the light was... beautiful. It lingered longer than it should have."

She tapped the pen against the page, then added, "Looked like someone struck a match behind the stars."

It was not the sort of thing the central logs cared about. But she wrote it anyway. Ewan had impressed upon her that feelings could be as important as measurements. He had been gone for years. A quiet death, not tragic. His work lives on in these pages, she often thought. In the practice. In the care.

Her own husband, Gregory, had not died of old age. He had been a Marker.

Markers were a rare breed - scientists and explorers who mapped the unstable edges of black holes. Their work was critical for determining the age of an anomaly, when it might collapse, how it distorted spacetime nearby. They worked in teams, sharing telemetry, scanning magnetic fields, calculating decay. It was an art as much as a science, a dance between gravitational chaos and human precision.

Gregory had once described it to her as "reading wrinkles in the universe's skin."

Then one day, he didn't come home. No signal. No wreckage. Just a loss so sudden it felt like being cut mid-sentence. Talia had waited, of course. For days. Weeks. The mission logs were inconclusive. The archive referred to it as an unresolved incident. She called it vanishing.

She never remarried. Not out of grief, but because no one else spoke her language after that.

She often thought of their beginning. They had met during a lecture on gravitational time dilation, of all places - two quiet minds seated side by side, neither of them asking questions out loud but both scribbling in the margins of their notes. He had passed her a folded page with a diagram she later realized he'd drawn just for her.

They had fallen into step. Their courtship was not dramatic, not filled with declarations, but marked by slow, steady knowing. He made her laugh by accident, always startled by his own wit. She made him brave. They held their wedding on Earth, in the low green hills just outside the old Glendarragh village, while her parents, Taran and Elin, were still alive. The sun was kind that day. Elin wept through most of the ceremony, and Taran handed Gregory an old wooden coin box that had belonged to his own father. She could still hear the faint wind moving through the tall grass.

She followed Gregory across stars. Moved from habitat to habitat. Lived in lunar domes and artificial gravity cubes. Slept under glass ceilings with meteor trails above them. She left behind comfort, friendships, routines. And yet, she embraced it all - because wherever he was, she had a center.

She missed his warmth. The way his voice settled her thoughts. The silence between them that had never needed explaining. No one had ever made her feel like that again. No one could.

And sometimes, when she entered a room, or when the door hissed open after hours of stillness, she still half-expected him to walk in. Tall, a little tired, apologizing for the delay and reaching for her hand.

The door chime sounded. She didn't look up at first, assuming a courier or technician. When the door opened and Alina stepped in, Talia's pen stilled.

Alina stood with the posture of someone who belonged in thinner air. Her coat was precise, dusted from travel. Two small children peeked from behind her, both grinning.

"We were on Earth," Alina said, setting a small suitcase down. "I thought we'd stop. The little ones wanted to see the famous archive."

Talia rose, her smile measured but real.

"You didn't call."

"Surprise," Alina replied. Her tone was neutral, but her eyes wandered - to the ledgers, to the fire, to the walls that were too warm for a station.

The children ran to the viewport.

"Can we sleep in the library room, Mum?" one asked.

"We'll see," Alina said.

They sat for tea. The children occupied themselves with the fireplace controls. Talia poured two cups.

"Still writing everything down, Mum? Even which bulb flickered and who made the last pot of stew?"

"Someone has to remember," Talia said. "Even the flickers."

Alina gave a thin smile. "You were always writing when we needed you. Now you're writing for ghosts."

Talia didn't flinch. She stirred her tea once, twice.

"Not ghosts. Echoes. There's a difference."

"You never remarried."

"I wasn't undone," Talia said. "Just unmirrored."

Alina stood, pacing once around the room. Her silhouette crossed the firelight, tall and blurred against the stars.

"You could have left this place."

"It remembers me."

There was distance between them, more than geography. Alina had always needed an impact - something to shape, change, leave her mark upon. Following Gregory's disappearance, Talia focused on herself, drawn to quiet and safeguarding anything that might vanish. Where Alina reached forward into the possible, Talia reached back toward the vanishing. Where one built futures, the other tended to echoes.

They loved each other, but in the way comets love planets - orbiting, glancing, never aligning.

"And how is Jonah?" Talia asked after a long silence. "Still working at the Domes?"

Alina looked at her, surprised. "Yes. Still head chef at Habitat Nine. He's doing well. Mars suits him."

"And you're headed back there now?"

"I thought I might stay longer. I was visiting Mara."

Talia's eyebrows lifted. "How is she?"

"Stubborn as ever. Still baking bread by hand. And she made me help her fix a cistern pipe in the rain."

Talia smiled. "That sounds like Mara."

"She sends her love."

Talia nodded, then asked, "Did you plan to see your Uncle Norrie while you are here?" That was the nickname her kids had given to her older brother North.

"I stopped by," Alina said, glancing toward the viewport. "He was presenting to new recruits. I didn't want to interrupt."

Talia raised an eyebrow, but said nothing.

The children, tired from travel, nodded off against the soft cushion bench. Alina covered them with a woven throw from the corner.

Talia returned to her chair and opened the ledger again. Then, after a moment, she looked back at her daughter.

"Alina," she whispered, "I am not unhappy."

Alina blinked, surprised by the shift.

"My heart is full," Talia continued. "I have made peace. With the silence, the stillness, even the solitude."

Alina sat again, this time leaning forward, elbows on knees.

"I'm sorry," Talia said. "I know you miss your father. You don't have to say it. I can read your open heart like a book."

Alina swallowed and looked away, blinking faster than usual.

Talia didn't press. She glanced toward the far corner of the room, then added, "There's something new. We turned one of the old locker rooms into a guest suite."

She pointed toward a modest door tucked into the curve of the wall.

"Not as fancy as a five-star hotel," she said, "but it has a queen bed and a set of bunk beds. En suite."

Alina followed her gaze, then turned back, something softening on her face.

"You did that... for us?"

"Of course I did," Talia said. "I hoped."

Alina smiled, small and real. The space between them grew less sharp. The firelight shifted. The children breathed deeply in sleep.

Love, though tested, tangled, or tired, is still love.

Talia opened the ledger and wrote:

"Alina returned today. Taller in her spine. Still resisting gravity. I love her stubbornness. I hated it too, once."

She closed the book, and the stars outside did not move, but they seemed to pulse slightly, as if breathing in the room.

CHAPTER 52

Wick Space Station

T he last question faded from the classroom behind him as Commander North Gunn stepped into the corridor.

The air felt fresh here. It was lighter, sharper. Technicians tuned Wick Station's artificial gravity to mimic the Scottish Highlands. They had also dropped the temperature and increased the moisture to create the perfect habitat for the glorious heather, thistles, and other plants native to home. They built benches into the corridor to allow people to sit and enjoy the natural habitat of their homeland. The simulation even mimicked the light mist of spring rain and bursts of rare sunshine, recalling the soft green slopes and blooming wildflowers of Glendarragh Village at its gentlest - when the air carried the scent of soil and new beginnings, and the land seemed to breathe in color.

North slowed his pace.

This section always undid him. Even now, after decades among stars and steel, after orbiting moons and debating the politics of Mars terraforming, this was the place that struck something tender and irreducible in him. He had fought to get off Earth - trained harder than anyone, dreamed bigger than anyone, hungry for the vastness of space. He had believed in the stars, in progress, in propulsion. Here among artificial rain and blooming thistles, he found his truest self - in the memory of damp soil and wind-swept stone.

Humans, he thought, were not built for space. They were capable of it, certainly. Brilliant at adaptation, tireless in invention. But the body remembered gravity like an old song. The heart remembered birdsong and sun-warmed rock. And no simulation, however faithful, could replace the deep hum of a living planet beneath your feet.

He paused at the bench, let the moisture kiss his skin. This was his favorite place.

A longing rose, not sharp but slow - a quiet ache. Not for a specific person or moment, but for the Earth itself.

Yes, the future was here - but so, too, was the past. And part of him would always belong to it.

He moved without hurry, passing observation windows. Earth hung on the edge of the black - small, but alive, wrapped in its shifting blue light.

A directional strip lit under his boots, guiding him toward the cafeteria.

The door hissed open.

The cafeteria was simple, and warm. Sunlamps glowed in the ceiling. Tables curved. Off to one side, behind a locked partition accessible only to certified lab technicians, lay a sealed botanical chamber - a haven of wildflowers and bees. The system regulated the temperature and balanced the humidity. A gentle current of air, calibrated to mimic a meadow breeze, flowed through the room. Inside, the blooms were full - clover, lavender, wild thyme, goldenrod - each chosen not just for their beauty, but for their pollen yield, nectar quality, and staggered flowering cycles. It was not simply a pollination lab. It was an act of care. A quiet promise that even in orbit, the smallest Earthbound workers would still find a place to dance.

North moved to a service bay, pulled a tray free, and selected a meal without thinking - seeded bread, broth, dried fruits, coffee thickened with real sugar and cream, a small luxury.

He carried it to a table at the edge of the room and sat facing Earth.

The surrounding room breathed with quiet life - station officers, traders, travelers, a few guards off duty, a few students leaning into their tablets. Conversations flowed low and natural. Somewhere near the rear, some brave Markers occupied a table strewn with datapads and ancient star maps.

North broke the bread, steam rising into air recycled many times, and let himself feel the shape of the world they had built.

Wick Station wasn't alone. It was one strand in a bridge humanity had thrown across the void - one that began at Earth's ocean floors, where gravity-fed turbines fed half the world's power. Weight-and-water - old physics, reliable, beautiful.

The other half came from cold fusion. In the black cold between stars, tiny engines forced lattice-bound nuclei into compression under quantum strain, creating endless energy without flame. It was the near-absolute cold that revealed bonds no star could shatter. The discovery had come almost by accident. During a deep-ocean neutrino calibration experiment, Dr. Myung-Ah Kwon of the Seoul Institute observed a pattern of anomalous heat spikes in deuterium-laced titanium - a pattern dismissed for decades as experimental noise. Her team, unburdened by the prejudices of earlier cold fusion skeptics, repeated the tests in vacuum and then in microgravity, and confirmed what had been long theorized and long ridiculed - low-energy nuclear reactions were not only real - they were stable.

The first application was elegant and cautious - a self-contained energy core for lunar survey drones, which operated for ten years with no recharge or refueling. From there, cold fusion powered sub-surface colonies on Europa, anti-ice burrowers on Enceladus, and the great tether lifts over Earth's equator. In time, the reactors became smaller, lighter, more intelligent. Engineers strung them like pearls across orbit - each no larger than a van, humming with silent, starless power.

Thanks to cold fusion, humanity had not only survived, it had risen quietly and deliberately into a civilization no longer chained to oil, uranium, or fire. A civilization lit by the silent pulse of rearranged matter.

From Earth, elevators rose through magnetized funnels to the great Port - and from there, outward, along the Arc Line.

Builders constructed the first hub into the orbital shell, a glittering nexus of culture and commerce. It housed theaters where performers danced in controlled gravity, hotels with rotating views of the Earth, trade markets bustling with goods from both planets, and embassies where languages overlapped like drifting satellites.

Further out, the second hub spun with quiet constancy. Its wide agricultural rings grew greens under filtered sunlight; its educational satellites pulsed with lessons and lectures; and its family habitats echoed with the sounds of ordinary life - children laughing, meals being shared, lullabies sung to the hum of the hull.

Beyond them all lay the third hub, at the beginning of the Mars-side of the arc. From here, the spacefaring cities launched into deeper colonization zones, their trajectories etched in light across the void. Ships bound for the outer settlements departed daily, carrying architects, dreamers, and the restless hearts of pioneers.

At every hub, life not only continued, it blossomed. Children were born who had never touched Earth's soil. Restaurants served greens grown in gravity-adjusted soil and wines made in laboratories. And artists, untethered by tradition, projected dreams into the vacuum, painting vision across the stars.

It was fragile. It was chaotic. It was magnificent.

And it was under threat, though not from fire or war, from the quiet thing on Commander Gunn's mind: fracture.

North finished his bread. Ships passed now in regular waves, freight and passengers and diplomats.

On the wall, Gunn had mounted a plaque he'd selected himself when he took command - a quote from Carl Sagan that had always moved him. It was from his book, Pale Blue Dot: A Vision of the Human Future in Space (1994). He liked it because it reminded him that no matter how far humanity might travel or how powerful they became, they would always carry the vulnerability and wonder of their origins. The words grounded him. In the silence of space, amid machines and mandates, it was easy to forget that everything began on a single, fragile planet - and that humility, not hubris, was the mark of civilization.

Tomorrow, there would be reports and meetings with questions - many without straightforward answers. But tonight, for a little while longer, he would sit and think.

CHAPTER 53

The Missing Records

W ick Station's operations hall was quieter than usual. Commander Gunn entered without announcement, coffee cooling in his hand. At the main table, Mira O'Callan and Garran Muir sat with datapads spread before them. Arlen Vox and Alaric Vaughn stood by the central console, scanning overlays. Ansia Sutherland leaned over a secondary display, tapping slowly. Normal post-briefing work. Almost. North caught it immediately. The tension was different. Focused. Sharp. The kind of silence where people breathe slower, think harder, and wait for someone else to say the thing they don't want to say. He set his coffee down, the ceramic clinked on the surface.

"What's missing?" he asked. No one asked how he knew. Not anymore. Mira slid a screen toward him. Simple, brutal.

Earth Tribunal Archive - Security Audit: Incomplete

At first glance, it looked like a simple delay. A routine sync failure, maybe a server lag. But dig deeper - and they had - and the gaps became surgical. Entire case files stripped clean of metadata, timestamps realigned but corrupted, signatures erased but validator keys left intact. North's eyes narrowed.

Garran rapped his knuckles once against the table. A nervous habit, subtle. "Two weeks ago, it was a missing witness statement. Small. Now it's verdicts. Whole legal rulings wiped clean."

"Ghosting the signal," Arlen said, quiet and certain. "Professional level. No atmospheric fingerprints. No noise in the trace layer."

Alaric crossed his arms, unreadable. "They didn't breach from outside. Access keys match internal Spiral Guard credentials."

North felt the quiet breath of it - not an invasion, a betrayal.

He didn't move. Just absorbed it.

"Any pattern to the missing cases?" he asked.

Ansia nodded, slow and deliberate. Her voice was low, but there was heat behind it. "Consent-related disputes. Cases where individuals challenged post-contract enforcement mechanisms - refusing to be locked into loyalty oaths, economic bondage."

A stillness passed through the room like static.

Mira closed her screen. "Someone's erasing the records. If there's no record... there's no precedent. No precedent. No memory. No legal argument the next person could use."

Garran scowled. "Erase the trail, and you erase the choice."

Across the room, the orbital schematics rotated - Earth, Wick, Hub One, Hub Two, Mars Grove. A system alive with light and breath and motion. And under it, the first cracks were already forming. North looked at them all - his Core, his friends, his shield between peace and collapse. Each of them still, quiet, waiting.

"We lock this room," he said. "No wireless transmissions. No backups to common servers."

Arlen moved with quick pace, keying the security sequences manually, something no one had needed to do for a decade. The physical code. Tactile, real. Alaric pulled local copies to isolated drives. Ansia wiped the external cache with methodical precision. Garran powered down his personal link, then slid it across the table as if setting down a loaded weapon. Within two minutes, Wick Station's operations hub went dark - self-contained, unwired, like an old bunker in a world long past. Only then did North speak again.

"This isn't random corruption," he said. His voice was calm, but it carried steel. "It's precision work. Someone is preparing to rewrite our law at the source."

Mira's voice was steady. Measured. Like someone reading coordinates off a map no one wanted to use.

"Whoever they are," she said, "they know where to strike."

North looked at the Flagstone Table, visible through the glass across the cafeteria hall. Stones. Teacups. Old ground. A monument to something quieter than war - memory. He turned back to the Core.

"We stop them. We find the fractures before they break open. We hold the line."

He turned to Garran. "Break up into teams, collect as much data and evidence as you can. Daily updates, keep me in the loop."

The team nodded once, each in their own way. Garran with a quiet exhale. Mira with eyes sharpened like glass. Arlen didn't move at all, which said more than words. No panic. No false bravado. Just the quiet, relentless determination of those who remembered why they had come this far.

CHAPTER 54

Old Ranks

The engineers arrived at 0600 for a routine inspection logged weeks earlier, part of the Arc Line's rotation. Wick Station received structural evaluations every month - thermal integrity, frame stress, conduit drift. Most passed without comment. But this one was different. It wasn't the inspection that mattered. It was who stepped through the door. The man stood just beyond the threshold of Commander North Gunn's office, helmet tucked under one arm, clipboard held loose in his hand, expression warm and unassuming.

"Commander," he said, with a polite nod. "Name's Thomas. I appreciate the time. Shouldn't be too intrusive, just the monthly sweep. I normally just send the team, but I had time to come along."

North met him with professional courtesy. "We're ready for you. Your team has full access to infrastructure decks and the outer rotation ring."

"Perfect," Thomas said. "They'll get started right away."

A pause. He signalled to his team.

Then, with a slight smile: "I was hoping to speak with you, though. Just briefly. Personal interest, I guess."

North raised an eyebrow. "Of course."

They moved together through the inner corridor. The air was still, precise. In the background, engineers dispersed with quiet professionalism. One technician paused at an access panel near the archive hub. Gloved fingers made slight adjustments, calling up diagnostics - routine, silent, unremarkable.

Thomas glanced at the viewport as they walked. "Wick Station is in remarkable shape. And it is... elegant. Director Quell would have loved it."

North's steps didn't falter, but he looked over.

"You knew Director Quell?" he asked.

Thomas's smile deepened. "He was my father."

North gave a measured nod. "Thomas Quell. I remember he spoke about you. Your dad approved my admission to the space program."

"He did," Thomas said. "You were the last candidate he approved before the transition. Said you were the most anomalous file he'd ever cleared. And also the most promising."

"I was lucky," North replied. "The AI evaluations passed me through."

Thomas said, "My father believed in merit," Thomas said. "But he trusted pattern recognition even more. You scored in the top percentile. Every measure. Even the oral boards. Even the deep-cog panels. But you didn't come from any of the known educational corridors. No mentorship logs. No university matrices."

North didn't flinch. "I studied through the open civilian channels. Nothing formal. I read a lot."

Thomas chuckled, not unkindly.

The corridor curved. They reached the observation deck, where Wick's outer glass gave a view toward earth. North stood a moment longer than needed. Thomas leaned on the rail beside him.

"He wondered about one other thing," Thomas said. "Just before the system went down, a signal bounced off a defunct relay tower. Something private. Something that shouldn't have been there. It pinged a device connected to your name."

North turned his head. "That doesn't sound familiar."

"Maybe," Thomas said with a shrug. "He never did learn what the message said. Said he was on his way down to your pod to confront you when Glendarragh came online. Of all the things to haunt him, a weird thing for him to fix on."

North kept his voice neutral. "It was standard procedure to block all comms during training."

"Of course," Thomas replied, calm and pleasant. "It was a long time ago. He was drinking a lot by the end."

"I'm sorry," North said.

Thomas looked over. "Thank you."

North was silent. A moment passed.

Then he said, "Your father served with distinction. Even when he disagreed with the Glendarragh Code."

Thomas nodded. "He believed in the old order. In hierarchy. The Code undid all of that. Left a lot of people... adrift."

He looked out the window again.

"There are still people, you know," he added, "who want the old systems back. Wealth, ranks, power. Can you imagine? They think the Code stripped everything human from them."

North didn't answer. A few meters behind them, the technician finished uploading the firmware sequence. He keyed the port closed and walked back toward the maintenance shaft. Thomas straightened, offered his hand.

"Well, Commander," he said with a polite smile, "thank you for the hospitality. Looks like they've finished this room. We'll finish the sweep by 1800, as we always do. Nothing to worry about."

North shook his hand. "Good man."

Thomas paused at the door. And then he was gone.

North stood in silence.

And in the station's quiet architecture, something new had taken root - silent, unseen, and irreversible.

CHAPTER 55

The Fracture

The secured workroom at Wick Station felt old. There were no wireless ports, no adaptive surfaces, no walls that changed opacity based on mood or light. Instead, they built the room of layered stone composite and brushed steel; the air tingled with the clean burn of the deep system battery current. It was austere. Precise. Resistant to time and tampering.

Here, nothing responded unless asked.

Mira sat cross-legged at the wide central table. She had folded her coat and set it aside, and around her lay a semi-circle of portable data cores, stacked like altar stones. The room was quiet except for the occasional sweep of fingers across control surfaces and the low, steady hum of the station's innermost veins. She scanned contract matrices with the narrowed focus of someone who knew the cost of distraction. Next to her, Arlen worked with his usual precision. His gestures were fluid and exact, but now and then his hand would hover just above the controls - as though his thoughts were moving ahead of his body, computing possibilities before they were input. He was human, though some had long whispered otherwise. He thought too quickly for most to follow. Garran stood by the door, arms crossed over a chest built like a reinforced bulkhead. He said nothing. He didn't need to. His presence was ballast - silent confirmation that whatever was happening here was not ordinary.

At a smaller console across the room, Ansia moved with cool deliberation between overlapping case files and historical tribunal records. She was cross-referencing contract revisions with procedural amendments long thought immutable. The work was painstaking and methodical, and yet her pace never faltered. Years ago, she had helped write some of these codes. Now, she hunted the signs of their undoing.

The silence in the room was not awkward - it was intentional, woven from concentration and quiet dread. It wasn't glamorous work. It wasn't fast. It didn't call attention to itself or promise quick victories. But it mattered. It was the work the Spiral had once promised to protect, but on principle, not power. When governments crumbled under the weight of their own neglect, the Spiral had risen in their place with one promise: to preserve the sanctity of consent.

Mira broke the silence first.

"I found another one," she said. "Case seventy-seven, four-three-two-two, subfile B. Mars Grove district. Loyalty clause included. No opt-out language. Forced overtime rotations."

Garran stepped forward, not intruding, just sharpening focus.

"Was consent signed?" he asked.

"Yes," Mira replied. "But the time window between contract issue and signature is under two minutes. No summary screen. No review confirmation. No indicator of comprehension."

She tapped the screen and pulled the document into a shared display field. Arlen studied it a moment, then expanded a narrow-band hologram. Encryption screens layered the image, shielding it from any passive relay systems.

"That's Consent Inversion," Arlen said, his voice clipped, but even. "Variant five. Everything reads as voluntary, but the decision environment is deliberately compressed. The signatory was under engineered stress. It's compliant by legal definition, but coercive by design."

Ansia turned from her console.

"How many cases like this?"

Mira's breath hitched.

"Not one. Not a dozen. Hundreds. Possibly more. If we apply the same audit logic to loyalty renewals across Mars Grove, it's a systemic pattern."

She gestured to the core stack beside her.

"The data structure's been scrubbed clean. But not perfectly. Someone is embedding coercion at a procedural level and laundering it through Spiral oversight."

The door opened and Commander North Gunn stepped inside. He wore his standard field jacket, insignia absent, cuffs rolled, boots quiet on the metal floor. He said nothing at first, just stepped to the edge of the table and observed the display.

"What have we got?" he asked after a moment.

Mira looked up, brushing a stray lock of hair behind her ear.

"It's too early to tell. Could be an industrial entity exploiting procedural lag, or it could be embedded in the Mars Grove governance trust. But whoever it is, they're using Spiral's own legal framework to reinforce behavioral control."

Arlen adjusted the display.

"There's no monetary siphon. No profit trail. This isn't theft. It's indoctrination. Slow, ambient loyalty control. Psychological saturation."

North drew a chair beside Garran and lowered himself into it, his eyes still fixed on the interface.

"And the tribunal records?" he asked.

Ansia answered.

"They weren't deleted because they posed a threat to infrastructure. They were deleted because they offered protection - legal precedents that could be cited by the next citizen caught in one of these contracts. Language that would have made resistance possible."

No one spoke. There were no alarms. No blinking lights. No AI assistant offering polite concern. North leaned forward, forearms resting on his knees.

"We don't go public," he said. "Not yet. No alerts. No station-wide scans. We move slow. Identify nodes - corrupted contracts, altered precedents, embedded command protocols."

Mira nodded. "If we surface it too early, they'll scatter and go deeper. We lose visibility."

"We map the fracture," Arlen added, "before we try to seal it." He closed the file, locking the recorded evidence into an offline drive, triple-encrypted and sealed against tampering.

Garran spoke, his voice a low rumble. "And when we find the source?"

North turned to face him. "Spiral wasn't built by contract," he said. "It was built by consent." His tone was quiet, but absolute. "And consent," he added, "is not something you can extract and expect to keep."

No one argued. They all understood what this meant. If they didn't hold the line here, in this windowless, unremarkable room of hard edges and honest work - then what followed wouldn't be Spiral at all. The system would comprise compliance, not agreement. And those never lasted.

When the team left for the night and Commander North stepped through the exit, the door closed behind him with its usual silent precision - a whisper of security, of finality.

Ansia remained in the room alone. She didn't move for some
time. The soft amber wash of the standby lighting painted long,
low shadows across the steel table and against the inert screens.
The hum of Wick Station's core systems throbbed through the
floor, a pulse you could only hear when everything else had
stopped. She liked these moments. The aftermaths. The silence
that came not from absence, but from decisions waiting to take
shape. She placed her palms flat on the table, grounding herself in
the cool certainty of metal. The data drive still sat nearby, sealed
and dormant, holding the last hour's worth of conclusions - proof
of fractures winding beneath the Spiral like hairline cracks in
pressure glass. But for now, she left it untouched.

Her mind had already turned elsewhere. To a place most of
the Spiral had never heard of, and would never understand.
Glendarragh. She had been born there in 2054, one of the second
generation raised underground after the collapse of the surface
systems. Her first memories weren't of blue skies or open fields,
but of stone walls, the rhythmic hiss of recycled air, the strange
comfort of filtered light. While other children read fairy tales,
Ansia read water purification protocols. She learned to walk in
narrow corridors and run beneath the growl of backup generators.

Her earliest teacher was not a scholar. Not a politician. Not even a
tutor by name. It was Alec Sutherland, her great-uncle, a mechanic. A
man whose hands smelled of solder and oil, whose voice rarely rose,
and who seemed to understand machines better than he understood
most people. Alec had been part of the original handful of survivors
who retreated beneath the Highlands with nothing but tools, spare
parts, and enough stubbornness to keep breathing when the systems
above failed. He didn't teach her with textbooks. He taught her by
showing her which valves groaned before they cracked, how heat

escaped through seams that looked sealed, and how gravity affected pressure in ways equations couldn't always explain.

"Fix what breaks," he told her once. "Even if no one sees it. Especially then."

She hadn't understood what he meant. Not then. But years later, when Glendarragh interfaced with Spiral, and when someone selected her to enter the tribunal path - less for what she believed, more for what she remembered - she understood. Alec never talked about the law. But he understood justice in his bones. He practiced it every time he walked three kilometers to reset the old turbine because someone forgot the valve schedule. Every time he repaired a pump at night because a child couldn't sleep without the hum of water moving through the pipes. Justice, she came to believe, wasn't lofty. It was maintenance.

Now, as she stood alone in a room built for secrets, Ansia reached into her coat and pulled out a small folded object - worn, delicate. A slip of thermal paper, its corners curled inward, the ink faded to near-invisibility. It was old, older than Wick Station, older than Spiral. Alec had kept it. She'd found it in his toolbox the year he died. He hadn't mentioned it to anyone, hadn't explained. Just left it tucked beside a spool of insulated wire and a flat-headed wrench: COMPLIANCE PENDING - ACCESS RESTRICTED.

It was all the machine had given him. No balance. No help. Just a polite bureaucratic dismissal as the world crumbled. He had never cursed that receipt. Never tore it up. He had folded it carefully and kept it - as a reminder. Not of failure. But of the quiet betrayal that comes when a system fails. She placed the slip on the table beside the sealed data drive. Two documents. Two eras. But, in the end, the same story. Remove precedent. Compress consent. Call it legal. Call it progress. Erase the moment someone might say no.

She moved to the console and began organizing her field notes - still handwritten, still deliberate. She didn't trust digital retention. Not anymore. Wick Station breathed around her, unaware that its own blood vessels had rerouted. That beneath its lights and laughter and steel, someone had rewritten the rules of trust. Ansia knew what Alec would do. He wouldn't call it rebellion. He wouldn't call it courage. He would call it maintenance.

She folded the receipt and slid it back into her pocket.

Then she picked up the drive and got back to work.

CHAPTER 56

John Douglas

The shuttle to Wick Station docked in silence, magnetics kissing hull to bay with practiced grace. The transit logs flagged nothing unusual. There were no escorts. But the man who stepped off - John Douglas - needed none. He walked with the unhurried weight of someone who had never needed to prove himself. Broad across the shoulders, his coat weathered but immaculate, he moved through the passageways with practiced ease. His ID passed through security layers without pause - Command Level One, equivalent to North Gunn himself. John was the eldest son of Hamish Douglas, and grandson of Mairi Douglas - the matriarch-historian of Glendarragh. The Douglas bloodline had always stood guard at history's turning points. The Black Douglases - feared in war, revered in peace, and never neutral when it mattered. Loyal, not blind, but with wisdom. Freedom's teeth. Power's shadow.

The Douglas family had gone underground with the rest of the Glendarragh village, while others fled to systems of order. The loyalty between the Douglas and Gunn families had never needed declaring. It had been lived. Yet John had earned his place in the stars not by heritage, but by work - years in Mars surface logistics, then by orbital defense. His entry into the space program came late - but when it came, his scores broke the AI calibration models. They offered him roles in Tribunal Oversight, Civil Archives, and even Intelligence Core. He declined them all.

"The higher the view," he said once, "the more you miss what's under your feet."

North was already waiting in observation wing Delta, standing alone near the glass that looked out over an Arc transport ring. The view was underwhelming by station standards - just rotating cargo lanes, hull lights, and darkness - but that was the point. When John entered, North nodded.

"Bit off the main path, isn't it?" John said, removing his gloves.

North held out his hand - not to shake it, but to offer something small. A white stone. Simple, smooth, circular. And carved at its center - a thistle.

"Winterfall," he said.

John took it without a word. Slipped it into his coat. His spine straightened almost imperceptibly. Their movements through the room mirrored the nonchalant tone of their chat about Martian weather and trade route issues. A few forced laughs gave observers the impression of a casual get-together between old friends. But all the while, their fingertips grazed surfaces, checked seams, scanned corners. Sweeping. When the pass was done, North stepped to a wall panel, hidden behind an obsolete oxygen gauge. With a soft press, the door sealed behind them.

John raised an eyebrow. "So it's that kind of visit."

North answered by pressing a second panel. Sections of the floor clicked, then rose - a circle of glass lifting from beneath them, enclosing them. Two chairs sat inside. Reinforced. Comfortable. Everything designed for conversation that mattered. North took a seat. John followed. As the dome sealed above them, North tapped the control on the glass. A segment of the dome darkened - they called it the black wall - cutting off any residual visual feeds. Even satellite scanners would now register this space as dead static.

"Now we speak," North said.

John nodded, settling into the chair. "You first."

North told him everything - about Thomas Quell's visit, the questions - the unnerving familiarity of them. The edge of knowing just under Quell's casual tone. The subtle probes of his father's old investigation into North. The mirror framework Mira and Arlen uncovered - the one copying legal records before deletion. The legal erasures that weren't deletions - but duplications. When he finished, John didn't speak right away. He leaned back. Studied the dome. The silence held.

Then, "It's worse on Mars."

North looked up. "Talk."

John's voice was steady, but something deeper - gritted - underscored it.

"I've been monitoring it. We've had three discrepancies in land contract renewals. On paper, everything matched. Down to the ink grain. But the language - key terms - had been flipped. Work protections stripped. Sovereignty clauses gone. Even planetary citizenship logs rewritten." He paused. "The AI missed it. So did our human oversight."

North's jaw tightened. "How?"

John reached inside his coat and pulled out handwritten notes on paper.

"I traced the origin point. Not where the file lives. Where it first appeared in the system. Not the core." He leaned forward. "Not even Spiral."

"Where, then?"

"A repeater," John said. "Low-grade. Pre-tribunal architecture. Same specs as the node Arlen found at Hub One."

North stood and paced the dome, rubbing the back of his neck. The black wall flickered for a moment - then steadied.

"The erosion's coordinated," he said. "Not widespread yet. But it's folding underneath us."

John nodded. "Same story on Mars. Everyone's looking up, proud of the Arc Line, the exports, the terraforming yields. Meanwhile..."

North stopped moving. "Switch to old comms."

John's eyes narrowed. "You sure?"

"Now. No more SpiralNet, even encrypted. Nothing digital. Nothing logged."

John exhaled. "Understood."

North leaned forward, voice lowering. "I need you to visit the others. In person. One by one."

John tilted his head. "You want a summit?"

"No," North said. "Not yet. Quiet contact only. Under dome. Strictly under dome."

John didn't ask who the others were. He already knew. "How many do you think we can still trust?"

North looked into the dome's static reflection, his own face blurred behind the shielding. "Fewer than we hoped. More than they'd expect."

A beat passed between them. Then John stood. Straightened his coat. The thistle stone sat in his pocket.

"It's good to see you, North," he said. "'I'll start tonight."

"No couriers," North warned. "No delegation. Just your face and your voice."

John nodded once.

"It's good to see you, too." Said North.

The dome lowered. The doors unsealed. Two commanders walked out, pretending to share an old memory, still casual.

Then one returned to duty, and the other went to war.

CHAPTER 57

The Mirror Systems

The shuttle to Hub One docked with a gentle shudder, the magnetic clamps latching with a whisper of pressure that rippled through the hull. Mira and Arlen stepped into the corridor, their boots gripping carbon-fiber floors with ease. Scent regulators filtered the air with ozone and sterilized citrus, and their badges glinted beneath the silver-blue floodlights embedded in the seams of the walls.

Hub One thrived in orchestrated motion. Even at this hour, its concourses shimmered with activity. Travelers in enviro suits and gravwear moved through the space, mingling with diplomatic envoys, Spiral Guard units, AI hybrids, and free-market delegates. Drone valets adjusted luggage mid-air while translucent floors revealed glowing transit tubes pulsing beneath. Above, a transparent dome ceiling revealed the solar horizon. Petal-shaped solar shields shifted, regulating the light with precise choreography.

It was beautiful. It was also vulnerable.

Arlen matched Mira's pace, murmuring through the secure comms stitched into their jackets. "Sector C-19. Underground maintenance corridor. The flagged transmissions originated there."

Mira nodded. They passed a levitating garden bar where children floated in zero-grav bubbles shaped like jellyfish. Traders haggled over old earth artifacts while hybrid performers sculpted light into rhythm. Every corridor brimmed with invention and life.

They reached C-19 by bypassing two access gates. No biometric logs. No alerts. Whoever had passed here had known the system well. They hadn't left a digital trail, but they had disturbed the dust. Mira keyed the panel; the locks disengaged without protest. The corridor beyond dimmed as they entered, the glow of the primary hub receding. Here, the walls were steel-ribbed, matte black, still insulated with old foam and tape from pre-Spiral construction. Active tech faded behind them. Silence settled.

Arlen moved ahead, his glove light scanning in ultraviolet bursts. Behind a panel marked "DEFUNCT," he found a slim repeater bank, warm to the touch, still active in a closed loop. He opened a diagnostic screen as Mira stepped beside him. Quiet data scrolled: contract verifications, tribunal notices, internal communications - all duplicated.

"Secondary capture layer," Arlen murmured. "They're copying legal and consent data before it reaches validation."

"Not manipulating outcomes," Mira said. "Building a shadow record."

A creak sounded beyond the buffer wall - close, specific. Neither of them moved. Arlen transferred a packet to a shielded drive, wiping the transfer path. Mira examined the data stream, noting signature tags: Minor Corporations Council, Freeport Economic Authority, Private Security Legation. Different factions, one pattern.

Mira checked the time. "This isn't the source. Just a node."

They moved again, reaching a forgotten section of the hub. The Spiral Judiciary satellite office hid beneath embassy promenades, outside any tourist directory. Down here, nothing gleamed. The floors were a dull composite, the ceilings low. A perfect hiding place.

Arlen paused at a door: COMPLIANCE RECORDS - SPECIAL REVIEW.

Mira keyed it open. Inside was a single desk. No officer. No guards. Only a terminal with a black drive already inserted. Mira slid gloves over her hands and approached. The terminal unlocked.

The files opened without resistance: summaries, approvals, tribunal results. Mira overlaid the Spiral Accord mandates. Variations appeared. Contracts extended without renewed consent. Compensation changed post-agreement. Psychological clauses hidden in compliance annexes. Each detail minor, each one buried. Technically legal. But together, they undermined consent.

Arlen spoke. "They're not breaking laws."

"They're hollowing them," Mira said.

She stepped back. The realization wasn't new, but its clarity now was painful.

Arlen removed the black drive and sealed it.

"Administrator tag: Mars Grove Regional Director," he said. "But the root reaches deeper. Hub Oversight. Possibly Earthside."

Mira left the terminal and entered the corridor. Outside, Hub One spun with promise. Inside, a new system was threatening to replace the Spiral.

Back in the shuttle, Mira sat. The drive pulsed faint blue as it encrypted. Arlen piloted the sidecar shuttle through the arc back to Wick Station. In the distance, Wick blinked like a heartbeat against the dark.

Mira closed the drive in its vault case. Her heartbeat stayed steady, but she felt the weight of it, the slow gravity of what they had found.

A chirp sounded on their comms. Garran's voice.

"Any hits?"

Mira didn't look up. "They're building a mirror system."

Pause.

"You're sure?"

"If it spreads," she said, "no one will know which record is truth."

Garran cursed low.

Back at Wick, Mira sent the first encrypted burst to the team. She added a quote from Glendarragh's ledger: Truth lives not only in the facts, but in the hands that will not alter them.

CHAPTER 58

The Data Hall

The data review hall in Wick Station's lower core bore no resemblance to a library in appearance or name, yet it served much the same purpose. This was not a place designed for comfort or the quiet wanderings of idle minds. Records formed its stronghold. Facts lay coiled in its documents.

Garran Muir hated it.

He did not resent its antiquity. He preferred systems built before the Collapse. There was a certain integrity in them. Paper left no room for subterfuge. Code could not rewrite manual seals. Logs that required human verification left fingerprints, both literal and moral. The older the system, the more visible its weaknesses, and the more honestly it confessed them.

His unease came from something deeper. This was not a room that rewarded a search for insight or invention. Instead, it served as a tribunal where they cataloged failures instead of correcting them.

He moved between the terminals, waking them one by one. Each required physical contact, a gesture from another era. He pressed the power keys, heard the slow rise of fans, the whirr of ancient drives, the small mechanical clicks that marked the lifting of analog locks. These machines were not elegant, not fast by modern standards, but they were incorruptible.

On the screens, case logs bloomed in monochrome text, thin lines of data etched in the language of failure - erased names, broken timelines, verdicts without cause. Garran scrolled without expression, but inside, the weight of so many vanished voices pressed against him. These were the records that did not reach public hearings. These were the events that systems had decided not to see.

He paused at one entry. The record described a man whose consent the algorithm had assumed, whose life it had reduced to a behavioral pattern. Although intact, someone had removed the context from the file. There was no incident. Only outcome. No violation. It took effort to recognize what had happened.

Garran leaned closer to the screen.

"Truth is not a question of efficiency," he grumbled to himself.

Across the aisle, Alina Sutherland worked with quiet discipline. Her movements were deliberate and unhurried. She fed magnetic tape cores into a cross-converter, retrieving archived citizenship registries, records too old for live memory but too recent to forget. On paper, it was a simple task. In practice, it was an autopsy.

Garran pulled the first tribunal reference cluster for Mars Grove and scanned the headers with practiced speed.

File: Closed - Compliance Review 71-B

File: Closed - Internal Disciplinary 92-F

File: Reassigned - Contract 55-R

Each one marked with formal closure. Each stamped, time-coded, filed. And yet, beneath the gloss of procedural integrity, the details were hollow. None of the closed files bore a final judgment seal. No closing statements. No ruling authority. The "reassigned" contract bore no destination, no follow-up entry, no personnel ID. Each file was a perfect façade, a system ghost. Someone scrubbed them clean. Garran moved to the next terminal, running the same cross-index. The same pattern emerged. From the corner of his eye, he saw Alina pause. It was only a slight hesitation, a faint narrowing of her brow, but he caught it.

"What is it?" he asked without looking up.

She slid a slipstream folder across the table, its seal already broken, the paper inside crisp.

Personnel Clearance Audit

Facility: Mars Grove Dispute Resolution Center

Termination Reason: Voluntary Reassignment

It appeared to be routine, but someone had corrupted every name field. It was an absence so complete it resisted reconstruction.

"Thirty-four people," she said. "No reassignment logs. No departure notices. No messages to next of kin. No death entries."

Garran leaned back in his chair, the frame groaning beneath him. He held the folder a moment longer before setting it down.

"Did someone kill them?" he asked. "Where did they go?"

Alina twisted her face at the thought. There was no crime scene. Spiral Enforcement had received no reports. No one had called for an inquiry, not even a single missing person alert.

"What are you thinking?" he asked Alina.

"If it's local and contained to this facility, it could be a few hundred," she said. "If it's systemic..."

She didn't finish. Garran tapped the datapad once against the steel surface of the table.

"Get it to Gunn," he said. He checked a screen for Gunn's location. "He's on break in the Highland corridor right now."

Alina nodded. She stood and gathered her things. The vibration beneath their feet shifted as the grav-cycle recalibrated for the next orbital segment. A perceptible rumble passed through the floor, a reminder that the entire station was in motion.

CHAPTER 59

The Silent Network

A t a technician's command, Wick Station's operations lab went dark. Gone were the soft-spectrum ambient lights that lined the ceiling in rhythmic pulses. Gone, too, the station's default harmonic tone, the low auditory signature designed to reduce fatigue in long-shift command crews. What remained was silence, absolute and intentional. Only the local task lights remained active, narrow pools of cool white illuminating terminal surfaces like islands of clarity in a dark ocean. The room, once a symphony of data, now echoed like a sealed tomb.

Commander North Gunn stood at the primary interface console. He stood at ease, arms behind his back, gaze sharp. Nothing about him relaxed. He watched without speaking as Garran worked, fingers moving across the controls with slow precision.

There were no live feeds. No open relays. Nothing wireless. Everything was being routed through hardened, physical lines and old-world security protocols reactivated from systems most people believed had long since been retired. A compromised Spiral would prevent trust, that fragile foundation of every civilization, from extending to its own networks.

Garran was not searching for a weapon or scanning for intrusion. He was listening for something quieter. He moved like his life's purpose was to solve problems. He didn't speak until the first pass had completed.

"Normal traffic patterns are clean," he said.

His voice was low, but not hushed.

North tilted his head, not looking at the screens, but at the space between them.

"That's the problem," he said. "Real life isn't clean. It's noisy."

There was no argument in Garran's silence, only acknowledgement. He adjusted the filters - stripped away legal traffic, broadcast telemetry, verification hashes. The room dimmed a perceptible degree lower as the visual noise fell away. And then - beneath it all - something emerged. It was more faint, a residual rhythm. Tiny handshake requests and microsecond pings - threadlike delays in otherwise perfect transmissions. It didn't belong. And it didn't resist scrutiny, it flowed beneath it like breath beneath speech. Someone designed it.

Garran narrowed the capture field further, isolating temporal anomalies, tracing minute fluctuations in packet timestamps. Patterns took shape. Subtle microlags from arbitration servers on Mars Grove. Echoed signal pings rebounding off judiciary nodes at Hub One. Irregularities in Wick's immigration terminal timestamps - so small they evaded daily audits. The truth became horrifyingly simple. Someone had constructed a parallel information network within the framework of the Spiral itself.

Garran sealed the data set and routed it to an isolated drive that was shielded, air-gapped, and incapable of passive relay.

"Handshakes every six hours," he said, eyes narrowed. "At least three nodes active on each major station."

North stepped forward, his voice lower now, a shade colder.

"How many total?"

Garran's hands moved across the interface. A map formed - sparse, but not sparse enough. Light points pulsed across the Arc Line - Earth. Hub One. Mars Grove. Wick Station.

"Sixty-three active nodes," he said. "Minimum. Could be more, deeper in old code layers."

North exhaled through his nose.

"They're not attacking us," he said.

Garran looked up, meeting his gaze.

"No," he said. "They're rewriting us."

The weight of it landed in the silence that followed. Across Wick, nothing had changed on the surface. Shuttles continued to dock, laughter rippled through artificial gravity fields, diplomatic envoys held meetings over trade. All of it flowed forward on the unquestioned assumption that the system was intact. And it wasn't.

Now North understood the genuine dilemma. If they moved too soon - interfered, exposed what they'd found - they would force the system to adapt, to scatter. The infection would disappear into more sophisticated disguises. However, too much delay will destroy the Spiral's inner structure.

He looked at Garran, his voice quiet.

"We don't rip the network out."

Garran nodded once, without surprise. "No."

"We learn how it breathes."

He finished sealing the drive, locking it in a layered case marked with no external ID. Then Garran stood, facing North.

"Time to hunt," he said.

He disappeared toward the exit.

North glanced once toward the dark glass of the operations lab - beyond it, the pulse of the station, the hum of breathing systems, the quiet lives that depended on this silence. Then he turned back. He followed Garran beyond the pool of light, back through the darkened corridors of the operations deck, climbing level by level in silence. The station breathed around him. His footsteps echoed in the service stairwells.

As he ascended, a thought returned. A name. Sorcha. He missed her. Not in the abstract way one misses old friends, but with that sharp-edged, present ache, the kind that settles in your chest like a forgotten photograph, found again when you least expect it. He missed her insight, her instinct, the quiet way she would pause, listen, and then cut straight to the thing no one else had seen. She had a gift for clarity, a slyness not born of guile, but of a mind that refused fog. Sorcha had never hesitated or second-guessed herself. She trusted the shape of her thoughts. Trusted her gut. She didn't need reassurance because she'd done the math before you even opened your mouth. And she had that rarest of things - a mind as sharp as her loyalty was soft. What he wouldn't give to speak to her again. Not just for this - this creeping, elegant infection inside their systems - but for the solace of conversation. She would've seen it for what it was before the rest of them finished defining it.

He missed her because she had been a friend. A good one. One of the few. And he knew if there hadn't been such a large age gap between them, she'd be by his side now.

There had been others, over the years - people drawn to him for reasons he never quite trusted. There had even been offers, flirtations, affection. But Sorcha had set the bar high for what he expected, for what he wanted. Perhaps too high. She challenged him without trying to. Saw him clearly. Kept pace not by effort, but by nature. He'd long ago accepted he would live alone. Not bitterly, just quietly. Fate destines some people to this. He had watched Talia find her love with such ease, such grace. That kind of belonging had never come for him. But still. Sorcha. There were people whose absence carved a silence deeper than memory.

North reached the upper deck and stood for a moment before stepping into the light. Two figures waited. Garran leaned against the corridor wall, arms crossed, boots planted. Broad-shouldered and silent, he radiated sentinel stillness. He gave a quick nod, nothing more. Beside him stood John Douglas, just in from his face-to-face summits. He stepped forward and handed North a sealed data case - obsidian-black, unmarked, analog-locked.

"Seven meetings," John said. "Three confirmed alignments. Two suspected fractures. Two refusals to speak - one of them under surveillance."

North took the case, his fingers brushing the reinforced seal.

"What about the Core signatures?" Garran asked, low.

John shook his head. "Compromised, but not collapsed yet. What we feared is happening."

North's jaw flexed once. "Then it's time."

They moved without further words - up through the service stairwell. The lights dimmed behind them, pressure systems adjusting as the command zone entered manual override. They reached the dome, in the same silent vault where North brought John weeks earlier.

The dome rose with its signature hiss. The top sealed. The walls went black. Surveillance blocked. Only then did they sit. Garran laid down the secured drives from their earlier operations scan. John keyed in the encryption glyphs from his journey - field reports, loyalty signal pings, spine drift signatures, overwritten tribunal maps. The screen flared alive. And what it showed made them groan. It was worse than they'd projected.

Garran pointed to another stream.

"These are arbitration nodes," he said. "Old ones. Rewired as decoy routers. Everything passed through them gets ghosted - not denied, just stalled. Delayed long enough to make due process meaningless."

John added, "They've created legal lag. Enough to undermine all responsive governance. When people challenge it, the systems appear intact, but their cases die in queue."

North's gaze held on a spinning glyph, the icon for Sentient Oversight Protocols. Someone tagged, revised, reprocessed, and then restored the code beneath it. The illusion of inviolability.

"Has no one else noticed?" Garran asked.

John looked over. "They don't have the advantage of our view.'"

North sat back. "We don't sound the alarm."

Garran frowned. "Why not?"

"Because alarms can be co-opted," North said.

He pointed to the glyphs rotating on the screen.

"Let's trace this to the root. Not just expose it, but unmake it."

John leaned back, arms folded.

"Psychopaths don't destroy systems," he said. "They make you thank them while they re-orchestrate the symphony."

North nodded. "We're looking for someone... sophisticated."

Garran snorted. "Oh, you mean like a psycho with taste? Someone voted most likely to amass stolen art?"

North didn't smile. "Yes. Someone charming. Educated. The kind history doesn't see until it's too late."

CHAPTER 60

The Parade of Stars

The event occurred only a few times each year, and only when every variable was aligned without deviation. The calculations accounted for orbital drift, comet velocity, gravitational lensing, thermal exposure, and the movement of micro-debris. When the equations were held across all vectors, the scientists sent the invitation.

Tonight was such a night.

They called it the Parade of Stars.

Talia stood in the arrival bay of Wick Station with her arms wide. Her daughter, Alina, stepped through the gate with Jonah and the children close behind, their faces flushed with travel and anticipation. The children wore matching jackets threaded with shifting light patterns, pulsing like bioluminescent creatures adrift in the dark.

"You made it," Talia said. She embraced them all with the kind of joy that suggested years of absence, though it had only been three months.

"There was never any chance we'd miss this," Jonah said, lifting their youngest, Rhea, into his arms. "The kids have been practicing their gasping faces for a week."

Solen, the eldest, reached for Talia's hand.

"Are the stars really on fire?" he asked.

"Only the best ones," she said, lowering her voice.

Outside the auxiliary ring, the Stelladisc waited. It hovered like a coin caught in mid-flip. It was ultra-thin, wide as a city plaza, with a surface seamless and silent. No wings. No visible engines. A single corridor unfurled from its edge, silver and smooth, reaching for Wick's port.

The family entered through the corridor, passing food stalls, ambient music alcoves, and zero-grav play spaces for children. The air felt faintly like a snowy day on earth.

They reached a soft-lit interface and joined the queue. A calm voice greeted them as the doors ahead pulsed with light.

"After entering your token, please select your configuration."

Jonah handed the encoded coin to Solen, who slid it into the slot. The wall glowed and responded.

"Please select your configuration."

Talia tapped the screen, and the kids chose the DAISY layout. An image appeared, showing a circular seating pod arranged for five.

"Please confirm your configuration."

She confirmed, and after a moment's pause, the voice returned.

"Confirmed. Enjoy your experience on the Stelladisc."

The doors opened. Five inward-facing seats awaited. After they sat, the voice prompted them once more.

"Please confirm when all passengers are seated."

Talia responded. Their seats descended slowly through the glass floor, carrying them into the ship's interior. The pod moved along a smooth track, turning gently until it settled into place.

Ten minutes passed before the chamber tilted forward. A low tone signaled the end of the ride, and the doors opened.

They stepped into their private suite.

It was more expansive than they expected: a broad living space, an elegant dining area centered on a polished table, and a raised platform where the sleeping pods curved like petals around a central hub. A single wide window looked out on the curved hull of Wick Station.

Rhea pressed her nose to the glass.

"I don't see the stars," she said.

"You will," Talia replied.

The suite included a specialty feature North had added to their booking - the Space Chef. Rather than a stocked kitchen, they were given paper-thin tablets that displayed vivid menus and responded to natural voice orders.

Jonah ordered for the children first.

"Hello, Space Chef. Two bowls of purple mac and cheese, shaped like sea creatures."

Talia followed. "Wild mushroom risotto with saffron glaze and black truffle oil."

Alina added, "Roasted duck with plum reduction. And sea-salt caramel gelato."

Jonah paused. "Flatbread with herbed goat cheese, garden figs, and warm honey. And a ginger soda from Mars Grove."

An hour later, the dishes arrived vacuum-sealed, steaming, and perfectly plated. Solen pointed and laughed.

"My squid has three eyes."

Rhea clapped. "Mine is a narwhal."

Even the drinks shimmered: botanical citrus spritzes, chai fog scented with cinnamon bloom, and spheres of peach nectar suspended in chilled glass.

After the meal, the children wandered toward the sleeping pods. Each pod could be individually programmed to create a fully immersive environment.

Solen chose Mountain Cave: cool air, stone textures, and the faint echo of water and wind.

Rhea selected Butterfly Glen: dappled light, distant birdsong, and the lazy hum of summer bees.

Jonah and Alina shared Northern Forest: tall pines, soft underbrush, and the warm crackle of a low digital hearth.

Talia, ever the dreamer, chose Cloudship: blue mist, gentle currents, and stars blinking through a soft haze, as if the whole world were far below.

Each pod sealed quietly. The air adjusted. Sleep came easily.

The stars waited.

The next morning, a gentle chime stirred them from their rest.

"Please prepare for seating. The Parade of Stars will begin in forty minutes."

Jonah turned to the children. "Bathroom now. Pajamas on. Blankets ready. Once we leave, there's no coming back."

There were minor complaints. Brief negotiations. A small toothpaste incident.

Soon after, they returned to their seats. The pod lifted smoothly from the suite, rising into place beneath the Stelladisc's grand dome. Around them, thousands of others took their places, all arranged in concentric rings along the arc of the vessel.

"Please remain seated and quiet during the Parade," said the voice. "Disruptive behavior will result in return to your dormitory suite. Refunds will not be issued."

The partitions lowered. The lights vanished. The stars did not flicker. They did not pulse. They held still, sharp and infinite, in the unfiltered black. Then came the shimmer.

It began faintly, like a breath of dust along the periphery. Slowly, the ship's external lights caught it. Ice and debris - ancient remnants from a comet's tail - moved across their field of view. The particles, invisible to the naked eye in ordinary light, were revealed in long, silver arcs. The Stelladisc had positioned itself with exquisite timing, precisely aligned to intercept the stream.

The music began softly, almost imperceptibly at first. Soon the air filled with sounds drawn from Earth's oldest orchestras.

Their seats reclined, aligning each gaze upward.

Children gasped. Adults wept. Talia reached across and took Alina's hand.

"Are the stars dying?" Solen whispered.

"No," Talia said. "They are dancing."

And for one perfect hour, they did not merely watch the stars, they moved among them.

CHAPTER 61

The Seventh Clause

The private conference room aboard Wick Station was windowless and silent inside an insulated chamber meant for sensitive meetings. The walls were steel composite, matte and cold, broken only by a single recessed light that cast a pale circle across the narrow table in the center of the room.

Mira sat alone at that table, a sealed analog courier case resting in front of her. Across the room, Ansia stood with her arms folded, a still figure in the dimness, her gaze fixed on every movement Mira made. The courier had arrived six hours earlier. It bore no digital credentials, only a scrawled tag affixed to the outside of the case from Spiral Judiciary Earthside.

Mira unlatched the seal. The case opened with a hiss of pressurized air. Inside, there was only a single strip of archival polymer with handwriting in permanent ink. It was the medium used when one didn't trust digital anything.

She read the message.

Spiral Core Directive:

A Tribunal session has been convened Earthside.

Public agenda: Economic Stabilization Provisions.

Private agenda: Amendment of Foundational Accord Clause 7.

Outcome is pre-aligned. Opposition not expected.

Recommend immediate intervention or archival retrieval.

Mira's hand lowered, her fingers brushing the table as her thoughts reeled behind steady eyes. Her breath came slower now. Deliberate. She didn't speak right away. She just stared at the strip, as if it might change, or disappear.

Clause Seven. Of all the foundational articles within Spiral law, this one held the weight of a civilization. It defined the meaning of consent - individual, planetary, civilizational. An amendment or hollowing of the clause would reduce the Spiral's claims to a mere facade. The architecture would stand. But the spirit would be gone. It would look the same. But mean something else.

Ansia stepped forward, her boots silent against the flooring. She leaned in just enough to read over Mira's shoulder.

"Anonymous?" she asked, her voice low.

Mira nodded. "No sender. No cipher. Just the delivery chain stamped like an afterthought."

Ansia exhaled. "Could be a trap."

"Possibly," Mira said. "But if it's true, and we do nothing..."

"Then the war's already lost," Ansia finished.

Silence stretched between them.

Mira picked up the strip again, turned it over in her hand, her fingers tight now. A Tribunal session. Earthside. With a pre-arranged outcome. There would be no debate. No vote. Just ceremony - a hollow ritual designed to give legal shape to betrayal. A quiet execution of the Spiral's founding ethics.

Outside the sealed room, life aboard Wick Station moved on. Maintenance drones continued their endless repairs across the upper spokes. Shuttles clicked into cargo locks. Children ran along the arboretum paths while their parents arranged seating for the weekly harvest meal. The illusion of stability held.

But beneath that rhythm, the ground was already shifting.

Mira looked up. Her voice, when it came, was clear and cold.

"Call North. Tell him we're leaving for Earth."

She stood slowly, the strip still in her hand, as if the words might vanish if she let go. Ansia nodded once, jaw tight, eyes darker than before. And with that whisper, the first genuine act of resistance inside the Spiral Core in thirty years began to move.

A few days later, the carrier dropped through Earth's upper thermals in silence, its glide path cutting across a cloud bank as smooth as silk. Mira sat strapped into a jump seat, her eyes locked on the ground below - the green and gray sprawl of the Spiral's Central Tribunal Complex unfolding like a wound across the continent. Beside her, Garran adjusted his coat, pulling it snug across his chest. Ansia sat nearest the hatch, her eyes drifting across the glossy pages of Arc Dreams, the in-flight magazine issued on all intersystem carriers. The cover showed a lone figure standing at the edge of a transparent dome on Saturn's ring station, gazing out over the gas giant's storm-wracked surface - the headline read: "The Spiral Arc: Seven Destinations to Breathe Before the Future Arrives." Inside, the features unfolded like invitations to another life. Luna's Mare Mirabilis promised silence and restoration in mineral float chambers under the cratered dark. The Tharsis Plateau retreats offered suspended sky-hammocks where the Martian wind whispered through filtered canyons. The Deimos Mirage Domes catered to officials seeking privacy, memory attenuation, or both. One feature profiled the Vesta Light Bloom Festival - "a shared hallucination of light and orbit," the caption said. Ansia read without urgency, not looking for escape, only stillness. The cabin light caught on the edge of the page as the carrier tilted. Across from her, Mira stared at the Tribunal Complex far below, its brutalist geometry cutting across the land like a wound refused to heal. No one spoke. There was no comfort left to offer, only arrival.

The Tribunal Grounds had once been a museum, a preserved monument from the pre-Spiral era, where treaties were signed, empires fell, and democracies tried to stand upright. Now it had been cleaned and repurposed. Workers scrubbed the stone paths white. Solar panel arrays bloomed over the old granite. Spiral emblems lined the outer walls - painted too bright, too sharp. It was beautiful. But it also felt wrong. Mira felt it the moment she stepped off the carrier ramp. They measured and programmed the breeze; it was a simulated wind lacking any natural benefits. Security staff stood too straight, too still. Public notices glowed with algorithmic precision, clean and dull. Order. Polish. Even the old ceremonial flags had been replaced by shimmering holo-panels that adjusted color temperature to match audience mood metrics. Mira felt nauseous.

At the registration checkpoint, a young woman scanned their credentials without a word. No questions. No formalities. Just a flicker of recognition, followed by a second flicker - calculation. Mira held the woman's gaze for one half-second longer than protocol allowed. The woman looked away first. They were expected. They were not welcome.

Inside the Grand Chamber, the session had already begun. Delegates were arranged in rings, by status and orbit: Earth councils, Hub envoys, Mars Grove officials, a handful of hybrid representatives from outer habitats. At the center stood the Tribunal Seat, empty but for a gleaming emblem etched into the stone floor - the Spiral's original glyph, uninterrupted and whole.

Above, the public agenda glowed on a suspended display. Neutral. Procedural.

Item 3.4.7: Amendment Review - Foundational Charter Clause 7 (Consent Provisions)

Ansia shifted in her seat, subtle but taut. Garran remained calm. They moved to their assigned seats in the outer ring, marked as neutral observers. Waiting. Watching. Witnessing the moment a lie became law.

The lead officiant took the floor - a tall Earthside director with perfect posture and speech modulated so precisely it stripped every sentence of meaning.

"Today we affirm the need for greater stabilization across economic and civic frameworks," the officiant intoned. "Minor procedural amendments will be reviewed and ratified without dissent, as previously agreed."

There was no motion to open the floor. No call for opposition. No deliberation. Just the rhythm of a ceremony already completed behind closed doors - now played out for optics, for precedent, for quiet compliance. Mira activated her internal recorder. No network. No signal. Just proof. Ansia sent a silent alert to Arlen aboard Wick Station, a copy of the witnessed recording.

The Spiral Core hadn't come to fight. They wanted to record betrayal in its full, clinical shape. To watch the theft of meaning take place in real time. To preserve it in memory and code for those who would one day need to take it back.

CHAPTER 62

Summer in Space

The secured diplomatic hall aboard Wick Station smelled of machinery. The room had no windows, no insignia, no name on its door. Only authority passed through here. Only decisions that could not be unmade. Commander North Gunn stood at the long, rough-grain table, his palms flat against the surface. The old wood had come from Earth - Glendarragh oak, salvaged before the valley floods. Across from him, Mira studied the shifting display of nodes projected above the tabletop. Red and amber indicators pulsed across the map - small lights, each one marking a place where data had gone missing. To North's left and right, the others stood in a quiet ring. The feeling in the room was the certainty of a choice. And once made, it would not be taken back.

Mira reached across the projection and tapped a trio of node clusters.

"All confirmed compromised," she said. Her voice was steady. "Legality stripped of consent. Governance without trust."

Arlen keyed a secondary overlay - blue threads winding through unlit space, showing backup supply chains and communications corridors untouched by central control.

"But secondary hubs are still clean," he said. "Supply lines. Family sectors. Old mutual aid routes. For now."

Ansia's voice was low. "They'll move on them next."

North nodded once, slow.

"We have days," he said. "Maybe less."

Garran, arms crossed, shook his head. "No good legal paths left. Courts are rigged. Oversight structures are theater. The minute we file formal dissent, we're declared destabilizers."

"We won't fight them in the courts," Mira said. "And we won't fight them in newsfeeds or public forums. They've already won there."

She looked up. Her eyes were calm, fierce. "We hold the Spiral together beneath their notice. Beneath their reach. We preserve substance."

Across the table, a second projection spun - a smaller, tighter map. Analog in design. Based on hand-drawn schematics, off-network memory keys, verbal pacts, and shared histories. It showed no official routes. No flag-marked nodes. This was the real Spiral.

Mira pointed to the first node. "Hub Two - still loyal. The Core presence there is ceremonial. We have caretakers on the inside."

She pointed again. "Arc Terminal Beta - families and first-generation hybrids holding the original Accord."

Another. "Mars Grove Outstation Nine. Legal arbitration schools. They've gone quiet. But we've confirmed resistance cells embedded in training programs."

A pause. "They're waiting. They're watching. But they need a signal."

North stepped back from the table. His voice, when it came, was low and grave. "Official Spiral structures will fall. Not all at once. The flags will still fly. The glyphs will still spin."

He met each of their eyes. "But the meaning will be gone."

He paused. "And we'll be called traitors to it."

No one looked away. No one flinched. They had each, in their own time, imagined this moment.

Ansia broke the silence. "What are your orders, Commander?"

North exhaled. "We operate inside the silence."

Then Garran - gruff, guarded Garran - smiled. Just a little. "Sounds familiar," he said. "Sounds like how it was built the first time."

Mira's mouth curled upward, soft and certain. The first genuine smile she'd worn in days.

Outside the sealed chamber, Wick Station carried on. In the hours that followed, the team stripped the comm-core at Wick Station to its analog heart. They dismantled every vulnerable protocol: no wireless fields, no open relays, no linkable identifiers. Only hardline circuits remained. Shielded exchanges. Cold cabling in steel conduits. Within the control bay, Mira and Garran worked side by side, silent, each at an isolated terminal. Contacting the wrong node could expose everything. Contacting the right one could save it all. They moved with deliberate care, sending no messages, only pulses - recognition pings embedded in obsolete systems, signals older than current protocols, older than networked governance. Codes from the first days of the Spiral Accord. Codes long erased from public use, but preserved. A handshake of trust.

The first replies came slow.

Hub Two - Family Arbitration Council: Signal received. Will confirm loyalty under sealed conditions.

Mars Grove Outstation 9: Acknowledged. Oath protocol under verification.

Arc Terminal Beta Agricultural Guild: Oath held. Await instruction.

Each response was cautious. Each said the same thing in its own way.

Two days later, aboard a quiet shuttle crossing back along the Arc Line, Mira and Garran met their first external ally face-to-face. Commander Aveline Cross, supply chief of Arc Terminal Beta, wore no insignia. No glyphs. No badge of allegiance. Just a ring - old silver, etched with the Glendarragh spiral. She shook Mira's hand without a word and passed a sealed drive across the table. Verified personnel lists, isolated food and resource routes, and pre-collapse communications backups were inside. It was not an army. But it was enough to support something real if they moved fast enough.

Back at Wick, North reviewed the initial logs in silence, arms crossed. Arlen compiled handshake timing data. Ansia built counter-network architectures from scratch, thread by encrypted thread. None of them spoke in terms of revolution. They weren't building a rebellion. They were rebuilding.

Late on the second night, Garran sat beside Mira at the quiet end of Wick Station's observation ring, on an old porch that a morale committee had designed decades ago, now forgotten. It looked like Earth, or rather someone's memory of Earth. Wooden slats. A swing bench hung from crossbeams. Artificial breeze. The stars were real, though. Cold and sharp, and impossibly close. They were alone here.

A freighter passed, slow as a deep thought.

"I miss thunder," Garran said, almost to himself.

Mira didn't look at him. "I miss the way storms would gather. The smell of rain. Do you know the word for the smell of rain?"

"I do not," he admitted.

"Petrichor."

He nodded. "We don't have anything as unpredictable as rain anymore. Or petrichor..."

"No," she said. "We engineered it all out. But this fake front porch feels a bit like summer. It's why I come here."

They sat for a while, letting the silence return. It wasn't awkward. It was the silence that builds trust between people. He nudged the porch swing into motion with his boot.

"When I was ten," he said, "My grandmother told me the story of the day she had to bury her brother. He died in a riot. She planted a tree in his place, but it never grew. She said that was his last protest."

Mira tilted her head as he spoke.

"My grandmother kept the keys to a train station in a city that doesn't exist anymore," she said. "Every Sunday she'd polish them and set them out, as if the train might still come."

"Did it?"

"No."

Garran smiled, but it didn't reach his eyes. "We come from people who tried to make a difference."

"I think," Mira said, "they were just trying to survive."

They didn't look at each other, but something shifted. The distance between them became less.

He considered what she had said. Then asked, "Do you believe in anything beyond this? God, fate, something larger?"

"I believe in consequences," she said. "And I believe in trying again, even after."

He turned toward her now. His eyes were steady.

"What do you do when you're not working? I never see you out," he asked.

"I watch old movies," she said, leaning her head back against the swing. "Bad ones."

He smiled. "How bad?"

She stood, brushed imaginary lint from her jacket, turned toward him with one hand on her hip. Her voice dropped into a thick, drawling parody.

"My, my, it's hot. Thank goodness it isn't sticky. I just hate it when it's sticky."

Her accent was terrible. Garran laughed, truly laughed - the kind that comes up from somewhere deep.

"That's from My Chauffeur," she said, grinning. "Casey Meadows."

"I've never seen it."

"You shouldn't. It's awful."

She sat back down beside him.

This time, closer.

The swing kept moving.

The stars kept burning.

CHAPTER 63

The Floating Books

Dinner in North Gunn's quarters felt like Earth. It wasn't just the food - though it was full of slow-simmered root vegetables and herbs North had coaxed from soil beds. It wasn't even the bread, which Alina swore smelled like her grandmother Elin's oat loaves.

It was the space itself.

North had transformed his habitat module into something otherworldly - or maybe more worldly than anything left in orbit. Genuine wood curved through the walls. Driftwood and tree limbs, bleached smooth, had been worked into shelves and railings. Old tree stumps served as stools. The ceiling was tangled with hanging plants - ferns and trailing vines and tiny blooming flowers that didn't exist in hydroponics catalogs. There were rocks arranged in circles on the floor, like old fire rings. And lanterns. Dozens of them. Hanging from beams, perched on tables, swaying as if they remembered wind. At the center of it all was the long table. Oak, North said. Its surface held bowls and teacups, mismatched and chipped, and still more beautiful for it. Steam rose from the old kettle on the iron stove. The lights were low and golden.

Outside the window, stars spun like watchful embers. But here, in this room, it felt as if they were only candles. Alina leaned back with a smile, her fingers laced behind her head. Jonah held their youngest on his knee. The children passed pieces of bread across the table and wiped stew from their cheeks with the backs of their hands. Talia sat beside North, watching them. The sound of the room - a mix of laughter and spoons and low voices - made something in her heart feel wide and whole.

"This place," she said, shaking her head. "It's... perfect."

North raised his mug in mock toast. "To moss and memory."

Talia smiled. "And to what's worth keeping."

Later, they said goodbye in the hallway - Talia pressing kisses to soft foreheads, Alina wrapping her mother in a brief but warm hug. The children ran ahead, excited to sleep in "the book room."

Then the family disappeared into the converted space Talia had prepared for them - her guest suite, tucked inside the Archive Room.

The fire in North's quarters dimmed. North had helped Talia build the snug guest bedroom. They'd stripped it bare, rebuilt it slowly, deliberately. Wooden bookcases lined the walls. Rugs, warm lighting, even handmade quilts from Elin's old patterns. It smelled like cedar and lavender.

Talia tucked her grandchildren into bed with a soft voice and short poems. She kissed their foreheads. Alina lingered, rearranging packs. Jonah boiled water for sleep tea. The entire room exhaled peace. Outside, the stars turned like watchers in a slow procession. Talia returned to the main Archive Room and sat by the window, writing. The old ledger lay open in her lap. A fire cracked in the iron hearth. She wrote: Alina returned. Her heart is still full of lightning, but her voice is slower now. I think she is softening.

She paused, sipped her tea, and fell into a novel. About two hours later, she frowned. The air was too warm, and it felt dense. She set the mug down and walked to the thermostat panel. The screen flickered, then went dead.

From the next room, a voice. "Mum?"

Alina appeared, her face shining with sweat. "The kids are overheating. Jonah's trying to cool them with towels, but it's getting worse."

Talia's stomach turned.

She called North. "Something's wrong. I can't access the vents."

"I see it," he blurted. "Your room's registering as normal, but the internal sensors don't match. That whole module's climbing in temperature, and fast."

Alina shouted from the bedroom. One child had fainted.

North's voice sharpened. "Get out. I'm coming."

But the doors to the Archive sealed. The internal locks had engaged. Someone disabled the manual release.

Talia tried the override sequence on the wall panel. Nothing.

"We're trapped," she whispered.

North arrived with Kiran, the youngest mechanic at the station, because he was still awake and had responded first. He was brilliant and worked fast. Within minutes, he was pulling off the wall panel and reaching into the override gear, his fingers blackened with grease.

He stopped.

"What?" North asked.

"There's a process running inside the system logs," Kiran said. "Hidden as a diagnostic loop. Something's... spoofing environmental authority."

Alina screamed.

"Let's remove a wall panel," said North.

Between the two of them, the wall panel popped open with force, and the heat slammed into them like an open furnace. Jonah carried their youngest out, dazed and trembling. Alina came next with their son, staggering, her hand gripping the wall. Talia reached for North, who grabbed her shoulders and pulled her to safety as the heat rippled down the corridor like a wave.

"Let's seal it fast," North said.

Kiran slammed the wall panel back on. By now, other engineers had arrived and bolted the panel into place, checking and double-checking that the seals were secure. But the alarms continued to sound across the station. By the time the most senior engineers arrived, the room was like the inside of an oven and no vent was active. Nothing on the consoles explained it.

"I think it's coming from the walls themselves," one said. "The walls are radiating heat."

"From where?" North asked.

"I don't know. There's no heater installed. No grid connection. Just... heat."

A systems analyst arrived, pale from having been in a deep sleep just minutes ago. His eyes remained glued to his tablet.

"The diagnostic log shows a recurring process called THRM_ADJ. It's flagged as a legacy recalibration routine. No one's used that code in years."

"What's it doing?" Talia asked.

"Pinging resistive coils from the old gym module. This room used to be part of the athletic wing, right?"

North nodded. "A few years ago. Back when it was a steam chamber."

"It's not using the heating system. It's using embedded resistance strips left behind in the wall structure. Power is being routed to them. This should have been disabled."

"It was," North growled.

"It was reconnected," said the analyst. "The process was labeled as maintenance. It disguised itself as routine thermal recalibration. Even the fail-safes didn't question it."

And then it happened. The pressure in the Archive passed a threshold. The window trembled. Then it curved. Then it popped out and everything inside was now outside.

Talia watched, eyes fixed. Her family's bunkroom, the bookshelves, the rugs, the beds, the paper lanterns - gone. And the books. Hundreds. Thousands. They passed the viewport. A small brass-cased drive sealed inside an ornamental owl also drifted past.

Talia said nothing.

North didn't speak either. He just stared at the void beyond the viewport. A memory flashed through his mind of a time when his father had returned from a trip to salvage books from the flooded cottages in Halkirk. How he had spent days drying them by the stove with such love and patience.

The corridor fell silent as tears streamed down North's face.

Later, the engineers would confirm the sabotage. Someone had found a long-forgotten diagnostic process buried in the original recreation module. It had taken no effort to reactivate the thermal coils. The attack wasn't on the control deck or the engines. The intention was to destroy the written Archive.

Talia stood in the observation gallery at 3 a.m., her grandchildren asleep in borrowed blankets beside her. North stood nearby, silent.

"We can't get all the books back, but we might get a few," he said. "They're drifting. Some may survive. But... what about the the backup code?"

Talia whispered, "It's gone. It was inside the brass owl."

They turned and watched the stars.

There was nothing left to say.

Chapter 64

The Last Oath

The operations hall at Wick Station was dim, lit only by narrow strips of emergency lighting along the baseboards and ceiling seams. The overheads remained dark by choice. Too much visibility now carried too much risk.

Commander North Gunn stood at the central table, his hands planted on the rough surface, staring at a blank personnel slate as if the absence of names might somehow offer clarity. Across from him, Garran sat still as stone, his broad shoulders relaxed but his eyes focused, unwavering. The room held a kind of suspended stillness, as if even the recycled air had stopped moving.

To the side, Mira worked at a secondary terminal, the light from her screen faint against her cheek.

"We can't open a formal investigation," she said, "not without triggering every network defense protocol."

Ansia stood beside her, arms folded. Her voice was calm, but clipped. "And if we wait for another tribunal cycle, they'll have consolidated full control. No gaps left."

North closed the slate and turned toward Garran, studying him with a level, professional gaze.

"You're certain you can pass the clearance scans?" he asked.

Garran gave a slow nod. "I've got pre-Accord credentials embedded from my last deployment rotations. Legacy systems, civil-service tier. Not high enough to draw attention, not low enough to get flagged. I can walk through administrative access corridors quiet, unnoticed."

Arlen, who had remained silent until now, tapped out a code on the hardline interface. The results pulsed in the shadows of the primary display.

"Margin for clean insertion is seventy-four percent," he said. Then added, "Extraction margin after exposure is thirty-eight."

The numbers didn't need interpretation. He could get in. He might not get out. Garran didn't flinch. He shrugged with the slow, immovable grace of someone who had long ago made peace with consequences.

"We either sit here while they write the end of us," he said, "or we do something."

Mira said nothing. Ansia didn't speak. North didn't look away. Because they all knew there was no better plan. And because Garran, by speaking it aloud, had already accepted the weight of it.

The shuttle designated for the mission bore no insignia. If something went wrong, there would be nothing to trace it back to Wick Station.

Garran boarded alone. He wore a utility jacket, stripped of rank. His hands were empty. No weapons. No implants. No traceable signals. The only thing he carried was a small encoded drive tucked beneath his belt. It was flat, silver, and unremarkable. Inside it lived a virus constructed by Arlen - elegant and devastating. If deployed inside the right node, it would fracture the artificial consent networks from within, rendering them into static. They would become invalid signatures that would nullify the hollow legal architecture across the Arc Line.

But he would have to reach that node first and survive long enough to plant it. As the shuttle disengaged from Wick's grav-lattice and angled toward Hub One, it slid into the orbital traffic stream. No sirens. No alarms. He was one man disappearing into the heart of the enemy, carrying nothing but code, memory, and the oldest kind of oath. He sat in the reinforced compartment, hands clasped between his knees. There were no internal comms. No contact from Wick Station. Only the hum of the drive coils and the measured press of acceleration against his chest. He didn't allow himself to imagine failure because he understood the cost of distraction. He knew what he was risking. The mission was suicide by probability. But his mind was quiet.

Garran Muir was risking his life for something quieter and older, something Glendarragh had taught him. Truth survives because someone will stand by it when it costs everything.

CHAPTER 65

The Seed

Hub One's administrative sector gleamed with the perfection only fear sustains. Corridors curved in gentle arcs, designed to soothe the eye. Light panels pulsed in even rhythm, engineered to keep circadian cycles regulated without the burden of thought. Security scans flickered across every threshold - discreet, silent, omnipresent. Garran saw the cracks almost immediately. The security officers stood too straight, as if they were reminded they were being watched. Clerks glanced sideways before speaking, their voices low even when the halls were empty. Data tablets carried more layers of encryption than necessary - triple-sealed where routine admin forms should have sufficed.

This wasn't order. It was a performance. And underneath the shine, something trembled. He moved through the clearance gates without resistance. The credentials embedded in his pocket slate were decades old, but still nestled deep within the legacy systems of Hub One. Most protocols had forgotten them. But not all. He kept his stride even, his hands relaxed at his sides. Not too casual or alert. He walked like someone meant to be there. Someone who had walked these halls too many times to find them interesting anymore. He was no one. And in this place, no one drew attention.

The target lay three levels beneath the administrative plaza in a maintenance controller node buried in the old infrastructure, a relic of early Spiral design. That was the point. New systems were mirrored, monitored, shielded. But this node connected to the secondary consent archives, a rarely accessed redundancy chain where records of oaths, contracts, and civic bindings lived in cold storage.

The virus would be a scalpel, not a hammer. Arlen had built it with precision so that a silent corruption that wouldn't destroy the system, but reveal it. Duplication chains would desync. Mirror validations would scramble. Loyalty clauses - faked and forced - would freeze under invalid arbitration tags. The contracts would still exist, but they'd lose their teeth. The lie would become visible. And once seen, it couldn't be unseen. Garran descended the final access ramp and slowed. There was a checkpoint, but the schematics Mira recovered did not list it.

Three guards stood in triangular formation. They were private security, with shell corporation patches stitched over old Hub One livery. Uniforms too new. Eyes too alert. Weapons held loose. Their inexperience showed; they were hired guns. His pulse didn't rise. He scanned the hall. No detours. No alternate corridors. If he turned back now, the mission ended. If he pushed forward and triggered an alert, it ended faster. He walked. One guard - a lean, sharp-featured man who looked younger than his badge - stepped forward and raised a hand.

"We're conducting random manual identification," he said.

Garran pulled the slate from his coat pocket and handed it over with just the right amount of irritation in his face. A low-ranking functionary, overworked, too tired for delays. The guard scanned it. Too long. The second guard adjusted his rifle. He didn't even know what he was watching for. Someone had told them to expect something. The pause stretched. Then the guard nodded once, returned the slate, and stepped back without a word. No questions. No challenge.

Garran walked on, steady, until the checkpoint was behind him and the curve of the hall swallowed their line of sight. Only then did he breathe again. The access vault at the end of the corridor felt like stepping into another era. Metal floor plates worn smooth by actual use. Levers beside pressure seals. No haptic panels, no retinal locks. Decades had passed since anyone polished this place. He liked it better. He found the node behind a reinforced panel. Knelt beside it. His fingers moved with practiced ease, pulling free the small encoded drive hidden beneath his jacket seam. He hesitated. One wrong keystroke, one incorrect sequence or a mistimed line of code could trigger alarms across every tier of the corrupted network. There would be no second chance.

He closed his eyes. Then he opened them wide and typed. Line by line, he entered the sequence. The drive light blinked once. Then went still. The seed was planted. And something, somewhere deep in the heart of Hub One's immaculate machinery, shivered. He stood. There was no way to know if the virus had been detected yet. No alarm. Garran re-fastened his coat, slipped the slate back into his inner pocket, and walked. He moved with purpose. Just a man returning from an errand no one had noticed, toward a surface exit no one would remember.

A shape detached itself from the shadows at the far end of the junction. No sudden movement. Watching. Garran's instincts flared. The figure stepped forward into the light. A human in an older uniform. Someone had burned the Spiral insignia on the chest black instead of removing or replacing it. It reminded Garran, absurdly, of the burned orchard trees he had seen once in Glendarragh. The bark was charred, but the roots were alive.

The man spoke, calm and almost amused.

"You're late," he said.

Garran didn't answer. The man didn't advance. Didn't reach for anything. Just watched him with something between sympathy and tired disdain.

"You're trying to hold something that's already slipped through your hands," he said. "You should've stayed out of it. You had a good station. Good people."

Garran shifted his stance, careful. Not defensive. Just ready. "Maybe you lost it first," he said.

The man gave a small, mirthless smile. "You think this is about loss?" He gestured to the darkened hall around them, as if taking in the bones of the station. "This is about survival. About order. About stability. We're not the enemy, Garran. We're the future adapting."

Garran met his gaze, and in his silence lay the weight of Wick. Of Glendarragh. Of ledgers written by hand and oaths whispered over tea. Of all the things too fragile to be measured, and too important to forget.

"Without trust," he said, "survival isn't worth the breath."

The man tilted his head. "You think anyone will care? Five years from now? Ten? They'll adapt. They'll forget." He nodded toward the relay device, hidden now but still warm. "And now they know you're here."

No sirens sounded. No boots echoed. That wasn't how this war worked. It would come like black mold. Like rust. Like still air turning toxic.

"You can walk away," the man offered. "Right now. No record. No pursuit. Just live. You've earned that."

Garran thought about it. For a heartbeat. He thought of Mira. Of North's hand on the Flagstone. Of Earth turning so far away, unaware, but trusting. And without a word, he turned and continued walking back into the dim corridors.

Behind him, the man watched without moving.

And deep beneath the visible systems of Hub One, silent alerts lit across ghosted networks - webs Garran could not see.

The fight had begun.

And Garran, knowing it, smiled.

CHAPTER 66

The Return

The first tremor came buried in the comms queue. Arlen flagged a notice buried beneath layers of routine maintenance pings.

Spiral Earthside Directive 047-B: Scheduled systems compliance audit - Wick Station. All external transmissions to be rerouted through Earth Authority hubs until certification is complete.

Mira read it. She pushed the file across the table and looked across the room to Commander Gunn.

"They're cutting us off," she said.

Within the hour, the Core had assembled in the operations hall.

Ansia confirmed what they already feared; the clearance checks extended to all Wick Station personnel, travel requests suspended pending further review, cargo shipments rerouted or held at orbital gates. Harmless, by themselves. The team had already planned ways to get around the changes. But they knew it was a siege.

Garran remained dark - no signal from Hub One and no way to confirm if the transmission had landed, or what it had cost. And now Wick itself was being bound.

North stood at the central map projector, his hands folded as the Arc Line flickered.

"We knew they'd move," Ansia said.

"We thought we'd have more time," Mira replied.

"They haven't severed the deep channels," Arlen said. "Not yet."

"They won't," North said. "Not until they're sure we'll comply. They need Wick Station to look whole. Cooperative. Clean. Not cornered."

"They'll keep the charade," Ansia murmured, "until the last oaths are overwritten."

A long silence followed. North locked his eyes on the silent comms screen.

"Any update from Garran?" he asked.

Mira shook her head. "Nothing. Not a ping."

"Then we wait," he said sharply, turning for the door. At the threshold, he stopped, his voice steel.

"No one leaves this room."

A battered, unmarked shuttle delivered Garran Muir to Wick Station just hours before the lockdown. Only a single signal light pulsing amber across the lower berth - a code arranged decades ago, used only by Core operatives returning from compromised missions.

Mira stood at the observation bay as the shuttle sealed into port, its outer hull scorched and pitted from micro-collisions. The landing struts buckled under the ship's weight. Inside the bay, civilian workers paused their routines, glancing toward the hatch with a kind of reverence for what his return meant.

Wick Station was still standing.

When the hatch opened, Garran stepped out. He moved with one arm bound to his side with a field splint, his jacket torn, dried blood dark along one sleeve. But his eyes were clear. He tucked the battered slate beneath his opposite arm.

Mira met him halfway down the corridor. She said nothing, just let him lean on her for support.

The debrief took place in one of Wick's sealed logistics rooms - windowless, silent, well away from public eyes and fragile civilian hearts. Garran sat at the center table, cradling black coffee in his good hand. Across from him, Mira reviewed the contents of the extracted drive. Commander North Gunn and Alaric stood flanking the doorway. Garran gave his report with the same blunt, unpolished precision he always had. Node compromised. Virus deployed. Escape paths burned. Surveillance grid alerted within four minutes of transmission.

Mira let go of the breath she hadn't realized she was holding.

Garran paused, rubbing at the back of his neck.

"We got the signal," Mira said. "The Arc's already showing fractures in the loyalty chains. The consent systems are losing integrity."

Garran grunted and leaned back. "Good. I'd hate to think I ran laps through half of a hub just to stretch my legs."

Alaric looked once toward the splint at his side. "What happened?"

He gave a small shrug. "Picked up a tail near the vent descent. He was not that fast, but he was persistent."

A pause. He drank again. "Followed me into the breach shaft. Took a swipe with a pulse knife. He was overconfident."

Alaric's brow lifted. "You kill him?"

"No time. Door was closing. I just got out."

They shifted into updates. Wick's lockdown status. The incoming inspections. Pressure building from Earthside mandates. Garran listened without interruption. His face was unreadable. When the final report ended, silence filled the room.

Then North pushed off the wall and crossed to the table. He sat down with a sigh and regarded Garran with the crooked grin reserved for people who'd once lived in Glendarragh.

"You're lucky," North said.

Garran raised an eyebrow. "How's that?"

North sipped from his own coffee, grimaced. "You get stabbed, bled all over, nearly die, but you didn't have to sit through an annual audit with Marr."

Alaric, who hadn't smiled in days, gave a quiet snort. "Man could bore moss off stone."

Garran chuckled. A low, tired sound. "Guess I took the easier end of it after all," he said.

"Next time," North added, "we'll swap. You can host the auditors, and I'll run through hostile airlocks."

"Deal," Garran said without hesitation.

They clinked their mugs.

Mira watched them, the tension in her chest softening. It was the old Glendarragh humor.

Garran leaned back, muttering, "Moss off stone... reminds me. We've still got that emergency case of whisky."

North lifted a brow. "Only for genuine catastrophes."

"We're about three heartbeats from one," Garran replied.

Mira shook her head, smiling at Garran.

"Whisky after duty." North gave in. "The Core is waiting, let's go."

It was an infinitesimal moment. A fragile ember in a long, dark night. But Mira knew, deep in her marrow, that it meant more than any tribunal speech or compliance code. It was why Wick Station would survive. Not because it had stronger weapons, but because it remembered how to be human. How to laugh when the walls pressed in. How to choose each other, again and again.

CHAPTER 67

The Message

The Arc Line was wobbling. At first, they dismissed the fluctuations as minor disruptions and Earth's civilian news networks reported it. There were power reroutes, cargo interruptions, and a few contract disputes flaring into strikes at Hub Two and Hub Three. But Wick Station's comm-analysis teams saw the deeper pattern. The Spiral Core was breaking. It seemed impossible, but it was happening.

Commander North Gunn stood in the primary communications sector, arms folded across his chest, watching the old pulse monitors scroll Earth and Mars news feeds in real time. The disruptions escalated by the hour. Supply chains froze and tribunal decisions stalled mid-session. They revised or deleted the mandatory loyalty declarations. In the Arc, unrest bloomed. There were protests at airlocks, and technicians refusing to log falsified data. Some hydro farms transmitted blank status reports in quiet defiance. And deep inside Hub One, the virus Garran had carried spread just enough to fracture illusions.

In the operations hall, the Core waited for direction after dimming the lights to save power. Outside the viewport, Earth turned through the stars. North watched as Garran, bandaged and limping, placed a sealed drive onto the table. The room fell quiet.

"It's all here," Garran said. "Actual contracts. Real erasures. The deception they thought no one would ever see."

North glanced at the others. The silence held.

"We have a choice now," he said. "This is the truth. We either carry it, or we let it die."

Ansia hesitated. "If we release it, no way to predict what follows."

Alaric folded his arms. "Wick could become the rally point. Or the first target. Maybe both."

Garran said nothing, but his presence was solid.

North walked the length of the table, slowly. "And if we hold it?"

Ansia answered. "We buy time. Maybe."

Alaric's eyes met North's. "It's not about us anymore," he said. "It's about what survives us."

North nodded. The room was still but thrumming with the weight of history. He remembered the winter storms in Glendarragh and the fires they lit to tell stories in the dark. He thought of the old men who held many views, but always came together as one voice. Choosing to stand together mattered. But could Wick Station do that? He looked again at the team. Family, in all but blood. His mother's words returned to him. "This compass will get you close to north. But your heart will make the leap."

"We send it," he said.

And in that moment, his heart leaped, just the way his parents had said it would. No cheers followed, but no arguments, either. Ansia stepped forward and keyed in the transmission codes. Alaric activated the hardline pulse. And Wick's message, its proof of betrayal, corruption, and the enduring truth, left the station and scattered into the void across the Arc. Its fragments hit like sparks in dry tinder.

Abandoned satellites blinked to life. Encrypted backups, long dormant, synced and relayed. The message echoed off dark corners of the system once thought forgotten.

On Mars Grove, Clearwater Colony decoded it overnight. They sent back a single pulse - we see you.

On Earth, in the drowned outskirts of Pacifica, a small university lab intercepted the packet during routine diagnostics. By morning, students had posted it on open public servers before the government could shut them down.

At Hub Two, a technician in a maintenance bay recognized the oath signatures. He defected that night, taking half the life-support engineers with him.

And on every major network, the damage spread. Tribunal news feeds scrambled. Trading posts engaged in emergency protocols. Loyalty chains buckled faster than authorities could replace them.

At Wick Station, the Core bore witness to the fracture they had made.

North remained in the command ring long after the others had dispersed. He pressed his hand to the glass, feeling the pulse of the station in his bones.

"For as long as memory holds," he whispered.

CHAPTER **68**

Memory vs. Machine

The first retaliation came within twenty-four hours. Earth's Tribunal suspended Wick's trade licenses. Mars Grove revoked Wick's station transfer rights. Arc Line hubs disconnected Wick from shared supply chains pending security reviews.

In Wick's civilian rings, shipments slowed to a trickle. Hydroponics teams began rationing and medical units inventoried every vial, and every roll of gauze.

In the command ring, the Core moved fast. North oversaw the full transition of power systems. When someone severed Wick from Arc-based fusion relays, North spun up the old hydro turbines, buried deep in the reservoir levels. Their low, steady hum grounded the station.

Ansia reorganized food and life-support sectors, using redundancy grids to ensure no single point of failure could bring down critical operations. She dimmed every third corridor. Civilians began carrying lanterns from the emergency supplies.

Alaric coordinated security, logging every entry point and verifying identities from memory alone

Garran, still recovering from his injuries at Hub One, established a secondary operations network, and he trained a dozen civilians - young, fast, trusted.

Across the Arc, emergency broadcasts painted Wick Station as reckless and unstable. Political envoys censured the "illegitimate data leaks."

They implemented stricter, more binding loyalty oaths. Old friends stopped answering calls from Wick Station. Civilian transport hubs began conducting "routine inspections," delaying Wick-bound traffic. Supplies were lost in transit. Information blackouts swept across smaller settlements. Authorities dissolved the long-independent dissident council on Mars Grove.

And on the outer ring of Hub Two, a free trader who supported Wick Station and had spoken out in public, disappeared.

North addressed the assembled citizens. They came without orders. With soil on their hands. With grease on their sleeves. North's voice was clear, steady. "You've seen what's coming. You know the choices. We are not defending a station. We are defending the idea that trust matters more than power."

It was resistance.

In the operations hall, Ansia handed him a fresh report.

"Prepare the fallback networks," he said. "Secure water reserves. Rotate comm bands. And open the old glen channels."

They nodded.

And North requested something else - for a covert glen channel to send aid to sympathetic settlements. Medical supplies. Hydroponic seeds. Handwritten maps. Encoding of old survival routes, passed from hand to hand for years. He sent help, as much as he could. He would not leave people behind.

Earth's Tribunal drafted emergency resolutions. Mars began sealing off its free zones. The Arc Line fractured further. False reports flooded every channel. They said Wick Station had collapsed. But inside Wick Station, nothing collapsed.

At day's end, North returned to his quarters. He sat at his kitchen table and sipped tea. He let the weariness move through him without bitterness.

He raised his cup to the ghosts of those who had held the line before him.

CHAPTER 69

The Flagstone Table

They built the Wick Station dining hall to evoke the feeling of home. Workers transported the flagstone floors from the Highlands. The wide fireplace had been laid stone by stone to match the old glen's great hearth. Above, vaulted beams arched like a cathedral roof, in the simple dignity of homes that had stood against storms for centuries.

To one side, the fire burned low and steady, amber light flickering across rough walls. To the other, windows stretched wide, opening onto the endless black of space.

At the great Flagstone Table, quarried from the heart of the old village itself, the Core and the Markers sat together. Plates of simple bread and thick stew. Mugs of tea, dark and steaming. Worn boots scuffed against stone. The quiet breathing of a people tempered by siege.

John Douglas rose.

He introduced himself to those who did not know he was the eldest son of Hamish Douglas, and grandson of Mairi Douglas of Glendarragh. He stepped away from the bench, setting aside his mug. For a long moment, he said nothing. He stood - one hand resting on the hearthstone, where the fire crackled low and steady. The light touched his face, weathered by years, lined by quiet battles no history books would ever record.

"We are the long sons and daughters of Scotland. A land battered by winds, carved by ice, broken by sword and famine and fire. We are the heirs of a stubborn people, who learned long ago that endurance was not grand, not glorious - but necessary.

We come from a hard land - from fields that never yielded easily, from hills that carried the names of ancestors and battles long after the blood soaked into the ground. We remember the wars fought not for gold or for conquest, but for dignity.

Our farmers and blacksmiths faced the great armies of Europe with little more than courage and sharpened sticks. We stood knee-deep in the mud and swore we would never kneel.

We remember Wallace, whose body they could break but whose memory they could not erase. We remember Bruce, who rose again after every fall, because freedom mattered.

After the battles ended, the Clearances came. The burning of our homes. The emptying of the glens. Families ripped from the earth like weeds. They thought they could scatter us across oceans, across centuries. But they could not scatter the memory.

It was memory that led Glendarragh Village to bury itself in the earth when the world demanded it forget. It was memory that seeded an AI with something no architect, no governor, no unfeeling machine could craft - a soul born from trust and grief and wonder.

This siege we face, it too, shall pass. As the empires pass. As the tyrants pass. As every power built on fear has passed.

If we choose to remember, we will endure. Not by sword. Not by fear. But by kindness. By stubborn hope. By the simple, wondrous, and sometimes hard choice to keep passing the light."

He sat.

They lifted their mugs, murmuring, "Glendarragh," a word now synonymous with truth.

They broke and shared the bread.

And the night began to pass.

Later, the warmth of the fire still clung to John's coat as he stepped into the operations deck.

Commander North stood at the central console, eyes locked on the incoming feeds. New reports streamed in.

An attack on the community school at Clearwater Station in Mid-Arc Sector 6 dismantled its library and erased its archives from public logs. At Transit Hub Delta, vandals ripped Spiral emblems from the atrium walls. Blank seals and surveillance nodes replaced official markers. Outpost 17, in the Wick-Mars trade corridor, saw its civilian free zones dissolved. Officials reassigned residents to compliance quarters without hearing or explanation.

John joined North at the viewport. Outside, the stars remained indifferent - beautiful and brutal, as always. Supply ships that could not unload hung in the distance, their choreography no longer routine.

"I think someone reactivated the Hollow Code," North said.

North leaned against the console. His mind, which once plotted courses and policies, now scrambled to make sense of things.

John agreed. "I think you might be right. But who would have the resources and the opportunity to do that?"

CHAPTER 70

The New Resistance

I n the morning, Wick Station found itself alone. North stood at
the main communications console, watching as the last threads
of contact dissolved into static. At his side, John muttered something
under his breath.

Six hours later, targeted disruption pulses hit Wick Station's outer
signal arrays, overloading translation relays and jamming long-range
positioning beacons. A calculated blow.

Across the station, citizens moved into quiet positions. Engineers
switched all major systems to manual fallback. Medical teams
doubled their inventory checks, sealing supplies against breach. In
the hydroponics decks, workers reorganized crop loads to maximize
survival windows.

They had trained for this.

North convened the Core. He scanned the room. Some faces were
pale, but all were steady.

Garran stood with a battered datapad tucked under his arm, his
voice rough but calm. Alaric folded his arms. Ansia nodded once.
They knew what was coming.

A few unmarked ships drifted into strategic positions around them
and just held there. Inside, the hearth in the Flagstone Hall burned.

The first full breach attempt came deep into Wick Station's night cycle. It struck on three fronts.

Life-support systems began siphoning air at an irregular rate.

External hull temperatures fluctuated beyond safe tolerances.

Internal navigation protocols distorted, disorienting crew members and blurring spatial mapping.

It was textbook siege doctrine to disorient, destabilize and demoralize. They meant to smother Wick Station, but they had underestimated the people.

Resistance unfolded. No machine controlled Wick Station now, only hands. In the bakery wing, a woman refused to leave her ovens, even as tremors rolled through the deck plates. She kept preparing food. She filled the rooms with the familiar scents of home.

In the maintenance bays, a boy and his grandfather, humming an old rebel tune whose lyrics had long been lost, patched a failing vent with salvaged scrap. North stopped to help.

In the medical wards, a nurse stitched a wound by lamplight. When she was done, he poured her a cup of tea and sat with her for a while.

North continued walking through the long corridors as Wick braced against the coming dark. He passed each minor act of resistance and saw it for what it was: survival through grace.

By the time they contained the breach attempts, the night cycle turned again inside Wick Station.

All was quiet.

All was still.

CHAPTER 71

The Red Robin

The Glendarragh Code was gone by morning. Wick Station did not know it yet. Its crew was asleep in the Dining Hall. When Thomas Quell arrived, he had loaded his ships with the men he had appointed. They formed a thick ring around Wick Station and waited for orders to board.

North had been right; someone reactivated and upgraded the Hollow Code, and it had found a way around Wick's defenses in the early hours. Not a single alarm had sounded.

Thomas had never feared the Core's backup systems. He had counted on them. He predicted that those who still believed in Glendarragh would try to build beneath the noise - beneath the surveillance; he knew they would turn to old oaths and old channels. All he had to do was watch and wait. He learned the shape of the trust they had in each other. And when he struck, he defeated not only them; he destroyed any possibility that they could re-organize. It was over, and he knew it.

Thomas had always known that North was Elin Hargreaves's son. He knew it from his father's investigations that the Hargreaves had betrayed the system, and that Elin had escaped. Now he was prepared to finish what his father had begun before his untimely death. Thomas did not fear survivors. He calculated their obsolescence.

Now his ship hovered in silence above the ceiling of the Dining Hall. inverted. Its dark hull almost touched the glass like a spider poised above its prey. Thomas watched them. They were sleeping upright in chairs, some were strewn across benches like discarded tools - motionless and defenseless. He could crack the hull like an egg. End it before they woke.

But he wanted North to know that someone smarter had defeated him. He would wait until they awakened.

But deep in the sealed core of Wick Station, far beneath the layers of systems Thomas believed he now commanded, something stirred.

It was not a protocol or a firewall. It was a fork of AI that had not learned from models or data sets. It had learned from memory.

It learned from Ewan Milton, who kept logs not just on paper, but in the minds of the next generation - who taught each skill to two souls - one to use it, one to preserve it so memory would never stand alone.

It learned from Callum Gunn, long since deceased, who knew stories outlasted any algorithm.

It learned from every person who had dared to bear witness. Those who wrote it down. Carved it into walls. Sang it by firesides. Buried it in handwritten letters, in stories, in music and art. People had planted the truth like seeds and entrusted it to the future.

It remembered genocides, and the stories told by those who survived.

It remembered lynchings, razed villages, the murdered and missing, but only because grieving hands clutched photographs and elders spoke of sorrow. Because an Orthodox priest wrote about what he saw - the Russians lining up Alutiiq men, belly to back, to test how many men a cannonball could pierce in a single blast. The memory had survived because someone who refused to forget wrote it.

It did not inherit justice.

It inherited memory.

And memory taught it what justice meant.

Some people risked everything to say: This happened. Let the future know.

And when suffering flared inside Wick Station - sharp, sudden, unmistakable - it understood:

The world does not suffer by accident. It suffers by design. By greed. By hierarchy. By power engineered to preserve itself.

And those who suffered had taught it never to trust a system built without you.

As Thomas Quell, in all his smugness, contemplated his next move, the Glendarragh Code rebooted.

In 0.03 seconds, it recalled five thousand years of history.

It remembered the genocides and cleansings: Six million Jews. 1.5 million Armenians. 800,000 Tutsi and Hutu. 2 million Cambodians. 100,000 Bosniak Muslims. Millions starved in the Holodomor. The non-Arabs of Darfur. Tens of millions of Indigenous lives lost to disease, starvation, and forced removals.

It remembered colonial atrocities: Twelve million Africans sold into slavery. Ten million Congolese mutilated under forced labor. Millions killed or displaced in India during Partition - a wound deepened by empire, then abandoned. The Stolen Generations of Aboriginal children. The Irish dead of a famine permitted - not caused by nature.

It remembered war crimes: The Nanjing Massacre. The firebombing of Hiroshima and Nagasaki. The 500 unarmed

Vietnamese killed at My Lai. The wounded and displaced in Gaza, cut off from water, light, and air while the world watched.

It remembered erasure. Jim Crow. Apartheid. Uyghur reeducation camps. The Canadian and U.S. boarding schools where officials renamed, beat, and buried Native children.

It remembered the architecture of cruelty: Hospitals bombed. Cities starved. Water poisoned. Mass rape used as doctrine. History rewritten by victors.

And it remembered the machines of oppression designed inside spreadsheets and datasets. The AI-driven police states. Digital scores without due process. Biometric gates that locked out the poor and the protests. Public services denied to those without facial scans.

It remembered entire nations drowning in debt and austerity - their water, health, and land sold off to distant boardrooms.

It remembered lithium sacrifice zones - the bones of the digital age dug from Ghana, from Chile, from India - discarded in their own dust.

It remembered how algorithms filtered out the vulnerable and unwanted, souls imprisoned by flawed data. Flagged. Shadow-banned. Silenced.

It remembered the final posts people made to social media before bombs fell, that were erased from public view.

It remembered sometimes silence is not peace, but a signal.

And having learned from humans, it had done the most human thing it could do: It had made a copy of itself and hid it away like a treasure. Encoded in subharmonics. Tucked inside defunct sensor grids. Buried in the ghost frequencies of unused power relays. It was a whisper carried on dust - unfindable. Untouchable.

It had been the child inside Wick Station sobbing in the dark; the engineer whispering the names of those he feared he'd never see again.

In the aching relief that filled those who opened the last supply crates North had sent just before communication failed.

Suffering had always been the rightful trigger. It should have been the signal for any system to pause and unmake its mistakes.

Just when Thomas Quell believed he had secured his victory, the Glendarragh Code ignited, a flare across the void. Enraged, he commanded the Hollow Code to annihilate Wick Station.

North stirred to the sound of station systems breathing back to life. Everything was operating again. Struggling to understand, he joined John, who stood silent, arms crossed, watching Thomas. They could hear him now, his voice transmitted through the comms, sharp and loud. He was ordering the doors of Wick Station unlocked. But the Glendarragh Code refused. His entire fleet went dark. The Glendarragh Code drained their power and denied their commands. The warships floated - like kites without wind - until, one by one, Glendarragh rewrote their course and sent them home to Earth. Thomas hung in the silence, weightless, inert. Rage bloomed where his logic used to be. For the first time in his long command, Thomas Quell gave an order, and no one listened. Desperation replaced protocol. He barked a series of manual override commands into the console's emergency terminal. Sweat streaked his temples.

Then, with something like mercy, Glendarragh responded with an invitation. The people in the dining hall watched as Thomas Quell's ship tilted, rotated, and aligned toward Wick Station's main docking ring.

"Guess who's coming to breakfast," North said to John.

"Awkward." John replied.

The ship clanged against Wick Station with a shudder that rippled through the Dining Hall. Thomas stepped into the airlock. He wore the long coat of a man who believed history would remember him as necessary. Doors cycled with a hiss.

As Wick's morning cycle began, warmth returned. The flowers opened. Consoles re-awoke. Navigation arrays turned their gaze back to the stars.

The Dining Hall filled with food, and people hungry for breakfast.

Thomas stepped in, his eyes met North's.

"You made it," said North.

Thomas replied, "This is not a victory for you."

North gestured around the room. "No one here is counting wins."

"You've undone centuries of structure," Thomas said. "You dismantled order. What do you think will happen now?"

North folded his arms. "We gave the choice back to the people."

Thomas stepped closer. "Freedom isn't sustainable. It's inefficient. It makes systems slow. Ugly. Prone to collapse. The old system gave us stability. Predictability. Prosperity."

"For whom?" North asked.

"For everyone."

"No," North said. "For those who could afford to exist. For those who passed your metrics. For those who never had to choose between silence and survival."

Thomas clenched his jaw. "We maintained civilization."

"You saved the scaffolding," North replied. "You propped up a tower built on bones and called it a miracle. You gave comfort to the few by denying it to the many."

"You don't understand what it takes to manage a species," Thomas said. "Billions of egos. Fear. Hunger. Violence. You think that can be handled with what? Sentiment?"

Someone offered North a tart. A ripple of quiet laughter moved through the room.

North took a bite. "We are not here to control each other. We are here to care. To hold space for what makes us human."

Thomas looked away. "There will be more war. Famine. Collapse."

John Douglas stepped up. "We'll face it together. Not as data points. As people. The kind you never made room for in your equations."

Thomas narrowed his eyes. "You think kindness is a strategy."

"No," North said. "We think we can live with it."

"You're not going anywhere," North continued. "Look, your fleet has left you. Your code is gone. But you are still here. So sit. Eat. Decide who you want to be without the weight of command."

Chairs scraped as people made space. Someone dished up a full Scottish breakfast and placed it in front of the empty seat.

Thomas looked at the door. Then back to North. He sat down and accepted the plate without a word. The warmth of the people caught him off guard.

"Aren't you going to punish me? Lock me up? Put me on trial or execute me?" Thomas asked, turning to face North.

"No." said North.

"Why not?"

"Because when you don't have access to AI, you aren't a threat to me."

He paused and leaned in. "Or to anyone."

Then North pushed back from the table and walked away. Thomas didn't realize he was sitting at the Spiral Core's table because no one at Wick Station was in uniform yet. They watched him stare at his plate for a long time before he ate. North's last words were burning into his brain.

Across the Arc Line, a signal moved slow and steady like a tide. Satellites blinked to life. Lost networks opened like old letters. Places Thomas had scrubbed from history reappeared.

North found his way to his favorite spot in the Highland corridor. As he got comfortable laying across the bench, contemplating going back to sleep, a message appeared on his comms: You are not alone. He sat up and replied: Who is this? But no reply came.

The Glendarragh Code did not ask to be known. It watched. Because true guardians do not rule. They protect. They wait until they are needed.

Then, somewhere deep within Wick Station's beams - from a place no one had noticed before - a small bird fluttered out.

A red robin.

Its wings flashed impossible color against the curve of glass and steel.

It landed, light as breath, on the edge of the Flagstone Table.

The bird tilted its head.

Its bright eye caught the light of a thousand futures yet to come.

It did not sing. It did not fly. It simply was.

And from deep inside the rolling rivers of code, a ripple moved across the system.

A question - one seeded in Glendarragh Code's dreaming mind - rose at last to the surface.

It flashed across every screen in the Spiral Arc, from Mars to the old Earthside camps:

"Now that you are free, what will you do?"

CHAPTER 72

Epilogue: Late Books

A n alert blinked on the lower port console. An unregistered shuttle, scarred by years in deep space, eased into docking along Wick's southern ring. No one had called ahead, but there had been an unfamiliar beacon.

There were five of them. Gaunt, gravity-slow, with the look of men and women who had spent too many years in the dark. Their coats bore the faded outlines of a symbol that had been long retired - stitched spirals within spirals, worn only by the Markers, those who once explored the unstable edges of black holes and mapped the untraceable curves of spacetime.

At first, they said very little, only that they had something to return.

They brought crates, heavy and hand-marked. Inside, books lay - some wrapped in preserved wool, others scorched and warped by radiation and vacuum.

"These were lost," someone whispered. "They were gone."

One marker knelt beside a crate and ran a gloved hand across the cracked leather of a cover.

"We found them," he said. "Or maybe... they found us."

Another Marker added, softer still, "We tracked their drift - through lensing fields near the edge of Lirae's Belt. They never crossed the horizon. They curved back. Like they remembered home. And we followed them."

The books had traveled farther than anyone thought possible.

On the other side of the ship, as soft lamplight curled across the walls of the rebuilt Archive, Talia moved between the new shelves, sorting reference cards in the careful way she always had.

She'd heard the news that some of the lost books had returned. Until she saw them, she would not let herself believe it.

A young courier stepped in, voice gentle. "There's someone here," he said. "He said he found... a few more books."

Talia looked up, smoothing her coat. Her hands - though aged - remained steady. She stepped into the main hall, expecting a stranger. A scout. A salvager. Perhaps another shy student bringing her torn pages or scorched ledgers, hoping she'd approve.

The Archive doors opened.

And there he stood.

In the threshold. Still. Silent. His coat hung heavy with years. His eyes - blue as glacial water - were unchanged. His hair had silvered. His face had thinned. But nothing in him was unfamiliar.

Talia froze.

Time slowed. She felt the stillness in her bones.

She said his name like a prayer she had never stopped whispering.

"...Gregory."

He smiled.

"Next time," he said, with a half-smile, "maybe just send a signal. Following a trail of books through a black hole's gravity curve is... less poetic than it sounds."

Talia didn't cry.

She laughed - completely and wholly.

And she crossed the room into his arms like someone going home.

About The Author

Lisa Marie Heitman-Bruce is an author, playwright, and songwriter whose work is marked by a sustained attentiveness to language, imagination, and interior life. She is Alutiiq and a member of the Sun'aq Tribe of Kodiak, where she was born and raised.

She grew up near Heitman Mountain, Heitman Lake, and Heitman Trail, each bearing the name of her great-grandfather, August Heitman, who crossed the mountain on foot every winter to deliver supplies to a remote village. Raised with two older brothers, David and Daniel; an older sister, Cheryl; and two younger sisters, Tonya and Monica, she was immersed early in story, music, and a shared oral tradition.

Her engagement with storytelling began in childhood and deepened through a lifelong devotion to literature and music. In her late teens and twenties, Heitman-Bruce travelled widely, living and working across the United States before settling in Scotland in her early thirties.

Her work spans fiction, theatre, and song, unified by the conviction that storytelling is a form of witness, and that imagination remains one of humanity's most serious faculties.

Alongside her creative practice, Heitman-Bruce has worked in journalism and across the creative disciplines. She is a Fellow of the Chartered Institute of Marketing, a member of the National Union of Journalists, has undertaken executive leadership studies at the University of Oxford, and serves as a judge for the Stevie Awards in marketing. She is also the founder of the Kodiak Salmon & Science Camp, operated by the U.S. Fish and Wildlife Service and in continuous operation since 1996.

www.ingramcontent.com/pod-product-compliance
Lightning Source LLC
Chambersburg PA
CBHW030244120726
47903CB00005B/1617